SAVAGE

A DARK BRATVA ARRANGED MARRIAGE ROMANCE

WICKED VOWS
BOOK 6

JANE HENRY

SYNOPSIS

Scarred. Overlooked. Tainted.

Born into the ruthless underworld, I've been cast aside. I'm locked in a cage of lies and betrayal, now framed for a crime I didn't commit.

But then he came for me.

Ollie Romanov, the savage enforcer, believes I'm a traitor.

He's ruthless, merciless, and prepared to make me pay for my sins.

To him, I'm nothing more than a pawn to punish. A traitor to be broken.

Yet beneath the cold, brutal exterior, I see something more —a darkness that calls to my own.

I shouldn't crave the twisted connection we share. I swear the man has no conscience...

Except when it comes to me.

Have I married a heartless monster? A psychopath?

Or has this Savage finally found his match in me?

CHAPTER ONE

Ollie

THERE ARE two types of people in this world: those who lie well and those who are shit at it.

Santiago Morales is the latter.

The goddamn pussy kneels on the rain-soaked ground, a thin trail of blood trickling from a wound in his forehead. His cheeks are hollowed, his dark-brown eyes haunted and gaunt. Isabella Morales's first cousin is a walking skeleton, haunted with terror of the devil he serves, in the custody of the devil he fears.

Sucks to be him.

But Jesus. Even I would feed the men who worked for me. The guy looks like he's subsisted on bread, water, and a steady diet of waterboarding. Carlos Carrera was a fucking narcissistic tyrant.

"Please," Santiago begs in broken English. "I don't know."

The shifting storm clouds over the late afternoon sky reveal his terrified eyes. I fucking hate the way he trembles. He knows where Renata is, and he deserves to die.

Blood thrums in my veins.

Renata Carrera is *mine,* and I'll burn this fucking world to ash before I let anyone harm a hair on her head. Others might say to let her go, to let her run and hide, but the beast in me wants her chained to me.

I walk in a circle around Santiago as his bloodshot, widened eyes track me. He licks his dry, cracked lips and swallows as if trying to gather up his courage.

"You have to understand," I tell Santiago in a deceptively calm voice. "The entirety of our operation hinges on finding Renata. If we don't find her, we're at an impasse. She has information on us that's incredibly time sensitive." I lean over and pat his cheek. He flinches as if I'm wielding a whip. "Doesn't that make sense to you? Hmm?"

At eight o'clock this morning, back in The Cove, our men holding Renata in custody were found dead with bullets between their eyes.

Just as well, really. I would have had to kill them for letting her go.

Renata's more than just a pawn in this game. She's the queen who slipped through my fingers, and every second I don't have her, the more my need to have her grows.

"I don't know. I swear to God, I don't know!" he sobs. I clench my jaw and glare at him. Jesus motherfucking Christ, let me go out of this world with my balls intact, no matter the circumstances.

I narrow my eyes and stand in front of him, my arms crossed. Emotions like this never move me. Some people think I'm the quiet one because "still waters run deep" or some poetic shit like that.

I keep quiet because I don't give a fuck about playing Mr. Nice Guy. It's just easier to shut the fuck up. Makes people wonder.

"You can kill me," the pussy says, looking away. Bluffing his fucking mouth off. "Do whatever you want to me; I swear I don't care! But you have to believe me, I don't know."

I sigh and shake my head.

A dog barks, and an angry woman screams something unintelligible at the market behind us. Worked out well that the marketplace was in full swing today because the muffled sounds of the people behind us mask our job. Even if they did see us, they'd keep walking. No one in this neighborhood gives a fuck about us, and they know better than to go anywhere near business involving the cartel.

I stare at him and shake my head again.

I don't care that he's covered in blood. I don't care that I'll instruct my men to make an example out of him, to bury him in pieces all over the place and spread the news of his death far and wide. All I care is that I'm looking for answers, and I'm going to find her no matter what.

In the distance, a siren wails, momentarily blocking out the chatter of the market.

I let out a belabored sigh. "It doesn't have to be like this, Santiago." The two men I brought with me stand stoically behind me. Loyal to the Morales cartel, they're now loyal to the Romanov Bratva by association since my brother's marriage to Isabella.

The one to my left has short gray hair and a neatly trimmed beard. His clothes are pressed, and the ink on his upper right arm indicates his affiliation with *Fuerzas Militares de Colombia*—the Colombian military.

The guy beside him is younger but larger, his muscles flexing when he clenches his fists. He reminds me of my brother Viktor—bulky, muscular, fearless. Both of these men hate traitors, and I don't fucking blame them.

One speaks in rapid Spanish to the other, and they both shake their heads. I speak Spanish, but poorly, so I only catch the gist. They said something about this taking too long. They would be happy to help me.

There was a time when the man bleeding out in the rain, begging for his life, considered these two his brothers. They would've died for Santiago and his family.

They want justice.

They don't care where she is. All they care about is making an example of this asshole so no one else gets the wrong idea again.

"If you tell me what I need to know, I'll make it worth your while." Now I'm the one lying. He's getting a bullet between his eyes no matter what he does.

"*¡Por favor, señor! No puedo decirle nada. Carlos fue el que me lo dijo. ¡Él es el que la persigue, es a él a quien debe encontrar!*"

Carlos? Even though I know Spanish, I shake my head. This doesn't make sense. "Carlos Carerro is dead."

Carlos Carrera was found dead before I came down here. Confirmed. We buried him beside Javier.

He realizes his mistake and quickly shakes his head. He jabbers on in Spanish so broken and rapid I don't quite get everything. It doesn't help I'm fixated on what he said either.

Carlos.

Carlos fucking Carrera.

Renata Carrera's brother. Our mortal enemy. If Carlos is alive, we've got bigger problems than we realized.

I take a step toward him and grip his hair. "Do you think I'm fucking stupid? You mean to tell me Carlos is still alive?" He's made a big fucking mistake telling me this.

The two men look at each other in wide-eyed terror. I can see the whites of both of their eyes. One of them whispers a rushed prayer as if on instinct. If Carlos is alive, they're fucking dead.

I don't want a sliver of misunderstanding between us, so I speak to them in their native language. My voice booms in the narrow alleyway so loudly that they both jump. "*¿Alguno de ustedes sabe algo sobre esto!*"

Do either of you know anything about this?

"*No, señor,*" they say in unison.

Santiago cries to himself. I turn and stare into his eyes. "You're lying. I know you are." I speak softly, almost gently, making sure he hears every damn word I say. "Carlos Carrera is dead. And you know exactly where she is and who took her."

He shakes his head, his full body trembling. "I don't!"

Jesus, he's stubborn. I glare at him. "Show him," I snap at the men.

In seconds, they pull up screenshots from Santiago's phone showing Renata's arrival. "We've been watching. We know," the older man says, his voice cold and unwavering. Renata's beautiful face is evident despite the grainy resolution. "This was taken today."

Santiago pales now that the evidence of his betrayal is undeniable. He turns his head as if looking away will make this all go away. The coward

I *hate* cowards.

"You thought you could hide her and get away with it. You thought you could be a hero for those who wish to betray us." I lean in closely. "You thought you could lie and survive."

He sobs, shaking his head from side to side.

"Do you know what happens to those who betray us?"

"No! No!" The whites of his eyes remind me of a rabid animal. I shake my head and stand up straighter.

I'm done. If Carlos is actually out there, we've got to fucking *move*. We're goddamn sitting ducks.

I nod to the men behind me. The gray-haired one pulls out his Sig Sauer P226 Legion and hands it to me. I love the heft and weight of it and how easy it is to pull the trigger. I love the feel of the cold metal in my palm and barely restrain myself from caressing it.

I aim the gun at Santiago's head. He babbles on and on in Spanish and then begins to plead in broken English. "No! No, please, I have family. You can't—"

I spit on the ground. "They're better off with you dead than knowing you're a traitor."

"I didn't— I'm not—"

The gunshot echoes through the alley. Santiago falls to the ground. His head hits the pavement with a sickening thud, blood splattering his gaunt face.

I'm told this is the part where I'm supposed to feel something. Remorse, perhaps? Regret? Something, anything that makes me human and not a robot conditioned to react and never feel… but no. I'm only mildly relieved one more traitor's gone and definitely pissed off we didn't get more from him.

I want Renata Carrera for myself.

Frowning, I turn to leave.

"Clean this up. You know what to do with the body. Make sure everybody knows what happens to traitors."

"Si, señor. Should we speak to Isabella first?"

"Yes. Ask her the best way to communicate this message, and do not take all fucking day doing it."

"Si, señor, si."

I walk into the shadows as the sun sets, rain beating down on Santiago's pathetic, lifeless body behind me.

It's all fucking behind me.

She's here. I know she is. I can fucking feel her here. And when I find her, *she'll* find out what happens to traitors too.

CHAPTER TWO

Renata

MY FAMILY really could've invested more in this godawful safe house. The floors are dirty, the light dim. The silhouette of tired, well-worn furniture shoved into a corner gives the whole place a dismal appearance. Rain tapping against the window only makes it worse.

I love my homeland, but right now, I'd give anything to be back at the Romanovs. I've longed to escape the ties to my family, to find freedom. But that dream is a nightmare and freedom just another word for survival.

Still, I sit upright in the chair I'm bound to and ignore the gnawing hunger in my belly and the stitch in my side from sitting here for so long.

He's coming. I know he's fucking coming. There's a reason I've been brought here, and everything in me knows why.

My brother is not dead.

I knew it was too good to be true, and I knew it was a lie because I felt no sense of relief. Only wariness and a deep, dark knowing that comes from sharing some part of the man's DNA.

And now, I'll wait until he comes to do whatever the fuck he plans on doing to me. I betrayed the Los Sangre Dorada. My brother must know that by now. My life is forfeit for what I've done.

Jesus.

The hefty old man with nasty garlic breath and rough hands, who dragged me here straight from the damn plane, chuckles mercilessly in the dim shadows. "He's coming," he taunts me. "You are in so much trouble."

I toss my head and pretend I don't hear him.

But I can't stop the way my skin crawls and the little hairs on the back of my neck stand. I hate how my heartbeat races on as if I'm being chased by an axe murderer.

I'd rather face a murderer than my brother.

Footsteps sound outside.

My heart pounds. I grit my teeth.

The door opens, and four masked men enter the room, each holding a gun by his side, all of them in strict military formation. And behind them, prowling like an angry, hungry lion, stalks Carlos Carerra himself.

Dressed in black, utilitarian clothing, he walks in with a familiar scowl and a newly adopted air of authority. I stifle a snort. Javier Morales, his former boss, is dead, which is the only reason he struts around like he's hot shit.

A lamp flickers on a bedside table as one of the masked men takes a chair and plunks it on the floor in front of me. But Carlos doesn't sit.

Holding my gaze, Carlos stands over me, his presence menacing. He wants me sweating. He wants me shaking.

I can't help it. I'm doing both, and I hate myself for it.

"*Hola,* little sister," he says, his voice cold and calculating. He leans down and brushes his thumb across the bruise on my cheek. I stifle a wince, but he notices. "Who did this to you?"

I jerk my chin at the hefty man sitting next to me.

"Such sloppy work," Carlos says. "This is the best you could do? You took a traitor here for questioning, and this is the best you could do? She isn't even bleeding." Shaking his head, he casually pulls a handgun from a holster at his side.

"Please, sir! I'll do better!" The man's eyes are wide, his hands spread, pleading. "Give me another—"

Boom.

I scream when the bullet lands right between the man's eyes. Blood pours from the wound as his heavy body falls to the ground, lifeless. I bite my lip until I taste metal on my tongue to stop myself from screaming, but my scream ends in a whimper.

"She's a traitor," Carlos says, reaching for me. I flinch, but I can't get away from him. Even if I wasn't tied to this chair, he's bigger and stronger than I am. I know that from personal experience.

He fists my hair and yanks my head back.

"If I send you to bring back a traitor, man or woman, and I tell you to punish them, I mean you fucking punish them," Carlos snarls. In one swift motion, he draws his hand back and slaps me, hard, across the face. Tears spring to my eyes, and my head jerks to the side. He slaps the other cheek. I cry out in pain. My jaw vibrates from the impact, my skin on fire.

He reaches for my chin and grabs it, appraising his work. "There. That's a bit better," he snarls, showcasing yellowed teeth.

My best friend Isabella always hated Carlos, and for good reason. She called him "homely and ugly," and she was right. "Too bad you got all the beauty genes," she said once. "Maybe that's why he's so grumpy all the time. It must hurt walking around looking like that."

But I know better. Carlos looks like evil incarnate because he is. The ugliness in his face is only a reflection of his heart.

"I'll take it easy on you this time, little sister, because I need you. And when I send you back to lover boy, things might get complicated if you have any broken bones."

Oh no. Oh God.

Lover boy? My heart beats so fast I'm sick to my stomach.

Now I know why it was so easy for Isabella to kill her brother, Javier. If I had a weapon and half a second, I'd pull the trigger so damn fast. I *hate* this man in front of me. The boy I grew up with, my brother, who was my confidant and partner in crime, is gone. I barely recognize this monster.

"Don't even think about lying to me, Renata. I know. I had eyes on you every minute you spent in New York. It's why I knew you were a traitor. I didn't miss the way you look at him. I saw the way you fell for him. I know."

God, how does he know? And how will I ever escape from this?

"So I'm going to make a deal with you." He sits in the chair and leans forward, his arms resting on his knees, his soulless eyes boring into mine.

He won't defeat you.

He won't.

I have to stay strong. I have to keep my head on straight. So what if he knows I fell for Ollie Romanov? So what if that's why he took me back here?

Still... what does he hope to gain from having me here?

He hasn't killed me because he needs something.

What?

Carlos presses his thumb to my throbbing cheek. My pulse threatens to choke me, but I don't move. He leans closer, his voice cold and cruel. "This is what you'll do. You're going back to your precious Romanovs in The Cove. They'll likely brutally punish you themselves, thinking you betrayed them, but the poor fools won't even know the half of it." He shakes his head. "You'll pretend I don't exist. You'll pretend you wanted to confirm my death here in Columbia, and you did."

My pulse is racing so quickly that I can hardly hear from the pounding in my ears.

I glare at Carlos, my cheek throbbing and my eyes watery. But my voice is steady and filled with resolve. "You underestimate me, Carlos. I won't let you use me like this."

Carlos leans in closer, his voice a dangerous whisper. "Oh, but you will. Because if you tell them anything... anything about me at all, I will murder the man you love in front of you."

One thing I've always been exceptionally good at was knowing when someone was lying. My mother used to call it my superpower. I was so skilled at it in fact, my father would call me into meetings with his friends and show me off like a circus act. People I knew would eventually learn that lying to me never worked. I knew there was no Santa Claus before I went to school, and I knew the truth about the birds and the bees much earlier than a child ever should as a result of this strange but undeniable talent.

And one thing I know for absolute certain: Carlos isn't lying.

My jaw drops. I quickly close it, but it's too late. He saw my reaction. I know he thinks he struck a bullseye when his eyes light up.

"I don't love anybody," I lie through gritted teeth. I'm an outsider in every world I've ever touched... at least they think I am. The daughter who betrayed her family, the lover who deceived her allies, the sister who let the devil take root in her own flesh and blood. My only home is a prison of my own making.

He shakes his head and laughs maniacally. It chills me. "I watched the way your eyes light up when he walks into a room. I saw the way you pined for him when he's not there.

I heard you ask for him. I saw you stare after him." He spits on the floor. "You're in love with a fucking Russian pig. Father would've killed you for less."

Also not a lie.

I look away, caught between the knowledge that he's found me out and the ultimatum he's issued.

Everyone will think I'm a liar.

Isabella. Her husband, Lev.

Ollie.

I close my eyes against another rush of emotions.

Carlos is cold and cruel, a vivid reminder of the brother I once loved, but another beast waits for me...one whose darkness I fear just as much as I crave. He'll find me.

I have to escape and leave all of them. I have to find a way out of here.

I have to start over.

All over.

There's no going back, no safe harbor. All I can do is run until there's nothing left of the girl I once was.

I reach a tentative hand to my cheek and work my jaw. Not broken. Good. It'll mend.

"You will find out what they know and report back to me. And when you are done—when you've done everything I've said here, we'll take the next step." He smiles. My stomach swirls with nausea. "I may even forgive you."

Lie.

He won't. Forgiveness to him is as foreign as kindness. He'd have to have a heart.

"And if I don't?" I ask. I want to know where I stand. I like it better that way and always have.

The men behind me make sounds of disbelief. Even Carlos needs a minute. He blinks in surprise. It feels a bit victorious.

"If you don't, I'll kill him first and make you watch, little sister, before you join him."

Little sister. It hurts worse than when he hit me.

A pang hits my heart when he calls me that. I remember being only three years old, cowering in fear in my father's study. I'd broken his prized possession, a hideous bookend his father carved into the shape of a serpent with a thick square base. I knew I'd get the belt for that. I wasn't allowed in his study.

Carlos saw me, his eyes wide in surprise when he found me crying in the study just moments before my father came home. I told him what happened in a rush of words seconds before my father came in.

He didn't even hesitate but spun on his heels and took the blame. "I'm sorry!" he said to my father. "It was an accident." I wept as he took the punishment meant for me, without a whimper, without a tear, and later nursed his wounds.

What happened to the brother who defended me? My father planted the seeds. Power and greed are insidious beasts that can destroy a man's heart. I blink, and a tear rolls down my cheek.

I can't help but pitch a final plea to the brother I once knew. "What happened to you, Carlos? We used to be friends. We used to love each other."

A flicker of something like humanity crosses his features but quickly evaporates. He laughs and shakes his head. "I grew up, Renata."

I stare at the lifeless body of the man on the floor, killed for not hitting me harder. I stare at my brother's cruel face, twisted in hatred and anger. I swallow hard.

"I'll do what you ask," I tell him. "But if you touch one hair on his head, I will kill you myself."

Carlos nods as if satisfied with my response. "There it is. The hint of Carerra blood you've kept buried under all those lies and deception." He shakes his head. "We'll meet again, Renata. Remember, I have eyes on you. Not a word to anyone about me. I'm dead to all the world. You know what will happen if you betray me again."

I wish he were dead. God, I wish he were *dead.*

I'll do what he tells me, but not for him. I'll play his game, because if I don't, Ollie will pay the price. But I swear to fucking God, when the time comes, it will be Carlos who bleeds.

He jerks his chin at me. "Take her. No more bruises, not today." I release a shaky breath. "Leave her on the street, crying for mercy. The American is here. He'll find her. Let him." His face twists in a cruel sneer. "Then leave the rest for me."

The American is here.

He's here.

And he thinks I betrayed them. For the first time in my entire life, I'm tempted to end it all. The crushing weight feels like too much.

"Remember, Renata. If you ever tell them, if I catch even the slightest hint that you've betrayed me, he'll die first. Then you."

No. I will never give up this one life I have to live for anyone.

I'll get away. I'll escape. I'll leave who I am behind and start all over, where no one will ever find me.

Carlos stands, and his men snap to attention. He jerks his chin at the one in front, who comes to stand in front of me.

"On second thought," Carlos says. "A little more blood might do well." He lifts his hand to strike me. I wince and brace for the blow I can't deflect, but it doesn't come. I'm gasping for breath and confused when I hear a loud *thump*. I look to find Carlos standing in front of me, the masked man's hand blocking Carlos from striking me. I notice a small scar on the inside of the man's wrist.

He speaks in rapid Spanish with confidence. He just watched a man die for not hitting me hard enough and had the audacity to block Carlos? "I'm sorry, sir. You should leave her, sir. It will make your story more credible. If she's beaten too badly, they might suspect a setup."

I hold my breath.

With a snarl, he shoves the guard, who topples into me.

"Fine. Get the bitch out of here. We don't have time for any more bullshit." I blink in surprise. One of his men defended me, and he... allowed it? Is there a shred of humanity left in him? Did my plea change him, or is he just wildly inconsistent?

I'll remember the guard with the mark on his wrist.

"Lover boy's not far off. When we get outside, hit her head and knock her out."

Something in me snaps. I'm not a rag doll to be beaten and abused. "No!" Panic sweeps through me. I struggle against the restraints and scream. I kick at the guard and try to get away, but there are too many of them and only one of me. I can't get away, no matter what I do.

They drag me out, blindfolded. I'm crying freely.

A blow strikes the back of my head and the world tilts. The last thing I see is the cold, bleak sky as I slip into darkness.

CHAPTER THREE

Ollie

MY MEN HAVE BEEN on the prowl now for two days, searching high and low for Renata Carerra. There are two things I know for sure: she's not far, and she's betrayed my family.

I've looked in every nook and cranny in Colombia to no avail, but Isabella says she hasn't left Colombia yet, so I keep hunting.

I pace in the living room of my brother Lev and his wife Isabella's Colombian home. They reside in both New York and Colombia, as they shoulder leadership roles as the bridge between the Morales family cartel and the Romanov family's Bratva.

"I can't find her," I tell Isabella, running a hand through my hair. "Maybe she's fled the country."

Every step closer fuels my anger, but beneath it, a darker

need coils tight. No matter what she's done, no matter what she still might do—she's mine.

Isabella, a bit older than Renata and a bit wiser, only smiles and shakes her head. "I have contacts, Ollie, don't forget, and I have it on good authority she's here." She takes a long sip from a glass of water. "Trust me."

Fine, fine. I'll trust her.

Jesus.

"I would know," is all she says. "Keep looking."

I'm about to leave when I finally get the call I've been waiting for. "Sir? We found her. I dropped a pin with her location to your phone."

My heart thunders, warring emotions choking me. Relief. *She's alright.* Rage. *The fucking traitor.*

Where has she been? What has she been up to? *What has she done?*

"Put it on speaker," Isabella says behind me. I give her a sharp look as Lev turns the corner. I'm not in the habit of taking orders from someone I hardly know, especially a woman, but Isabella is the one in charge of the Los Sangre Dorada, and she's borderline insane to boot.

My brother levels his gaze at me, so I tap the speaker button.

"They have her." I swallow. "Is she alright?"

Why do I care? She betrayed my family. I don't look at Isabella and Lev when I ask.

"Not that badly. A little beaten up, but conscious." A

shadow crosses Isabella's face. In the not-so-distant past, the two of them were best friends.

I frown. This isn't adding up. If her brother was alive and had her in his custody, she'd be dead by now.

"I'll be right there."

I disconnect the call and turn to Lev and Isabella. "You were told about Santiago?"

Isabella gives one sharp nod. "Good riddance." Loyalty to the LSD is of paramount importance to Isabella, for good reason.

"Were you debriefed regarding the conversation I had with him before I put a bullet in his skull?" I take my gun out and check that it's loaded. Isabella casts a quick glance down.

"We're not in the Wild West here in Colombia, Ollie. You must be careful. There are very strict gun laws in Colombia. We don't have the connections and immunity you do in the States."

Fuck.

I grumble and tuck it away.

"No," Isabella says. "I have not been debriefed."

I blow out a breath. "They said Carlos isn't dead."

Lev and Isabella share a look before she glances my way again. "Is that so?"

I look at her in surprise. Did she hear me correctly? Carlos Carerra, Colombia's most wanted next to the late Javier Morales, Isabella's brother, was once thought dead.

"You aren't surprised."

She sighs and shakes her head. "Not at all. I half expected as much. First, it was too good to be true that we ended both my brother's reign of terror and Carlos's in one fell swoop. Second, Carlos is too fucking mean to die."

We'll fucking see about that.

"Bring her back, Lev." Isabella's gaze grows cold as ice. "I need to have a...talk...with my former friend. Woman to woman."

Lev eyes her thoughtfully. I nod to them both and head to the car.

I park a block away from where the pin marked their location, conceal my weapon, and march down the street. My anger toward Renata grows with every step I take.

I have to take her back. If what we've been told is true, Carlos will be on the prowl for her. Hell, he might be the reason she's here.

The two men Isabella assigned to me stand in a darkened doorway at the end of the street. There. They've got her. She's here.

I'm going to whip her pretty ass and tie her to my bed to interrogate her. I'm going to use every fucking tool I have to teach her a lesson she won't forget. I'll make her beg for mercy and crave the punishment I'll deliver, so she knows exactly who she belongs to.

I'm taking her home.

Home.

I don't like being here anymore. Everything feels borrowed and tired. I liked traveling for a while, but it's come to the point where I miss my home. I want my own bed again. I want to see the rest of my brothers and my sister. I want to see my mother. Wanderlust can sometimes make me itchy to move, but I want to be home again.

And I want my own damn bodyguards with me.

They see me coming and give me a wide berth, revealing the small, prone body of Renata on the ground several yards in front of me.

My world comes to a screeching halt, and my mind goes blank. All of my anger. My need for vengeance and blood. My frustration with Renata's escape and my need to make her pay. All of it evaporates.

I take one look at her small, crumpled body on the ground in front of me, and one thought erases all others: *mine.*

I snap at the men in Spanish. "How could you fucking leave her on the ground like that?" Jesus. It's cold and dirty. "The next fucking asshole who treats her like trash will dig his own fucking grave. She's *mine* to punish."

One of the men blinks at me in surprise. It takes him a minute to unfreeze. I'm running, my feet pounding on the pavement, when he reaches for her. But when I see him almost touch her, every nerve in my body shrieks.

"No! Leave her. I'll get her."

He looks at me, unsurprisingly shocked at my contradiction. Do I want him to touch her or not? I don't want her on the ground, and I don't want any other man to come anywhere near her. So the next step is obvious.

I fall to my knees in front of her and lift her up. She stirs in my arms and blinks up at me. Even broken, even dirtied and bruised, wearing a tattered top and torn jeans, she's the most beautiful woman I've ever seen. Long, glossy dark hair hangs about her shoulders, her piercing brown eyes haunted and sad. The hollows of her cheek make her look thinner than the last time I saw her.

She needs food, water, and a doctor.

Punishment can wait. Right now, I need to bring her back to life.

I lift her to me and tip my hand under her chin. I tilt her head to the side. Her complexion's darker than Isabella's, but even in the dim light, I can see a bruise along her cheekbone and jawline.

"Who did this to you?" I'll fucking kill them. I run my thumb as lightly as I can along her face, checking for marks, but when she winces, I realize even my light touch is too much for her.

Of course she doesn't reply.

"Your brother? Was it your brother?"

Her eyes flutter closed. "Carlos is dead," she croaks out.

I can't tell yet if she actually believes that.

I push to my feet with her against my chest. "You shouldn't have left," I growl and give her a little shake. "You were safe in The Cove."

Safe with me.

"You think I left?" Her voice is silky and soft, and it makes me want to kiss her.

"Don't lie to me, Renata."

My footsteps thump on the rain-slicked streets as I carry her to the car, purring a few paces away. I pause before I slide her in.

Someone's watching. I can feel their eyes on me.

But when I turn to look, we're alone. The two guards follow at a close distance, weapons drawn. Colombia's conceal and carry rules are strict as fuck, but these two don't care. They hold their Brügger & Thomet MP9 sub-machine guns right out in the open. Maybe I don't miss my men as much as I thought I did.

Thunder cracks overhead, followed immediately by a bright flash of lightning nearby. I bend and put her in the car just as the rain picks up again.

I fold myself into the seat beside her as the taller of the two guards takes the driver's seat. "Get us back to headquarters," I snap. "Isabella's waiting."

We drive at a breakneck speed. I watch her out of the corner of my eye. If she says Carlos is dead, there are only two possibilities: she believes it's so, or she's lying.

If she's lying, we can narrow it down further: she's either on his side or she's afraid.

I'll find out the truth. But first... Isabella.

She sits beside me, her back as straight as an arrow, her gaze fixed ahead of us.

I want all the answers. *Now*.

"Look at me."

When she turns to me, her gaze is sadder than it was the last time I saw her.

"You said you didn't escape. Who took you, then?"

With a shake of her head, she turns away. "You're a fool if you think I can tell you anything, Ollie."

Why does her voice have to sound as soft as velvet? Why does my name on her lips sound like prayer and heartache?

I swallow hard and grit my teeth. "I saw the footage. I saw how you got away from our guards. No one *took* you."

She looks away.

"Are you hurt anywhere else?"

For the first time, a hint of a smile ghosts her lips, but it flees as quickly as it comes. "I don't know. Why don't you check for yourself?"

My dick stirs at the innuendo.

I can't trust this woman. She's as sneaky as they come.

But I can play right along with her. I lean forward and tuck a piece of hair behind her ear. "Oh, I will. And you won't fucking like it."

She rolls her eyes.

"I want answers, Renata. Who hurt you? You know I'm bringing you to Isabella. She'll demand answers too."

When she doesn't respond, I grip her arm and bring her eyes to look at me. "I asked you a question. Answer me."

I ignore the wince of pain on her face and remind myself who she is. Why we're here. Her sneaking around and conspiring with our enemies put the lives of my entire family at risk. I can't allow that.

"I have enemies, just like you," she says through gritted teeth, squirming to get her arm out of my grip. "You should know that."

"And you ran to them at the first chance, didn't you?"

"They took me. I had no choice."

Fucking little liar. "I saw the videos, Renata. I know what fucking I saw."

We come to a stop outside of the LSD headquarters. Renata shoves her chin in the air and presses her lips together. Are her eyes watering? I look harder, but when she blinks, I think I've just imagined it.

"You're in big fucking trouble for this, woman. You'll pay for your betrayal."

"Betrayal?" she scoffs. "When did I ever give you the impression I was loyal to you? I owe you nothing."

We're wasting time. Her fate, at least for now, lies in the hands of her former best friend, who just happens to be the most ruthless, cutthroat, cunning and loyal woman I've ever met. She'll easily handle the intricacies of this.

Someone opens the door. I step into the rain and drag Renata with me. She keeps up with my long strides, and if she's afraid, she doesn't show it.

Isabella's men stand guard on either side of us, weapons drawn. One of them spits on the ground in front of him.

All of them are loyal to Isabella and Lev, we've seen to that. They believe Renata betrayed them, and for good reason. But none of them will harm a hair on her head.

I keep my face impassive as we march down the brightly lit hallway to the antechamber.

"*Traitor*," one growls in Spanish.

"Fuck you," she snaps back. I don't respond, but my pulse quickens. I grit my teeth.

These are Isabella and Lev's men, not mine. We're associated, but they're not under me.

"Lying whore," another snaps.

My face burns with fury. I clench my free hand and swivel my gaze to the men beside us to see who said that, when she glares at a short, stocky man. "At least I didn't suck Carlos's dick to get to where I fucking am."

He lunges at her, and I shove her behind me. I grab him by the shirt and throw him back. He falls back, screaming in Spanish. He knows better than to throw a fist at *me*.

"What is going on here?" Isabella's sharp voice cuts through the commotion. She stands in the doorway of the office in front of us, her hands on her hips.

"Some of your men don't know how to shut their fucking mouths."

"She's a traitor!" one of them screams.

"*Enough!*" Isabella's voice rings with authority.

Lev materializes beside her, his voice harsh and merciless. "Ollie has brought Renata here for questioning. Her fate lies in the hands of your leader. Anyone who has a problem with that can take it up with *me*." He stabs a finger in his chest.

And me.

"Into the office," Lev snaps, jerking his chin at me and Renata.

I yank Renata in front of me, push her through the door, and follow behind her. Isabella gives orders in rapid-fire Spanish, and they all disperse. The door shuts behind us with a loud *bang*.

It smells of whiskey and old wood in here. I'm told it once was her mother's sewing room, and she converted it into an office. Her father's old office has been made into a bathroom. She smiled when she told me and shrugged. "I can be petty like that."

I silently push Renata into a chair and watch her reaction. She stifles the wince. Yeah, she's hurt.

"My friend," Isabella begins in a tone of voice that is anything but friendly, it's downright serpentine. "We have some catching up to do." Isabella Morales Romanova is a force to be reckoned with, utterly, irascibly feminine and as cruel and vindictive as a king cobra. In other words, she's got this.

"Is she hurt?" Isabella asks me.

"Yeah."

Isabella nods and lifts her phone. I expect her to call a medic, but instead she sends a text. "Where is she hurt, Ollie?"

"Not sure yet."

Isabella's eyes cut to mine. "Find out."

Renata's eyes grow wide. I won't strip her in front of my brother. I'd cut his fucking eyes out if he saw her naked, but I can be discreet. I'll have to.

I reach for Renata and draw her onto my lap so she's facing me. The memory of her with me, alone when she was under my watch back in The Cove, floods me. I thought she was on our side and only had to keep her under observation as a matter of protocol. I had no reason to believe she wasn't loyal to us.

I got to know her. It felt sacred and secret, our friendship.

And then she left and ruined everything.

"Ollie," Lev snaps. "We don't have all day."

Renata swallows, and her eyes meet mine. She feels it too.

Good. I hope she knows what she lost. I would have burned the fucking world for her.

"Where are you hurt?" I ask her. "Tell me where it hurts, Renata. And if you fucking lie to me, I'll find every bruise, every mark, and make you confess where each one came from."

She stares at me through gritted teeth. "Go ahead, Romanov. Find out for yourself. Why don't you strip me?"

I narrow my eyes and begin.

First, I run my hands through her hair and press my thumbs to her scalp. Nothing. I run my hands along her shoulders next. Her skin is warm, her lithe, curvy body evident beneath the tattered, form-fitting clothes she wears. I run my hands along the length of her spine, and she winces when I get to her side.

"That hurt?" I ask. She flinches and nods. I press harder, and she cries out. "Right there?"

"Yes, you asshole," she hisses out.

I slap her ass hard. "Behave yourself," I say in a low drawl. "You wouldn't want me to have to punish you in front of my brother and his wife, would you?"

Her narrowed gaze tells me she would *not* like that.

Too bad. I would.

Next, I run my hands down the length of her legs, ignoring the way my dick hardens at the feel of her skin on my palms. With her facing me, I grasp her hips, circling her inner thighs. I note the way her breathing hitches and the way she bites her lip with a scowl as if she's angry at me for turning her on here, in front of her former friend and my brother, when we aren't friends, and she's being inter-rogated.

I stroke my thumbs over her breasts, lean in and whisper in her ear. "Does that hurt? Did they hurt you there?"

She squeezes her thighs on my body as if she wants to squash me to death and doesn't respond. I chuckle and keep on investigating. When I get to her belly, she cries out in pain.

I lift her shirt and grit my teeth when I see a mottled mess of bruises on her abdomen and sides.

"She's fucked up all around here." Looks like someone kicked and punched her.

"Good," Isabella snaps. "That's where you'll hold her while I ask her questions."

"Bella," Renata cries out, her voice shaking. "You think I betrayed you? Why would I do that?"

"I know you did. Don't ask stupid questions," Isabella snaps. "Keep your hold, Ollie."

I hold Renata firmly, feeling the tension in her body as Isabella steps closer, her eyes cold and calculating. Renata's breaths come in sharp gasps, her fear tangible despite her efforts to conceal it. Isabella crouches down to eye level with Renata, anger and sadness etched on her face.

"Why do you think you can lie to us?" She grabs Renata's chin and forces her to look at us. "Tell us the truth now, and maybe we'll consider not making this worse for you."

Renata's eyes dart to mine in a silent plea, but she has no ally there. I'm not immune to the look, though, no matter how hard I try to pretend otherwise. I squeeze her side as a reminder to tell the truth.

"I didn't do anything, Bella," Renata whispers, tears brimming in her eyes. "I was the one who told you everything I knew. Please. You have to believe me."

"Then why did you escape?" Isabella snaps.

"I didn't! I was taken!"

Isabella nods at me. I tighten my grasp and press my fingers into her bruised skin. She gasps, a sheen of sweat breaking out on her face.

"We found the messages, Renata. We know you've been in contact with our enemies."

Renata's face pales, and her eyes widen in surprise. "That's not true! Those messages weren't from me! Someone framed me, Bella."

Isabella and Lev share a look. "We saw the footage," Lev says in a low voice that rings with authority. "We know you escaped and want to know why."

"You have to believe me," she says, shaking her head. Isabella raises her hand as if to slap her. I feel a surge of anger but force it down. Now is not the time to intervene. I can't let a pretty face, and a plaintive plea sway me from the truth.

"Hold her tighter, Ollie," Isabella commands, her voice ice-cold.

"I'll tell you everything I know," Renata says, her voice cracking. "I didn't escape The Cove. I was taken... against my will. I don't know what you saw or heard, but I'm telling you the truth. I promise I am."

"Who took you?"

"Your enemies, obviously," Renata snaps. I apply more pressure to her side, and she cries out. Jesus, I feel like a dick, but I want this over with.

"That's all you're going to tell us? What did you tell them about us?"

"Nothing!"

I press her abdomen now, and she hisses in a breath as a tear rolls down her cheek. I'd rather beat a man to death than make a woman cry. I'm well aware it's a weakness of mine, but that doesn't change the facts.

Isabella leans in, her voice dangerously low. "You expect me to believe that? After all the shit we've been through, Renata. After everything I've done for you. You think you can turn your back on me, and I'll just take your word for it?"

Renata shakes her head and doesn't reply. If she's lying, she's fucking good at it. I look at Lev. He holds my gaze and nods.

"Please," she finally says. "I came to *you* in The Cove. I helped you bring down Javier. You couldn't have done it without me."

Isabella doesn't respond. This is the truth. "They tried to get me to talk. Why do you think I have these bruises? I said nothing, I swear."

Now it's Isabella's turn to look at Lev. He crooks a finger at her, and Isabella walks over to him.

Jesus. I'm glad *someone's* got a grip on her. They have a hushed conversation, half in English and half in Spanish, but I don't catch what they say.

Renata's gaze flicks to mine. "I don't know why you all believe that you can be victims, that you were manipulated and lied to, but I'm the traitor here." Her gaze pleads with me. "You have to believe me."

I lean in, my voice softer than I intend. "There's too much at stake, Renata."

I can't fucking help it. She's breaking my heart.

The safety of everyone I care for and everything Isabella and Lev built hinges on whether or not Renata betrayed us. I look to Isabella.

"Do we have any evidence that we've been compromised?"

"I'll look," Isabella says, taking out her phone.

"Compromised?" Renata says. "What could I have possibly told them that they couldn't find out themselves? Your location? Well known. Your part in the death of Javier? No one's hidden that. What else would they have asked me?"

Isabella crosses her arms, her eyes narrowing. "It's not just about what they could find out on their own, Renata. It's the details, our plans, the timing. Did they ask about our operations?"

"No! They don't care about that."

"Then why are you here? Why didn't we find your body in a ditch somewhere? They let you go."

She cries out loud now, tears streaming down her face. I can't help it. I'm not immune to her tears, not even close. I look away, but her pleas...

"I escaped. My brother *was* alive, I saw him. But his own men turned on him, they killed him. I had my chance. I ran, and I hid. And I knew where you had a watch set up."

I turn and study Renata's face, searching for any sign of

deceit, but deciphering the truth isn't my strong suit. Ironically, it's hers.

She could be telling the truth. She could be lying.

Isabella shakes her head. "Nothing reported here or in The Cove that would indicate anyone's been compromised."

"See?" Renata says, her voice breaking. She lets her chin fall as fresh tears stream down her cheeks. "I am not lying."

Then why isn't she looking in my eyes?

"What if she's telling the truth?" I ask, my voice calm but firm. "We need more than suspicion to make a call like this, Isabella." We need cold, hard facts.

"Would you be saying the same to me if she wasn't a beautiful woman?" When I look at Isabella, there's a twinkle in her eyes, and her lips quirk upward.

Well, no, but I don't know what that has to do with anything. I discreetly give her the middle finger behind Renata's back, which earns me a chuckle from Isabella and a warning glare from Lev. I give him a look that tells him, *Relax, asshole, your wife can hold her own just fine.*

Isabella releases a sigh. "Fine," she concedes after a moment of silence. "We're going to trust you're telling us the truth. But if I find out you lied to us, Renata, you'll beg for death before the end..."

She'd better not be fucking lying.

My voice is a low rumble. "One wrong move, Renata..."

Renata's shoulders slump in relief, but there's still a shadow of fear in her eyes. "Thank you. I promise I won't let you down."

Trust is so damn fragile in our word. One misstep and all that we built can come crashing down around us.

Isabella turns back to us, her gaze steely. "We'll release her, but I have conditions. I want her brought back to The Cove, immediately, where we can keep her from any contact with our enemies and make sure she's safe from any insidious blowback from the men here who believe her to be a traitor."

Renata nods, and I do believe she looks relieved.

Isabella turns back to us, her expression stern. "Oh, and one more thing." I look up at her, so damn ready to get back home.

"Yeah?"

"Tomorrow, you two will be married." Her eyes are as black as obsidian, cold and merciless. "This time, there will be no escape."

CHAPTER FOUR

Renata

"*¡DIOS MÍO!*"

Ollie and I stare at each other. He looks as stunned as I am.

"What?" I manage to eke out. "*Married?*"

"You act as if it isn't the next perfect step," Isabella says with a toss of her head. "You, my friend, need to be watched *very* closely. While there's no evidence of any lying *yet*, we all know our suspicion you and our enemies are playing a long game is valid. We can keep you under watch for a time, but do you really want the alternative—to be kept prisoner here in Colombia?"

I stare at her, disbelieving. My whole world has crashed down around me, and I hardly know who I am anymore. I shake my head.

"But I *will* be a prisoner. A prisoner with a ring and his last name."

"Yes," Isabella says, her voice like steel. "A prisoner to the Romanovs. But isn't that better than being prey to the circling wolves outside this room? And Ollie will keep a much closer eye on you if you're his wife, I'm sure," Isabella says with a smirk. "I ought to know."

Lev winks at her. I stare, still practically frozen in shock. I'm well aware I'm sitting on Ollie's lap. I'm further aware that he's hard as fuck, his dick pressing into my ass. I swallow hard.

"If you tell them anything about me at all, I will murder the man you love in front of you."

Do I still love him?

I look back at Ollie. His bright-green eyes are fixed ahead of me. My heart breaks a little at how devastatingly handsome he is. I half expect the man's a psychopath based on what I've learned about him and seen with my own two eyes, but there's a rugged sexiness about his quiet aloofness that calls to me. He has a calm, commanding presence, fearlessness, and a predator-like grace that call to me.

I've always been attracted to the villains. There's something about knowing I could tame a beast like him... It's like my personal challenge, even as his piercing green eyes see right through me.

If I tell him about my brother, Ollie is dead.

I'm a puppet on a string, and my brother holds the string.

"You want me to marry her," Ollie says, shaking his head.

Lev sighs. "You know you have to be married soon anyway, brother." He does. He's the last single man in the Romanov family and has a sworn duty to marry within the year. At least, that's what I've heard.

"It's the perfect move to solidify the alliance between the Romanovs and the cartel," Isabella continues. "And if Renata is indeed working with Carlos, this will infuriate him beyond all reason and bring him out of hiding."

"It's hard to be in contact with a dead man," I mutter, but I don't know if anyone believes me. *I* don't even believe me.

A part of me's so relieved I can hardly breathe. There's a reason why Carlos believes I'm in love with Ollie.

But I have to protest. "I can't believe you are doing this to me, Bella. You're marry me off like I'm cattle. Are you serious?"

Isabella steps over to me. "Deadly serious. This isn't just about us anymore but the future of the Los Sangre Dorada and the Romanov family. A hundred years from now, we'll be nothing but rotting bones, but our legacy will live on. This marriage will strengthen our position and force Carlos's hand... if he's still here."

Ollie looks between us, scowling. My God, I half convinced myself I still loved him, but the look of utter disdain he gives me makes me think otherwise.

He will never love me.

I will never love him.

Our marriage will be what every other marriage in my family has ever been and ever will be—nothing more than a manipulation tactic.

"And what if Carlos doesn't take the bait?" Ollie asks, his gaze on Isabella.

"He will."

"I told you, he's dead," I snap. "Don't waste your time."

I might as well be invisible.

Ollie's lips thin, and he tightens his grip on me, a silent reminder that I belong to him now, whether I want to or not. *Goddamn,* that hurts. I hiss in a breath, and he loosens his hands as if he didn't really mean to do that, but he doesn't look at me.

"He will," Isabella says with certainty. "He won't be able to bear seeing Renata ruin his reputation with such flair. You'll see."

Oh, they'll see, alright. They'll watch as Carlos murders Ollie, then me, in succession. I shiver and turn away from all of them. This marriage is a death sentence.

My shoulders slump as I process the gravity of all of this. For the first time, Isabella softens. "Just do your part. We'll do the rest, Renata. If what you say is true, that you haven't betrayed us and you're not in league with our enemies... time will prove that to be true." She sighs and swallows hard. "I sincerely hope it is."

She places a reassuring hand on my shoulder, and I meet her steely gaze. "If this is what it takes to prove myself to you all, then I'll do it." I don't have a choice, of course, but at least it makes me feel a bit better.

Ollie shoves me off his lap. "Let's go." His voice is rough when he doesn't look in my eyes.

I was mistaken. If I ever thought I loved this man, I was a fool. How could someone like me ever love a man as cold and heartless as Ollie Romanov?

"Your ride awaits you," Isabella says. "Go. We'll meet when Lev and I return to The Cove for your wedding."

Our wedding... which is *tomorrow*.

As we drive toward the airport, the silence in the car is suffocating. Finally, he turns to me. "Are you hungry?"

"No, those huge servings of humiliation and disbelief have me pretty well satisfied." I roll my eyes and look away.

He grips the steering wheel, his knuckles white. I fold my arms across my chest and wince, remembering my damn bruises. I turn away from him and look out the window, my heart beating faster.

When will Carlos realize I'm marrying Ollie?

What will he do?

I hate the position he's put me in, and I don't know any way out of it. How do I prove myself to Isabella and Ollie without sentencing Ollie to death? It's impossible.

Impossible.

A lump forms in my throat. I swipe at my eyes.

"Are you crying? Are you even serious right now?" He has the nerve to sound affronted.

"*¡Cállate la puta boca!*" I seethe through gritted teeth.

Ollie slaps his hand on my leg and squeezes. "You think I'll let you talk to me that way when you're my wife?"

Damn. I forgot he spoke Spanish, and I just told him to shut the fuck up.

"Oh, that's right, you Romanov men are all *heads of the house* and all that," I say with as much disdain as I can muster. If I didn't hate him right now, I'd have to say I kind of like it. They're so dedicated to their wives, so steadfast and loyal. I've seen the way Mikhail, his older brother, half worships the ground his wife Aria walks on — he's set the precedent for the rest of them.

"Whatever." Very mature, Ollie. Very mature.

"What's your problem, Ollie?" I snap, my frustration boiling over. He doesn't respond immediately, his muscles clenched. I'd guess his jaw is clenched, too, but he's decided to grow a beard again.

Whatever.

When I was back in The Cove, he was my caretaker. Mikhail assigned him to me... to keep watch over me and find out if I was trustworthy. I was the one who came from Colombia as an inside source to Isabella when she sought to overtake the throne from her brother. *I* was the one who put her life on the line for the Romanovs, who should be dead right now and would be if Carlos hadn't gotten so greedy and decided he wanted to use me more than he wanted to kill me.

And this is my reward?

When he finally speaks, his voice is low and dangerous. "You really want to know, do you? Fine. I'll tell you. I don't do *vulnerable*. I don't do *love*, Renata, especially with someone linked to my enemies. I've seen what happens to my brothers when they let their guards down. When they let themselves become weaker by falling in love, and I won't make that same mistake."

I snort. "You think loving someone makes you weak?"

"I don't think it," he snaps. "I know it. I've seen it happen over and over again."

"And weakness is the ultimate failure in your book?"

He gives me a sidelong glance. I can't help it, my heart does a somersault in my chest. I look away.

"Of course it is."

His words hit me in the solar plexus. Why do I feel that bite so deeply? I need food and a good shower and some sleep. I feel like I've been put through the wringer and hung out to dry in the midst of a thunderstorm.

"So what am I to you, then? Just a means to an end?"

"Yes," he says coldly, his eyes a good stare on the road ahead of him. "You're beautiful, I'll give you that. And cunning as fuck. But that doesn't change who you are to me or the purpose of our marriage."

With that, any candle I held for this asshole just went *poof* in the wind.

I won't roll over and take this though. "You're a fucking coward. Hiding behind your walls because you're scared to feel. I know how this works." I turn my head away. "I've done it myself."

"Oh, you have me all figured out, do you?"

Not all, Ollie. Not all.

I don't respond.

"Don't pretend you know me, Renata. All you know is the man who kept you prisoner. That was back when I thought there was a shred of goodness still left in you."

Now that stings.

"I see right through you," I say, talking through a haze of tears, but he doesn't see. "You're terrified of being hurt. Guess what? We're both damaged."

He scoffs. "I'm not afraid."

I stare at him in surprise because, for the first time since I met him, Ollie just lied through his teeth.

"You're lying," I say softly. I can't help myself. My voice trembles slightly. "There's more to this, isn't there?"

His eyes widen slightly before he catches himself. I caught him off guard. "What the hell are you talking about?"

"I can sense it... when people lie to me," I insist, my heart pounding. It's more than sensing—it has to do with body language and the eyes, but it's the easiest, simplest explanation. "You don't want to admit it, but you *do* feel something for me." I pause and rest my hand on his leg. "Don't you?"

His face hardens as if his defenses all just snapped right back into place. That only confirms my suspicions. "You're delusional. Take your hand off of me." We pull to a stop near the runway. "This conversation is over, Renata."

"For now," I say in a singsong voice.

I struck a nerve. The truth is there, *right there,* hanging between us, and if there's anything I'm good at, it's uncovering the truth.

CHAPTER FIVE

Ollie

I HATE THIS. All of it.

Being in such close proximity to Renata Carerra, all five foot, one hundred pounds of dynamite, sitting next to me. She'll be my *wife*. And while I know exactly why my brother and his wife decided this was the best move, I'd rather marry a total fucking stranger than this woman.

Before her betrayal... this would've seemed like the best gift, all neatly tied up in a bow. But now that she can't be trusted, I've just been given the world's worst assignment: Keep a close watch on a woman who gives you a reason to breathe. Make sure she doesn't betray us. Oh, and also, have sex with her, but you'd better not goddamn enjoy it because that will only make you weaker. Deal with her in your bed, in your thoughts, in your fucking dreams, but make sure you don't fall in love with her.

Sure thing, guys. I'm fucking on it.

I take our bags and jerk my chin at the plane. "Go," I snap. The air is fucking tense.

"What did you take with you?" Her voice is a challenge, a test of her will against mine. She wants control, answers, but *I'm* the one that gives orders around here.

"Does it fucking matter? Get on the plane." The sooner we get to The Cove, and the more distance we put between Renata Carerra and her homeland, the better.

"I want to know what they packed," she says, standing on the tarmac with her arms crossed on her chest.

Is she fucking kidding me right now? "And I want you on that plane before I count to three, or I'll drag you on that plane, and you'll be in big trouble."

Yeah. Good one, Ollie.

She narrows her eyes at me. "Just because you're going to be my husband doesn't give you the right to boss me around."

I kick up my foot and dust her ass with it. "Fucking go. And yes, it does."

"You just kicked me!"

"I didn't kick you. I encouraged you to move your ass before I blister it." I'll fucking take her pants down right here if she keeps this up.

The sound of tires screeching on pavement is our only warning. I toss the bags to the side and dive into her, knocking her to the ground just as the sound of gunshots explodes around us. My first thought is to keep her safe, to shield her. If anything fucking happens to her, the world will *burn*.

My men snap into position. Gunshots ring as we scramble for cover.

One, two, three men are on the attack.

I'm gonna guess Carlos got the word.

The first man goes straight for the jugular, his gun aimed in my direction. My shot hits him straight between the eyes. As he falls to the ground, I nail a second. The third is a fighter though. He manages to dive beneath the oncoming fire and lunges straight at Renata. I roll to him and pull the trigger, but someone grabs me from behind, and my shot goes wide.

I try to keep my gaze on Renata, but whoever's got me won't let me go. I elbow their ribcage and hear them scream in frustration, but I can't get out from under them in time.

Renata's scream rents the night air. She's fighting like a rabid cat, scratching and clawing. Finally, I get a grip on the man who's got me. I roll over on him and deck him, and my gun skitters to the side. I hit him again and again, blood spurting onto the ground. His eyes are swollen shut, and his lip is bloodied. I lift his head and slam it onto the concrete.

I quickly look around us. Everyone's down. Renata's bleeding heavily from a slashed cut on her arm. I bend, lift my gun, and shoot the passed-out asshole between the eyes once, twice, three times.

"I think he might be dead," Renata deadpans, her lips pursed. She's holding a hand to her bleeding arm, blood seeping through her fingers.

"You never know. You alright?"

She rolls her eyes. "Got a little paper cut, but I'm otherwise fine. Sorry about that. I suspected someone would attack us, so I wanted to delay. If they attacked when we were hitting the air, we'd never get out of here."

I gawk at her before responding. "You did that shit because you thought someone was coming?"

She frowns. "Yeah. You have a Band-Aid?"

I blink and stare at her arm. "Jesus, woman. Put your hand down." I kneel in front of her and assess her arm. "Are you insane?" My voice is harsher than I intend, but she doesn't flinch. If anything, she stands taller, daring me to do something about it. And fuck, I want to. I want to bend her over my knee and show her just how fragile that defiance is.

"Why?" she asks, looking down.

"Because you referred to this gaping wound as a paper cut and asked for a Band-Aid."

"It's not *that* bad. And can I have a sense of humor, or no?"

I growl in response.

"Please translate that into English. Or Spanish."

"I'll translate that," I say wryly. "My wife is going to learn to behave herself. And if she doesn't, I'll make sure she does."

A smile plays on her lips.

"Hold still. It's not deep, but it needs to be cleaned. We need to get to the plane now."

"Aw, handsome, I'm so glad you're with me. I never would've known what to do next."

I narrow my eyes. "Ahhh, I get it now," I say as I get to my feet and lift her up.

"Get what?" she asks. God, she's a mess, but even now, she's the most beautiful woman I've ever seen.

"You're taunting me. I see right through your little fucking games. You want to push me, see how far you can go. But be careful, Renata. Push too hard, and you'll find out the hard way exactly how far I'm willing to take this."

Her jaw drops open.

"I see where this is going, how you're going to act the brat and defy me, so I turn you over my knee." I nod as we step onto the plane. "Fair, fair. But really, honey, you didn't have to play me. You could've just asked."

I love the way her cheeks flame pink. "I do not! And you will *not*!"

I snort to myself. "Now who's lying? On the plane. We need to clean you up." I don't need any lie-detection skills to read her this time.

With a quick, haunted look around her, her eyes dart every which way before she moves, looking as if she expects an army to attack us before we leave. It makes me uneasy myself, so I take another minute, weapon drawn, to scout the area. But we're clear.

This attack seemed spontaneous.

The sooner we get out of here, the better.

And we won't come back until I personally stare into the lifeless eyes of Carlos Carerra.

"I'm dripping blood everywhere," she says, her voice choked. I can't help it—the sound of her vulnerability undoes the knot in my chest.

"Here," I say, more softly than I intend. I reach for her hand and help her into the seat. I know she's more than capable, but I can't help but want to protect her. What if she *is* telling the truth? What if she is innocent in all of this?

Unfortunately, I'm not the one with built-in lie detector senses.

I get a first aid kit from the flight attendant, who's as unruffled with my request after an attack as he would be if I asked for a bottle of water. It's not the first time my family suffered an attack trying to leave this country, and it won't be the last.

I kneel in front of her and press folded gauze to her arm. The feel of her skin sends a jolt through me. Crimson quickly saturates the pad. I look more closely at the wound and press harder. She hisses in a breath but doesn't move. She's bleeding, in pain, but all I can think about is how close she is, how easy it would be to make her mine.

"Hurts like a motherfucker," I mutter. "Doesn't it?"

"Mmm," she hums.

I signal to the flight attendant, an older gentleman with short gray hair and a trim frame. "Sir?"

"Give me a shot. Anything. Something hard and strong." I hold another square of gauze to the wound while we wait for him.

It takes effort not to look into her eyes, but I feel them burning into me. Even now, with blood seeping through the makeshift bandage, Renata Carerra is the most beautiful woman I've ever known. Her long, dark hair hangs down her shoulders in crazy waves, making her look like a half-wild woman. Her skin, sun-kissed and dark, contrasts sharply with the white gauze.

Her eyes, a deep blend of hazel and brown, are filled with a mixture of pain and determination. I'm not so sure that the pain is from her wound. When she was my prisoner back at The Cove, we spent day and night with each other. I feel as if I knew her, and now I question which Renata is the real one. The witty, self-deprecating, quirky woman who talks with her hands and sings when she showers? Or the sullen, guarded woman in front of me now?

Her full lips, usually curved into a smirk or smile and rarely anything in between, are now pressed into a thin line as she tries to control the pain. My God, even now, she's stunning, and I'd be a liar if I said I was immune to her. No. Renata Carerra is a witch who cast her spell. A wave of her fingers and I'm helpless and must follow.

I swallow and focus on her injury—getting another piece of gauze and replacing the first one, saturated with her blood. "Let me look you over," I murmur, pulling her closer. My eyes travel down the slender column of her neck, her bare collarbone. I want to kiss and lick my way down her body until I get to her perky, full breasts. I want to hold her body against me and show her she's mine.

Her petite frame is deceptively delicate; I know there's a strength and fire within her that rivals any man's. I catch a glimpse of the scar on her right cheek, a reminder of the battles she's faced and survived. A memo to me of who my enemies are and why they will die a slow and painful death. I swallow again. Her vulnerability, coupled with resilience, makes her more attractive to me than ever.

Every inch of her screams of raw, untamed beauty that pulls at me, no matter how hard I fight to resist her. The curve of her waist, the slight rise and fall of her chest as she breathes through the pain—she's magnetic, enchanting, and it's fucking driving me mad.

I'll kill Mikhail and Lev for putting me through this.

The flight attendant returns with a fistful of small glass bottles. I take the first one with a nod of thanks and hand it to her. "Drink." Holding my gaze, she twists the top off, tips her head back, and downs it in one go. I stare at her throat as she swallows and finally comes up for air.

"Another."

I take a second and hand it to her. She quickly downs it and finally sighs with contentment. Wordlessly, she gives me a nod to continue.

"Hold still," I order, opening a bottle of antiseptic and pouring it over her wound. I swear to God, I feel it in my own nerves when she gasps and grits her teeth, but she stays still.

"Good girl. Just like that. We don't want this to get infected. Any pain relievers in that kit?" I ask the attendant.

"Yes, sir." He gives me a flimsy pack of pain relievers. I open it with my teeth and tap them into her hand. She chases them down with a third shot and finally drops her head back.

"Strange how he cut your arm. Why not somewhere more vulnerable?" If I were slashing to really hurt or kill, I'd have gone for the back or neck. "This might need stitches."

She nods. "Fine. You have what you need in that kit?"

I look at her in surprise. Jesus, she's ready for me to stitch her fucking arm *here*? With nothing but whiskey and vodka to numb the pain? These Colombian women are made of goddamn steel.

I shake my head. "No, we'll get you home."

Renata lifts her chin and clenches her jaw.

"You can bring me back to The Cove, but it will never be my home."

That's what she thinks. She's mine now, and soon, she'll be my wife.

Her home is where I am.

"Right," I mutter, taking my seat next to her. I call Isabella and Lev to fill them in.

"Well done," Isabella says. "Are you sure she's alright?"

"Yeah. It was strange, and they left really quickly, so maybe he just wanted us to know he hasn't forgotten us."

"Mmm," Isabella says. "Or something else."

"When we get back, I'll talk with Aria." My oldest brother's wife, Aria, is a world-class hacker and computer whiz. The woman's insanely intelligent and capable of finding people and places invisible to the rest of us mere mortals.

"Good idea. We should step up security back at The Cove too."

"One hundred percent."

"Ollie, one more thing," Lev says as the plane begins to taxi down the runway.

"Yeah?"

"You let us worry about your landing and security when you get back. We'll have a team waiting for you. Before you get back to your house, we'll have you stationed at a safe house."

I shake my head. "No. I want to go home. I've got this."

I watch Isabella and Lev engage in a subdued conversation. The tension is palpable.

Finally, Isabella breaks the silence, her tone decisive. "Mikhail will make the final decision."

Lev nods, his expression resolute. Before I can respond, Isabella turns her attention to me, her gaze sharp and unwavering.

"Ollie, we'll handle security details. Your sole focus right now is handling Renata."

I look over at her. Her eyes are locked onto mine, a silent plea for assurance.

In that moment, the weight of responsibility feels heavier than it's ever been... but I'm more resolved to do *exactly* what I've been commissioned to do.

Handle Renata.

CHAPTER SIX

Renata

ONE THING OLLIE doesn't know about me but will soon learn—I *cannot* hold my liquor. Fortunately, Isabella, the only person who does know, isn't here.

The flight from Colombia to The Cove is a good six hours, and I fully plan on sleeping the entire way. But even though the shots he gave me are thrumming through my veins, the pain relievers haven't kicked in yet, and my arm is fucking *throbbing.*

I won't give him the satisfaction of knowing I'm in pain though.

Or would it even be satisfaction at this point? He looked genuinely *concerned* about me back there, as if this twisted marriage was more than just a strategy, more than just a means to an end. But I know better. This isn't love—it's survival.

Ollie. The name alone cuts like a blade. I have to look away, to force myself to breathe, because if I don't, I'll remember how it felt to trust him. To want him. It's a temptation I can't afford.

A pang hits my heart, and I have to look away to compose myself. There was a time when we'd swiftly become each other's confidants, and I'd give anything to have that back.

I hate that my brother has forced me into a position of looking like a goddamn traitor to the two people I actually care about. I hate that he's turned me into this—an outsider in every world I belong to.

I stifle a sigh. Sometimes, I wish I wasn't so good at detecting truth and lies. This might all be easier if I didn't know he cares about me.

My brother wanted me to know that he's watching. He wants me to remember what I promised, and he wants me to know—one slip up, and Ollie's a dead man.

I close my eyes and fight against the well of fear that threatens to consume me whole. I don't know how I'm going to get out of this.

"How's the pain?" Ollie sits next to me.

I shrug and don't answer. For a minute, I feel as if I do, I'm actually going to cry.

Unlike me, covered in dirt and blood, my hair askew as if I had just walked head-on through a wind tunnel, Ollie looks perfect.

He always looks perfect.

I swear to God, the Romanov men could be models, and it is *not* fair. Gods among mortals. Strong genes in that family which probably has something to do with their status in The Cove. They get everything they want—King Midas with his golden touch. Everywhere they go, women fall all over themselves, trying to get them to look their way. It isn't fair, really. Filthy rich *and* the picture of ancient gods?

Like a creature carved from stone, he's unyielding and untouchable. But I've seen the cracks beneath the surface, the beast lurking in hiding...I want to coax him out of hiding, tame his inner monster.

I shake my head and take a look at my enemy...also known as my soon-to-be-husband.

What the hell is Isabella *thinking*, throwing us together like this?

My God, he's every bit as handsome as I remembered.

His jawline, sharp enough to cut glass, is covered in rough stubble. Those green eyes that see right through every layer I've built to protect my heart. Others say he's cold and merciless, and while I wouldn't deny it—there's more to Ollie Romanov than others think.

I *hate* how my pulse races just by looking at him, a reaction I wish I could control, but I'm only human. His presence fills every room he enters, commanding attention and respect without uttering a word. It's infuriating how effortlessly he exudes power and dominance.

"Are you going to keep staring at me, or do you need more painkillers?" Ollie's emotionless voice breaks through my thoughts, snapping me back to reality.

I scowl at him, trying to mask the involuntary flutter in my chest. "Oh, I'm fine," I say sweetly. "I need nothing more from you, sir. Thank you very much."

"Ah. Good to know you're practicing how to respect your husband."

I give him the middle finger... just to set him straight. His eyes spark at me, and he sobers, leaning closer. "Do that again, Renata, and I'll test my theory about my fiancée and her spanking kink."

I gape at him. "What?"

"You heard me." Oooh, the *nerve*. I want to wipe that self-satisfied, smug look right off his face, to see the man beneath the mask. The man who might actually feel something more than cold, calculating detachment.

I flop back in the seat, and the small interior of the plane swirls in front of me.

"Is that turbulence?"

He snorts and raises an eyebrow, a hint of a smirk playing on his lips. Oh, fuck you, Ollie Romanov. I'm helpless when he smirks.

"No, I think it's the shots. You probably shouldn't mix alcohol and painkillers."

Oh. Right.

Well, fuck.

I hate that he's right. I hate that despite everything, I'm going to have to rely on him, and that makes me even more vulnerable than ever. The thought makes me want to scream and break things.

"I don't trust you, you know," I say. My voice is steady, but when he gives me a stern look, my heart races faster.

"You don't have to." He leans in closer. "It's really very simple, Renata. All you have to do is marry me. Let me fuck you. Take my name and have my babies." He shrugs, as if all of this is so simple—all I have to do is marry him, give him everything, and let him control the rest.

But this is more than a marriage. This is war.

"I'll handle the rest, Renata."

Oh, is that all?

I narrow my eyes at him but don't give the smug prick the satisfaction of a response.

"Fine," I snap. "But don't think for a second I'll let my guard down with you." I whirl a finger in a circular motion around my face. "See this? This is all you'll get from me."

What the actual fuck am I saying? What was in those drinks?

His dark, rich chuckle sends a shiver down my spine, confirming my suspicion that my comeback line was as lame as it sounded to my own ears. "I wouldn't expect anything less."

My head feels as if it's three times the normal size, and the throbbing pain in my arm has begun to fade a little.

"Fine," I say. Then I wonder if I said that out loud. "Did you hear that?"

"Hear what?" he asks, getting that adorably confused look he gets when he's thinking about something, like a curious puppy. For one tiny minute, his guard drops, and he's utterly disarming.

"When I talked to you." I stifle a giggle. "Did I say that out loud?"

Oh, God, here we go. I should not have had those drinks, especially not on an empty stomach.

"What the fuck are you talking about?" For some reason, I find his confusion hilarious. I burst out with another giggle and cover my mouth with my hand.

"Nothing."

"Are you drunk?" He shakes his head.

"Oh, honey," I say on another giggle. "I'm fucking plastered. I can't hold my liquor at *all*."

"Jesus." He stands up, towering over me, and I can't help a feeling of dread and anticipation. This guy is going to be my *husband*, my protector, and my biggest fucking challenge. And somehow, I have to make sure I navigate this new reality without betraying him to Carlos and without losing myself in the process.

This will be impossible.

"Look at me," he snaps.

I open my eyes as wide as I can and stare up at him, my head swaying lazily.

"Mmm?" His face swims in front of me.

"Have you eaten anything?"

I shake my head. "Somewhere between being captured by our enemies and then dragged to the LSD headquarters, questioned, then dragged to this plane and attacked I forget to eat my three square meals." I shrug. "Oopsie."

He rolls his eyes and signals to the flight attendant. "Orange juice, two ice cubes. Something sweet. And a chicken sandwich, no mayo."

I turn my head away when tears prick my eyes. Of course he remembers exactly what I like. It feels like a lifetime ago I was detained for questioning, and he was the one in charge of me... but in reality, it was only a week ago.

The flight attendant hands us our food, and we eat in silence. I watch him discreetly.

I'll kill the man you love.

I have to look away.

What have I done to give an onlooker like my brother the impression that I love Ollie Romanov? I think back to my captivity with him.

The way we talked for endless hours, and I told him all about my childhood. He talked about his trips to various countries as the international consultant for the Romanov Bratva, and I asked questions, intrigued. Ollie is a quiet man to others, but he opened up to me.

My brother hit me where it hurts. He knows I'm vulnerable when it comes to Ollie Romanov. I wish I wasn't so easy to read.

My head feels light, and my arm aches as I finish my sandwich and eye a chocolate chip cookie.

Ollie glances at me, his eyes softening. "Is your arm still bothering you?"

"Only when I use it," I reply, my words slightly slurred. "Which is all the time because it's... one of my most favorite limbs." I glance down at the bandage. "You doctored it up damn well though. How'd you get so good at that?"

He shrugs. "I was the Bratva's medic before Mikhail took over. We all tried out different positions. I wanted to go into medicine when I was a kid." He takes a long sip of a bottle of soda. I watch his Adam's apple bob up and down and swallow hard. He lifts the second half of his sandwich and takes a large bite, chews methodically, and swallows. "I study things and aim to become an expert." He shrugs. "It's sort of my thing."

"I've noticed."

Languages, cultures, traditions and locations—he keeps it all in his head as if cataloged. Once he learns something, it's there to stay.

I wonder if his skill at mastering things translates to people too.

I shove the cookie in my mouth before I say something stupid again.

Ollie leans over, gently reaching for my arm and examining it. "Looks swollen."

I look down. "I doubt human flesh is made to be slashed and bandaged like that. I'm fine."

"Renata." The sober tone of his voice catches my attention. God, I love it when he says my name. The thoughts in my head come to a stop, and my pulse quickens in my veins. "I'm serious," he continues, his brow furrowed in concern.

I swallow hard. My brother was right. I'm madly in love with this man, and it will kill me... if he doesn't first.

I wave my good hand dismissively. "Relax, Ollie, I won't fall apart. I've suffered worse." I lean in closer, whispering loudly. "And I bet when we get back, you'll kiss it and make it better, won't you?"

I lean back and giggle when he growls, then hold my hand up to the flight attendant.

"Another shot, please."

"I think you've had enough." Ollie scowls.

"Not quite yet," I say with a sickly sweet smile. I push my plate away and stare hard at his cookie.

The flight attendant looks back and forth between us, and Ollie gives him a firm shake of his head. He scurries away before I can put his life at risk again.

"You gonna finish that sandwich?" Ollie asks.

If he thinks he's going to boss me into eating more food... I glare at him. "No. I could use another cookie though."

Wordlessly, he leans over me to grab it. That clean, woodsy scent of his tickles my nostrils, and I stifle a groan.

Not fair. *Not fair!*

I watch as he annihilates my sandwich in two huge bites, then eye the cookie still left on his plate. Cookies are my favorite. Wordlessly, he slowly hands it to me. I nearly clap my hands with glee.

It's rich and buttery, and I savor every bite.

"You're like a kid," he says, but there's a softness to his voice, something almost protective...

"Mhm. You got a problem with that?" He's not wrong. Healthy food is all well and good, but give me a cookie, and I'm a happy girl.

He snorts. "I like drunk Renata."

My heart thumps madly. Maybe he doesn't despise me.

I grin at him and twist the top off another shot. "Do you? What do you like about her?"

He watches me, amusement dancing in his eyes, but there's a hint of sadness in them. "She's playful. Uninhibited. And maybe a little vulnerable."

"Is drunk Ollie playful and uninhibited? Or would that require a lobotomy?"

He snorts and shakes his head.

We finish our food, the tension easing as we fall into an almost comfortable silence. Despite everything, this feels somewhat normal again. We found a groove with each other back in The Cove. Maybe... despite everything... we can find it again.

Maybe.

I lean back and close my eyes.

It's safer for me not to love him. If the time comes when Carlos makes good on his promise, it would kill me.

We have to find Carlos. We have to get to him before he gets to us... or neither of us will survive this.

CHAPTER SEVEN

Ollie

I WORK THE WHOLE FLIGHT, catching up on what I missed during my trip down to Colombia, but mostly, I'm trying to ignore the beautiful, captivating, infuriating woman beside me. She snores adorably in her sleep, and there's a little bit of drool in the corner of her mouth. I smirk and take a little video. That could come in handy.

I frown when I rewatch the video. She'll wake up with a throbbing arm and a hangover. I'll have to watch for that. I shouldn't feel bad for her. I can't.

Early morning sunlight peeks through clouds as we land at our small, private airport right outside of The Cove. I scrub a hand across my eyes, grateful to be home but fucking exhausted. While Renata slept most of the six-hour flight home, thanks to the drinks and meds, I haven't slept more than a few hours in days.

Still, I have to stay alert. Moving from one place to the next is always when we're most vulnerable.

She needs her sleep, so I don't wake her until we've landed. I hate being the one who drags her back into the present and back to being in pain.

"Renata." Her head's on my shoulder, her beautiful face so peaceful. I feel like a dick. Maybe I could carry her off the plane and get her to the car without waking her—

"Mmm?" She sits straight up, and her eyes fly open.

Maybe not.

"Why didn't you tell me we were almost here? I like to know these things." It's true—she hates being left out of the loop and surprised. It's partly why her brief captivity before was so maddening to her.

"You needed sleep. How's the arm?"

With a sigh, she looks down as if just remembering what happened. "Still there, I guess. It's fine." She looks ahead when the door opens. "Ride waiting?"

"Yeah. Mikhail said straight to family headquarters." I have to do what my oldest brother and *pakhan* of our Bratva tells me. I want her alone. I want to take her away from everyone, just the two of us, to the moon if I had to. I blow out a breath. "The closer we are to family headquarters, the better."

She grumbles and shifts in her seat. "Alright, I got ya." She looks groggy and confused. "That was fast."

"Time flies when you're fast asleep." I pull up the video on my phone and show her.

"You made me do that! Delete that, Ollie!"

I snort. "Not a chance. This is prime blackmail material."

She tries to look annoyed but gets this little look where her lips twitch, but her face quickly contorts in pain when she holds her arm. "Ugh, my head. My arm. What the *fuck*. Little slash like that shouldn't hurt so much."

"It wasn't a little slash, but we'll have you looked at when we get back."

When we exit, the familiar sight of home brings a sense of relief. While my brothers have settled in nicely here, my job hasn't afforded me that luxury. For years I've been a nomad, moving from place to place.

Until now.

I look at the beautiful woman beside me. We're getting married. Does that mean I'll actually get a chance to put down roots?

"Is that your driver?" she asks, pointing ahead to the car that's waiting for us. I stifle a yawn. God, I'm fucking exhausted.

I shade my eyes from the sun and squint. "I think so."

I take our bags and head out while the flight crew begins their cleanup. I'm eager to get her back to my house.

"Where did they decide we're going?" she asks.

"Family headquarters."

Renata nods but doesn't offer much. She's focused on the driver. I can't see him from here, but everything looks legit. That's our car. He's standing in front of us, as is protocol.

I take our bags, and this time, she doesn't argue with me about it.

Good. I just want to get home. Back to safety, where I can drill down security and make sure she's safe again.

"Who's back at the house now?"

"My mother and sister, I know that, but I'm not so sure about my other brothers. We'll have a meeting this morning and decide what's next."

The driver approaches. "Welcome home, sir. Ma'am. May I help you with your bags?"

"I've got them," I tell him. He should know that.

Renata shakes her head and gives the driver a curious look, not meeting my eyes. "Were you already given the location of the safe house by security?"

We aren't going to—

"Yes, all set, ma'am. Your location is secure."

Renata smiles sweetly. "Perfect." She turns to face me and beckons for me to come closer. Her sweet, warm breath on my cheek, she whispers, "He's not your driver."

I whisper in her ear, "No shit. I'm going to kiss you like we're in love, then pull my gun. You dive for cover. Do not fuck around."

She nods.

I kiss her cheek, her soft, sweet skin to my lips like honeyed butter.

I want her.

I want all of her. It's like the first hit of an addict. One taste, one touch of Renata Carerra, and I need more.

With reluctance, I pull away, my weapon drawn.

The driver takes one look at me and dives into the driver's seat. I pull the trigger.

Glass shatters as he peels away. Adrenaline courses through my veins as I toss Renata my phone. "Call Mikhail, get eyes on him!" I shout as I chase after the vehicle. I shoot again and again, hitting one tire, but the exit is so close, he turns sharply, and all I see behind him is a cloud of dust.

"Mikhail?" Renata's eyes are wide beside me.

"Who are you, and where the fuck is my brother?" Mikhail thunders.

"I'm here," I shout so he can hear me. "I had Renata call you. Our driver was replaced by someone and he tried to kill us. I tried to get him, but he got away. We need eyes on him."

"Aria, did you get that?" Mikhail asks his wife. With Aria's skills, she can find anyone, anywhere, anytime.

"On it. We've got a drone on Seventh, and I can tap into the security cams on the interstate in one... two... *Come to Mama, baby.*"

I look wildly around the parking lot. I need to get her the fuck out of here immediately.

"We need a car."

"Viktor's ten minutes out. Keep her covered until then, Ollie."

Renata frowns. "Wish I had a gun too."

"There's no fucking way I'd give you a gun."

"Well, what the hell am I supposed to do? Stand around and look pretty?" She looks down at herself in disgust. "As if I even could, covered in blood, my clothes all ripped, my hair like a neglected, abused Barbie doll."

Jesus. Women. They focus on the wrong damn things.

"No," Mikhail snaps on speakerphone. "Do what he fucking tells you. Hang up and get cover. *Now*."

He disconnects the call, and she throws her hands up in disgust. "My God!"

I scan the area.

"There. Over by the hangar. Follow me."

"Yes, *sir*. Whatever you say, *sir*."

Not drunk anymore. Good. She'll feel every smack when I give her the spanking she so obviously deserves.

"Why are you being so miserable?" I ask her, tugging her hand down so she sits on the pavement beside me.

Frowning, she doesn't answer. I didn't expect her to.

She's not usually so difficult. While I'd hardly call Renata Carerra submissive or compliant, she's rarely so exhausting.

She sits beside me cross-legged on the pavement, playing with her hair. Fuck, but it's sexy watching her delicate, graceful fingers sweep the hair off her neck and begin to braid it.

"I don't want to talk, Ollie. You have no idea what I've just been through. Let's stop with the third degree."

I grit my teeth. "You're right; I have no idea what you've been through. Our only goal right now is to stay alive until our ride gets here."

"Why?" she snaps.

"Why stay alive?" I look at her in surprise.

"Jesus, no," she says, shaking her head. "I've got that sorted out. I like being alive." She gives me a sidelong look and swallows hard. "At least most of the time, anyway. I've had my moments."

What does that mean?

I nod, listening, but I'm still hung up on *I've had my moments*. It's a stark reminder that there's so much more about Renata that I don't know, and I want to know it all. I have to.

"I meant, why do we have to wait for a ride? We're sitting ducks here. My brother's not like Javier, you know. I mean he—he wasn't like Javier."

A look of panic flits across her face. I play it off like she didn't just fucking admit he's alive.

"What was your brother's method?"

"Javier was all about strategy and manipulation. He had his tentacles far and wide and thankfully burned all his shit to the ground before he got to power. My brother was wild and reckless." She stammers a bit. "He'd...he'd strike hard without thinking about the consequences, and anyone who's taking over for him would be the same."

"I get your point about us being sitting ducks and all that. I don't want to sit here any longer than you do. But I trust Mikhail with my life and now yours. So I'm not interested in doing anything that will put either of us in danger."

She frowns. God, she's beautiful when she frowns like that.

Correction. She's beautiful no matter what she says or does.

"We're staying here. It's the safest bet."

She wraps her arms around her legs, her eyes darting around the space outside the hangar.

"Is this what my life is going to be like?"

I stand beside her, my weapon drawn. She seems so small sitting beside me. I feel like I tower over her.

"What do you mean?"

She shrugs a slim shoulder and shakes her head. Unruly hair dances over her back and shoulders, and she swallows hard. "It's just... I hate feeling like I'm out of control. Like someone else is managing my life for me, yet that's exactly what happens when you boss me around and tell me what to do."

I can't risk taking my eyes off the view outside the hangar, so I scan again before I crouch down so I'm closer to her. The coast is clear. If we were at a regular airport, we'd be fucked, but luckily for us, we can do this kind of thing here.

I'm going to be married to Renata. It doesn't matter. She'll be mine whether she likes it or not.

"Ollie—"

I look at her. When her eyes meet mine, the guarded wall around my heart cracks. I feel it crumbling. A part of me wants to do everything in my power not just to protect her, not just to make her mine... but to make her fucking *happy*.

Jesus. I'm a goddamn pussy.

"What?" I snap, sharper than I mean to. I look away.

I can tell the moment she shuts down. Her eyes shutter, and her jaw clenches. She looks away as if she's given me the taste of her vulnerability and needs to snatch it back now.

"Forget it." She turns her face completely away from me.

I want to force her to look at me, to tell me what she's really thinking.

"Stop playing fucking games with me, Renata. Tell me what you were going to say."

"It doesn't matter."

Jesus.

"I'm not fucking playing this game." I want to shake her, but my need to get her to pay attention doesn't outweigh my need to protect her. I keep my eyes in front of me, staring so I don't miss a thing.

"Is this what you'll expect me to do? Shut up and do what you tell me?"

I clench my jaw. "When your safety's at risk? Fuck yeah."

"This is gonna be one fun marriage, isn't it?" The spark in her eyes is a warning sign, but I've never been one to heed those.

"What the fuck are you talking about?" A shadow moves to the left in front of me. I cock my gun, but a second later, a pigeon bobs its creepy head and walks along in front of us.

The wind outside the hangar is the only sound as seconds stretch into minutes.

"Nothing about this is easy, Renata. None of it. You know that."

She hugs her legs tighter. "I know that. But you take a difficult situation and only make it harder."

She's not wrong. I've always done that. Not on purpose, I know, but I can't help it. It's who I am.

I remember the first time I came home after Mikhail and Aria's wedding. She was forced into marrying him, and they were enemies at first. She was pregnant by the time I really got to spend any time with her, and Mikhail doted on her like she was made of spun glass. I still remember standing in my mother's dining room, nursing a drink. Mikhail sat at the head of the table, having a heated discussion when Aria walked into the room.

Mikhail's entire focus shifted to her. He held a finger up for Aleks to hold his thought. She walked to him and stood beside him. He rested his hand on the small of her back and inclined his ear to her so he could hear whatever it was she whispered to him.

Something hit my chest with the force of a freight train. Mikhail had changed. He'd met a woman who'd changed him, and he would never be the same.

Later, I talked to him about it. "What happened to you?" I asked. I couldn't keep the bitter tone out of my voice.

Mikhail was my idol, the one I looked up to, and seeing him cave to a woman felt like a form of betrayal. That wasn't what we did. It wasn't how we were taught. It wasn't who we were.

"What do you mean?" he asked.

I shook my head and shoved my hands in my pockets. "She says 'jump', and you say 'how high'. What the fuck, Mikhail?"

I half expected him to deck me or at least shake me down and tell me to mind my mouth or something shitty like that. The old Mikhail would have. Instead, he only half smiled. "One day, you'll see. Until then, telling you won't make much of a difference."

"What do you mean?" I asked. It felt like some shitty "when you're older, you'll understand" speech.

"Mutual respect for your wife isn't a form of weakness. It takes a real man to learn humility and meekness. A good leader—leader of the home or leader of the Bratva or leader of a country—knows that bullying is a form of cowardice, not strength. A true leader learns from everyone. A good man knows he's nothing without the strength of a woman beside him."

I felt frustrated. Angry, even, that he'd lecture me, but I did truly want to know what the hell had changed.

"I'm not talking about bullying," I snapped, still so fucking angry.

"I *am*," he said, steel in his voice reminding me that he was still in charge.

Yeah, I didn't forget that. But I don't know if Renata betrayed us. I do know that her best friend doesn't trust her anymore, and she's orchestrating this so that she doesn't get away from me.

"Did you put an offer in on a house yet?"

My gaze snaps to hers, then back to surveillance.

"A house?" I never told anyone else I was looking for a house. It felt sacred. Special. Something only the two of us knew and talked about.

"Yes," she says softly, not meeting my eyes. She's playing with a strand of her hair, twisting it around her fingers. "The last time we talked, you were looking at houses. You said you were ready to put down roots and thought you might put an offer down." She swallows. "You particularly liked the one with the Brazilian rosewood floors and those quirky little stained-glass windows."

How does she remember those details?

"No," I say, shaking my head. The sound of a car approaching makes us both go silent. My phone beeps with a text. "Got a little distracted with an escaped hostage."

> Mikhail: Ride approaching. Sent cuffs for Renata. Cuff her on the way here

"That's our ride."

"Why not?" she asks, standing. "Why didn't you put an offer in? It's one phone call."

I frown, watching the approaching car. "I don't want to put down roots only to pull them up again, and I wanted to see what my wife thought about moving before I did."

I don't want to talk about me. I don't want to talk about us. I have to cuff her and bring her in.

"Your wife?" she asks sharply, meeting my gaze. The car comes to a stop in front of us.

"Yeah," I mutter. The driver opens the door and hands me a set of cuffs. I don't want to talk about this. "Now come here."

Renata looks puzzled.

I hold her in front of me, her hands on my chest. "You said your brother's watching. I want him to know exactly what's happening next."

"So we are going to a safe house?"

"Fuck a safe house. No. We're going to make your brother come out of hiding. We're going to piss him off and throw down the gauntlet. You game?"

Her eyes spark with excitement, though she can't hide her fear either. "Hell yes, I'm game."

I thread my fingers through her hair and cup the back of her head. Our breaths mingle. The chemistry we had before felt like an old dream, something poignant and meaningful but fading with every breath that I took.

But now... with her so close to me, our wedding on the horizon, and my need to claim her pushing me forward, I lower my mouth to hers and brush her lips with mine.

I stifle a groan. She tastes as good as I remembered—sweet and addictive, like whiskey on the rocks after a long, hot day.

I lick her tongue, and she lets out a low moan. I slide my hand along her lower back and draw her to me. I want her so close that I don't know where she begins and I end. Her lips are soft and her body pliable as I deepen the kiss, losing myself in the heat of the moment, her body next to mine, our connection undeniable.

I pull away when our driver clears his throat. *Shit.* I lost myself there.

I have to stay alert.

She's pressed up against me, momentarily disarmed. I snap the cuffs on.

CHAPTER EIGHT

Renata

"YOU ASSHOLE!" The fucking nerve of him to kiss the hell out of me then sneakily put those damn handcuffs on me. "Why?"

"Mikhail told me to."

"Mikhail told me to," I mock, even though I'm well aware of how important it is that he does what Mikhail tells him to.

"Maybe I like the way you look handcuffed," he says with a casual shrug as he fastens my seat belt like I'm a child. The glint in his eyes makes my heart leap into my throat. I swallow hard.

"That's your grand plan? Take me back to your family home, with your mother right down the hall, and tie me to your bed?" I wrinkle my nose, pretending my cheeks aren't flaming hot. "Is that what you do with all the girls you bring home to Mama?"

"No, baby," he says with another characteristic smirk. "Only you."

I want to hate him. I want to separate us, at least superficially, with a wall between us so that I don't ever have to worry about him hurting my heart. I started falling for him —I know I did, but I can't give my brother any more fodder.

I turn away and stare out the window, looking for any evidence at all that we're being followed. I can't see any.

But I know they're there.

My arm burns from my injury. I'm tired. My eyes feel scratchy, and my mouth is dry from dehydration. I'm a mess. But that doesn't stop my heart from soaring when I see the Romanov family home looming in front of us, as bright as a brilliant daisy underneath beaming rays of sunlight.

For one small moment, I felt like I belonged, that I was wanted and needed. I felt something like love.

The thick walls, heavily reinforced with steel, weapons, and a convoy of alpha males, make me feel more secure than I've felt in a long time.

My brother is brutal and ruthless, but he's only one person. Only one.

"Ollie," I say tentatively as the car comes to a stop.

"Yeah?"

"Do I have to talk to everyone now? I don't want to see any of them, especially since we're getting married."

He looks out the window and gives me a curt nod. "I'll get out first and make sure we have privacy."

I feel strangely emotional as I watch him exit the car and walk straight toward the front door, his mouth already up to his phone.

I don't know what he's saying, but he looks serious as his lips purse, and he gets into a heated discussion. Finally, after a moment, he heads back my way, opens the door, and unlocks the handcuffs. "Coast is clear. Let's go."

"Can I just get some rest first?" I ask as I walk beside him. I'm on edge, expecting one of his many siblings to come find us or, at the very least, some of his younger nieces or nephews, but thankfully, we're alone as we head inside.

"You can see a doctor first," he says in a tone of voice that brooks no argument. "Before anything else happens. I won't make you socialize or anything like that, but you do have to take your health seriously."

I grumble under my breath. I don't want to see a doctor. I've been to hell and back and want a warm bed and time alone to process what I'm doing next.

"Renata," he growls under his breath.

"What?"

"I'm not going to let you fuck around with your physical health."

"I got a scratch on my arm. It's hardly in need of amputation. Mikhail told you to make sure I see a doctor, and God knows you can't go against anything he tells you to do." I don't know why I'm being so ornery. It isn't like me. Honestly, it isn't.

"Is that Renata?" I hear his sister Polina's voice in the background, but someone quickly hushes her.

"After some rest, you will have to see them," he says. "There's no getting around that, you know."

"I know."

I can't get past the fact that they all think I betrayed them.

I want so badly to be a part of this family. I want them to know they can trust me, but I'm not sure how to reveal the truth about my brother and what I know about the Romanov family. I have to pretend I *am* the enemy, even if it will kill me.

"We're going to the bedroom," he begins. I swallow hard. It feels intimate and dangerous to be alone with him. He continues, undisturbed. "You'll see the doctor. I'll make sure you get food and something to drink, then you can take a shower and rest. But for now, don't fuck around."

It's the smartest thing to do because even though we are on fairly friendly terms at the moment, I have seen firsthand how quickly that can change.

He leads me to the third floor, a place I've never been. The house is huge and often bustling, but the married men have homes of their own now, so it's not as chaotic now as it once had been. Mikhail and Aleksandr, the two oldest brothers, are firmly established and married with children. They own houses not far from here. The third brother, Nikko, married Vera Ivanova, a doctor often stationed overseas in various countries. He travels with her. Viktor and his wife, Lydia, also live nearby, but not quite as close as Mikhail and Aleksandr. Lev and Isabella go back and forth between New York and Colombia.

Ollie is the only one who doesn't live on his own.

Before I was taken back to Colombia, we would talk about this. I wanted to know what his plan was, what he dreamed of, and he wanted to know mine as well. He told me, in great detail, and it meant something to me that I was his confidante.

I want to get back there.

Ollie opens the door to the bedroom and gestures for me to go in. I'm tired and weary and have no more power to resist.

Before I can even sit down, there's a sharp knock on the door. Ollie has his weapon drawn.

"You don't need that here," I tell him, my belly twisting. It's so instinctual for him to draw his gun when something unexpected happens; it's like a hair-trigger reaction.

"I know," he says quietly. "I don't want anybody else to hurt you. Not again."

I look away as something in the wall of my chest breaks a little. He doesn't want me to be hurt. It's not just his instinct but his instinct to protect me. My God.

"Who is it?" he snaps.

He told his family to leave me alone, so I don't expect Mikhail.

"Dr. Agostino," comes the response.

An adult Latina woman with short gray hair enters the room. I've never met her before.

Ollie glares at her. "ID, now," he snaps.

I don't know how he thinks this woman actually got into the family home if she isn't legit. Without batting an eyelash, she flashes her ID at him.

"What happened?" she says sternly, her gaze fixed on me. I look like a wreck... I know that. Her eyes flash back to Ollie. "Did you do this to her?"

His eyes are immediately on her. "Of course I didn't. That's my fiancée. Did you come in here to interrogate me or to check on her?"

A muscle ticks in his jaw as he stands at his full height, at least a head taller than her, but she's unfazed. "I was hired to check. I need to know if you're an immediate threat."

Huh. She's lying. He said nothing to her about Ollie being a threat. That's all on her. Mikhail vouched for her, and she's lying to our faces. I can tell by the shift in eye contact, and her facial expressions betray her. She's good at it; I can say that much. I'm guessing she's concerned about these guys, and for good reason.

"You can leave now, doctor," Ollie snaps as he opens the door.

"Mr. Romanov instructed me to come here," she says. "I am not leaving."

What the fuck? Ollie takes his phone out, places a call, and starts speaking in Russian. I don't understand what he's saying, but a minute later, Mikhail himself steps into the room. "Is there a problem here?" he asks. The tension is so thick in here it's choking me. I lean back on the bed, exhausted. I don't say anything to anybody. They wouldn't believe me if I did.

"She's giving me shit about whether or not I hurt her," Ollie says.

"A legitimate question," Mikhail replies evenly. He doesn't make eye contact with me. "She betrayed us. She's a prisoner. You're marrying her to cure that. Don't forget it."

Ollie locks eyes with the doctor. "Fine. Continue," he says.

"This is what you're concerned about?" she asks, jerking her chin at my bandaged arm. "Who did the bandage?"

"Ollie did," I say, giving her a wary look because I don't think I like her either. "You did a good job," she says without meeting his eyes. She removes the bandage easily and inspects my arm.

Mikhail and Ollie have a hushed conversation, something to do with competency and trust and respect. I'm not sure who they're talking about. Maybe all of us.

"Fine," Ollie says to Mikhail.

The doctor looks over my arm. "There's nothing concerning here," she says quietly. "It looks like it was properly disinfected. You can use this pain-relieving cream and take an oral pain reliever as well if you need to. Is there anything else you need from me?"

"No, you may leave," instructs Mikhail.

I wait until Mikhail leaves us alone, and then it's just me and Ollie. I'm exhausted and so hungry. I feel like I've been to hell and back.

He's going to be my husband, so I might as well pretend that I can trust him, even though I still need some time.

"Ollie?" He brushes a hand through his hair and releases a breath. God, he's stressed as fuck.

"Yeah?"

"She lied to you."

He turns to unpack our bags. His muscles flex with masculine perfection.

God.

I love watching his body move. I lick my lips and swallow.

Focus.

"What are you talking about, Renata?" he asks.

"She said she was hired to check to see if you were a threat. I can tell she was lying."

He turns around fully to look at me and anchors his hands on his hips. "I know. My brother wouldn't do that. Seems the doctor has her own agenda. We'll note that. How do you know somebody's lying?"

"It's a good instinct, an intuition," I tell him. "Sixth sense, you could call it. And if I had to really explain it, it has more to do with expressions. The way people look at you. I just know."

He frowns. "Are you saying she's not a doctor?"

I shake my head. "Her lying was very subtle. She probably is a doctor." I swallow hard, staring at my arm. "It's when she inspected me that she lied. First, she expressed concern about my safety and played it off like that was her job. It wasn't. Second, she lied about my arm. My arm is not okay."

"Fuck," Ollie says. This time, when he runs his hand through his hair, it sticks up on end. "*Jesus*." He shakes his head, disbelieving. "Alright, I'll look into it," he says. "You're safe. Do you believe that she's a threat to you?"

"No, I didn't get that vibe at all." I look away, my voice betraying my emotions. "You're the one who tells other people they're insincere, aren't you? You're the one who thinks everyone else is lying."

Like me.

"The fuck, Renata?" he snaps. "You know that's not true."

He sits on the edge of the bed, his large frame causing it to sink. "You're safe here. I'd bet my life on it. No one's going to hurt you. Take the pain relievers she gave you." I nod, my throat tight. I'm not going to fight him this time. I'm too tired, too weary.

"Then strip. I'm going to run a bath for you, and I'm going to bring you some food. You're going to be my wife, Renata. We might as well pretend that you and I like that idea."

Maybe I do. Maybe I fucking do. Why would he know?

I've never been on this floor before. From here, out the window, I can see houses beyond us, but the Romanov family home and headquarters are firmly established right here in The Cove. I know we're going to get married soon, probably tomorrow. Does it matter? Does anything matter? I feel as if I want to throw everything to the wind and just forget about it.

Exhausted, I head to the bathroom and do what he said. The hot water feels good. I allow myself to sink into the tub and imagine it's washing me clean of everything.

I close my eyes and dip my head back. The hot water on my scalp is soothing. I sink beneath the surface and let it take me.

I could... just end this. I could stay under the water and never come up again. I hold my breath and contemplate what that would look like. A few moments of struggle... the water would fill my lungs, and I'd... sink... never to surface again. And then all of this would be *over*.

Ollie knocks at the door. I ignore him.

I want it all just to go away. It's heavy and painful, and I am so damn tired.

I surface and gasp for air, my lungs expanding.

"Renata?" His tone is sharp. "Are you alright in there?"

"Yeah." I try to sound normal like I wasn't just fully under the water contemplating drowning myself. "What do you want?"

At the sound of his deep voice, I'm suddenly very, very aware of the fact that I'm naked, and he's standing just on the other side of that door. That I'm here. Still breathing.

Still fucking breathing.

"You hungry?"

I swallow. "Yeah. Starving."

"Finish up. Get dressed. I'll get you something to eat for now, but later you'll eat with my family."

When I don't answer, the door flies open. I gasp and sink into the water.

Not as far as I went before.

He stands in the doorway, all alpha male perfection, and I'm vividly aware of the contrast in power between us.

I swallow... hard.

"Go ahead, cover yourself up with water. It doesn't make any difference. I'm going to see you naked whenever or wherever I want." His eyes narrow on me. "Did you hear me?"

I nod. "Yeah."

When he gives me a sharp look, I decide it's time to push boundaries a little bit. "Yes, *sir*. That better?"

"Yeah, Renata." He pushes off the wall and heads my way. "Much better. I like it when you obey me. I like it when you submit." He rubs his thumb across the apple of my cheek and down to my lips. "I like it." Then I bite his thumb, and his eyes flare with temper and excitement.

"To think. You're going to be my wife. Who would have expected?"

I turn away. My eyes feel so heavy, and I know it's just exhaustion, but also the weight of carrying what I have for so long. All of it. When I close my eyes, I see my brother's face, and Ollie's—one threatening me with death, the other with life.

The back-and-forth roller coaster of my emotions between the two men is killing me. I'm halfway between waking and sleeping when the smell of fresh food wakes me. The world could be falling down around me, but when I'm hungry, I know only one master. I blink, surprised to find I'm still in the tub.

Ollie sits beside me. Watching.

"Were you making sure I didn't drown?"

"Someone had to."

He did.

"Get out of the tub," he says in a soft tone that disarms me all over again. Heat thrums through me at the low sound of his voice, the primal need and want he isn't even trying to mask.

I step out. Water cascades down my body in rivulets, and Ollie doesn't miss a thing. My nipples pebble under his hard glare. I shiver, and this time, it isn't just fear.

He holds a thick, plush white towel like we're at a hotel, and he's here to serve me. I swallow and lick my lips.

I know better.

"You're the last brother to get married," I say, my voice husky. "Aren't you?"

He's going to want children soon, very soon. It's how the Romanovs operate. My brother is going to get in touch and demand I tell him everything I know. I'll need to have something to give him, but I'm not sure what. "I do wish that you would—" I turn around to face him and stifle a gasp when he's suddenly right in my space, his green eyes burning into me. The towel falls to the floor, forgotten.

Unnecessary.

He grabs my wrists and pins them above my head, backing me up until my back hits the bathroom door. My skin burns under the heat of his gaze.

"No one is watching us in here," he reminds me.

I smirk at him. "Only if your brother is a much bigger creep than I thought."

His mouth descends on mine, branding me, annihilating me. I melt under the heat, his tongue tangling with mine. I reach for his clothes as he reaches for my naked body. His hand fists in my tangled, wet hair. When he pulls away, he grabs my chin in his big, rough hand and holds my gaze.

"Did you betray us?" he growls.

I want to slap him. I want to claw at his beautiful, heart-breakingly handsome face and make him scream. I want to shake him until he sees the truth.

Instead... my voice breaks. My heart aches. I blink back tears of fury and tell him the truth. "You *know* I didn't."

"Then who took you from here?"

I pinch my lips together. He grabs me by my shoulders and gives me a hard shake. My teeth rattle, but I still manage to glare at him.

"I can't answer that question, and you know it."

He curses in Russian and shakes his head. "I need your body checked. What if you're hiding something on your person?"

"Like in... a body cavity? Oh God. *Ew.*"

Panic slices through me.

"I could have my brother search you, but I don't want anybody near you. Do you understand?" His hand is on my jaw, his grip firm. "You belong to me, Renata. I was the one who went down to Colombia to find you. I was the one who questioned you. I was the one who bled for you." He shakes me again. "Do you understand me?" he repeats.

My eyes widen, and I nod, not knowing what to say. Tears prick my eyes.

"You're going to be my wife soon, Renata. From now on, I expect you to act like it. Am I clear?" Bright-green eyes hold my gaze with his, the tone of his voice implacable.

When I don't answer right away, his huge palm cracks against my naked ass. I scream, choking on my breath as he shakes me again.

He's losing his mind and is going to snap, a man pushed to his absolute limits.

"You'll do what I say. I know who you're dealing with. Everyone else believes your brother is dead. I know better, don't I?"

Shit.

I look at him pleadingly. If there's any chance we are being watched, I can't risk acknowledging this.

"He's dead," I whisper. I blink, and a tear falls down my cheek. We're all dead. Renata Carerra, the little girl who grew up in Colombia under her parents' thumb. Ollie Romanov, the boy who grew up a homeless scrapper on the streets of New York before the Romanovs took him in. Carlos, the brother who once loved me.

He kisses down the side of my jaw, down to my neck, and bites my shoulder. A moan escapes my lips, and heat blooms between my legs.

"I believe that you were taken against your will," he whispers in my ear. "But I don't know why you're back here and not dead. I don't know what his endgame is, but I know this—anyone who comes near you has to go through *me* first."

I nod and swallow. "Good girl," he whispers in my ear. "You're going to be punished for disobeying me... for everything." He spins me around to face the door and plants both hands flat on the surface. This is a large, spacious room, but there's not enough air in here, no matter how hard I breathe.

It's too much. I shiver against the door. My fierce determination to survive has protected me in a world that constantly threatened my safety, and I am haunted by feelings of guilt for what I've done. But if I'm a survivor, I will survive again. I will not let Ollie Romanov take all that I am, and I will not let the fear of what my brother will do hold me back. Just minutes ago, I considered ending it all. There's a certain freedom in staring death in the face and not giving a fuck about it.

I have to protect myself. I have to find my brother. I have to make sure that I'm not destroyed in the process. So I tilt my head to the side and catch Ollie's gaze over my shoulder.

My voice is shaky. I don't recognize myself.

"I don't know what you mean. Why don't you clarify it for me?"

Ollie's palm slams against my ass, and heat floods my veins.

Again, he spanks me, and I have to swallow the pulse of unharnessed need that filters through my veins.

Spanking kink? Yes, sir.

He spanks me again, this time plunging thick fingers in my pussy before he slaps my ass again. I can't think straight.

He spins me around and pushes me to my knees.

Oh, hell yes.

I war between fear and elation. My heart pounds so hard it threatens to choke me. I want to please him. I want to have this small measure of control. I want to somehow break whatever walls are between us and show him the truth.

His blazing green eyes meet mine as if fueled by fire, a world of unspoken words hanging in the air between us. He's going to punish me—I know this, and a part of me wants him to. I want to feel his dominance and control. I want him to feel my sincerity, to know how badly I want him to believe me. If I can convince him, if I can get him on my side, then that's all that matters.

Nothing else matters. *Nothing.*

I respond eagerly, my hands trembling as I reach for his belt, unfastening it with swift, deft movements as his fingers rake through my hair and he yanks my head back. Pain skates down my scalp, and my head falls back. I cry out. He takes the belt from my hand and fists the buckle before he shoves my hands away. "Put them behind your back," he orders. He gives me a sharp crack of the belt, the tail end hitting my ass. My heart pounds as I obey, and he reaches for his zipper. I shiver at the sound it makes when he pulls it down.

This is happening.

"I've never done this before," I whisper, hoping he can hear my plea for mercy without making me beg.

I love the satisfied smile that ghosts his lips and the possessive way he holds me even tighter. "I'll teach you," he says quietly, pulling his hot, thick cock out. "And if you don't listen, I'll punish you." He flicks the belt over my ass again to remind me that he can and will.

Jesus. My skin's on fire, my pussy throbbing, and he isn't even touching me.

I've thought about this. Wanted this. The Romanov men are virulent, sensual alpha males, and Ollie is my favorite. The blend of quiet and stern intrigues me, calls to me, and makes my heart beat so much faster.

I want to be the one who ruffles his perfect composure.

"Open," he says in a coaxing whisper. "Lick the tip and suck." At the first taste of his hot heat on my lips, I stifle a moan that mingles with him.

I close my eyes and lose myself to sensation. I lick and suckle, in tune with the way he responds. If he moans and curses, I do it again. He gives me low commands, and I do everything he says. "Like that. Yes. You're doing great. Jesus fucking Christ, you're a natural."

He groans when I lick his veined length, making my way up to the very tip. I lick and suck, then take him in and bob my head up and down, stroking him with my tongue and mouth. I'm so lost to this, the intimacy and connection, I don't realize it's my own moans mingling with his.

"Take me," he growls with a hard snap of the belt. "Fucking swallow."

His cock pulses, and hot, salty come hits the back of my throat. I swallow and suck, eager to please him, eager to take back control. I love the sound of his moans of pleasure. I love the deep groans that are *all male*. I love knowing that we're connected in this way, that a part of him is infused with *me*.

I love all of this. My salty tears mingle with the taste of him on my lips.

His heavy hand comes to rest on my head as he pulls out.

"Good girl," he whispers softly, stroking my cheek. "Good girl, Renata. You did exactly what I told you."

Heat flares across my chest. I love it when he praises me. I feel like we've crossed a small bridge, but there's a yawning cavern we still have to cross, yet we've moved forward.

I did that. I made him groan. I earned his praise.

I did that.

The belt falls to the floor, the metal buckle clanging, as he lifts me in his strong, powerful arms. My legs wrap around him, and his cock, still hard, presses into me.

"Come here," he says softly. My head falls to his shoulder. He holds me and walks me back to the room, laying me on the bed. "My good girl. That's my good girl. Jesus, Renata. I'm sorry," he whispers.

I blink up at him. He believes me. There's not a deceptive bone in my body. I'm resilient and fierce, but a liar? Never. I can't. I won't.

It's partly why I hate that my brother has put me in this position to begin with.

"Come here," he repeats, pulling me to him as if he wants us to be fused together. He holds me and kisses the top of my head. "Spread your legs," he says in a ragged whisper.

I'm throbbing with need, and we both know it's so, so much more than just sex.

I obey him, spread my legs, and he shoves his thick fingers into my pussy. No preamble, no warning, he plunges into my wet core and groans. "You're fucking soaked. You got off on that, didn't you?"

I nod and moan when he thrusts again.

"*Khristos*, woman." He flicks his thumb over my throbbing clit. My hips buck, my pelvis rises, and I stifle the need to cry out.

"I want to eat you out. I want to taste your pussy," he whispers.

I shake my head. "I want that, too, but right now—"

"You want me to hold you," he finishes, his tone surprised.

I nod. There's a knot in my throat, and my vision's blurred. I hate how easily he undoes me, but Ollie Romanov is going to be my husband.

For better or for worse.

"Let me taste your nipples," he says. "Move this way, Renata."

My vision grows hazy with the first stroke of his tongue on

the hardened bud. He circles my nipple and suckles, and a spasm of absolute bliss flashes through me. Oh my *God*.

It seems like he's everywhere at once—his mouth at my nipple, one hand between my legs. It's hot and consuming, and I'm on the cusp of coming when he comes to a sudden stop.

"Beg me. Fucking beg me as if your life depends on it," he commands.

"Please," I whisper. "Fucking hell, Ollie, please—"

He gives me one powerful stroke as he sucks my nipples, then freezes again. I'm right there, right on the edge, about to explode, and he's taking his sweet time.

"Ollie! Jesus, *please*," I sob.

"Are you going to be a good girl?" he asks, his hot breath on my nipple the most divine torture.

"Yes," I promise. "Fucking *yes*!"

"That's it, baby," he says, licking my nipple again. "Come on my hand, Renata. Come, baby."

Another stroke of his tongue to my nipple, perfect pressure to my clit, and I explode into ecstasy. I scream with pleasure, my body writhing next to his, the power of my climax making it impossible to even breathe. He strokes until I come back down, and my panting slows. Another stroke and it's nearly painful.

"Okay," I whisper. "Please..."

He gives me another stroke. I'm so sensitive my hips buck.

"Remember who owns you, Renata," he whispers darkly with another stroke on my too-sensitive clit.

"Ollie!"

He strokes again and again, and I can't take it anymore. It's too much, and I'm too sensitive.

"Lean into it. Tell me you'll obey me. Promise me, Renata."

"I will," I say, my voice breaking.

He bends and bites my nipple, and a second wave of pleasure floods me, this one sweeter, more intense, and so powerful my muscles tense beneath him as I scream with pleasure. "I promise," I say weakly.

Ollie bends and slows his stroking. I sigh, and my eyes flutter closed. I'm exhausted. Spent. And for some reason I can't even explain myself... I wouldn't have it any other way.

If only we could stay here. Right here, in this tiny space of safety, cocooned in each other. But I know that's only a dream... only a wistful, wishful dream.

CHAPTER NINE

One month ago...

THE SUNLIGHT FILTERED *through the curtains, casting a warm, golden glow across the room, as if the world was granting us momentary peace. If my past was any indication, it was a peace that wouldn't last but goddamn, I'd enjoy it while I could. It was the fifth day of her captivity, and Mikhail said in two more days, I had to let her go.*

Her best friend Isabella was back in Colombia with Lev, and everything she reported back to us corroborated what Renata had told me thus far: her brother worked alongside Isabella's brother Javier to destroy our Bratva, Javier was dead, and Carlos was as well. Neither woman showed a shred of remorse about their brother's deaths, solidifying what I knew to be true—there was no love lost between them.

Renata sat by the window, her long, thick, dark hair catching the light like strands of chocolate silk. Her fingers danced absentmindedly over her thigh, her serene expression masking the storm I knew raged inside her—the storm I was desperate to calm. How could I, a man who straddled the line between life and death, bring peace to a woman like her? Still, I couldn't help but watch her, mesmerized by how beautiful she was. I held myself as motionless as I could, as if moving too fast or breathing too deeply would break the peace.

Finally, I cleared my throat.

"Renata," I said softly, not wanting to break the spell. But I had a job to do, and we had more to discuss.

She turned to me, her eyes wary, always on guard. "What is it?" she asked, her voice steady and sharp. If she were on her feet, she'd be ready to take a fighting stance. I fucking loved that about her.

I walked over and sat beside her, close enough to feel the warmth of her body and smell the fragrance of vanilla and warmed cinnamon.

"Where do you want to go from here? Have you given it any thought?"

"From here?"

Mikhail had suggested a warmer line of questioning, something friendly to build trust. "Talk about her future, hopes, and dreams," he had said with a sardonic grin. "Let her believe you actually give a shit."

Problem was? I did.

She gave me a small, almost imperceptible shrug. "I haven't given much thought to the future. So far, it's been wildly *unpredictable. I'm more of a live-in-the-moment kind of girl." She swallowed. "I've had to be."*

If that wasn't something I fucking loved about her. I was forced to be a live-in-the-moment kind of guy, and I didn't like it either. It was exhausting, never having a promise of tomorrow. Dreaming of the future was a luxury we couldn't afford.

I reached out and took her hand in mine. I expected her to pull away or, at the very least, recoil, but she did neither. She stared at our hands. "If I were to think about it," she began hesitantly, "I might think about a time when... all the violence and bloodshed is behind us—me," she corrected, looking away from me. Maybe she didn't mean to include the two of us together.

I loved that she did.

"I could just be... normal. Maybe have a little home some-where quiet, away from main roads or noise or... everything. A quiet place to sit. Maybe with a little deck or rocking chair. Somewhere I could just think and not have to answer to anybody. I grew up in the city. I grew up with a lot of money. I don't want that anymore."

"You grew up with a lot of money?"

She corrected herself quickly. "According to my father, earning money was the best thing he could do for anybody, the best thing any of us could do. What bullshit," she said, shaking her head.

"Your mother?"

"I didn't have a mother." She gave me a sad smile. "When I was little, before my father became completely corrupt, he

would tell me the story of how I grew in the garden next to the cabbages."

She paused, thoughtful. "Eventually, I found out the truth, of course, that my mother did have me but died in childbirth. I wondered for a time if my father blamed me for her death, but he never did. My maternal grandmother, though, she was another story."

I'd have to keep that one in mind.

"Do you really think something like... a house, a future, is possible?" she asked, her eyes wistful as if my answer held the key to hope in her future.

"I have to," I said, squeezing her hand gently. "It keeps me going. The thought that one day, I can leave the violence behind and be free from all of this."

She sighed, looking out the window. "I've learned that expecting too much only brings sadness. Dreams have a way of getting crushed."

"I know," I said, my own voice tinged with sadness. "But that doesn't mean we can't hope, or want more, or even plan for it."

She looked at me, her eyes softer but still tinged with caution. Still guarded. I knew then it would take a lot more than mere days for her to trust me. "I want to believe in that too," she said quietly. "But it's hard. It's hard to let myself believe that it could happen."

"I understand," I said, brushing a strand of hair from her face. "But know this, Renata—I'll fight like hell for that future, for us, even when you can't believe in it yourself."

She frowned slightly. "Then how can you make it sound so simple?" she asked, a note of acute accusation in her voice.

I sighed. "I don't know if it has to be that complicated."

Did everything have to be?

For a moment, the walls she had built around herself seemed to crumble, and she leaned into me, resting her head on my shoulder. We sat there in silence, the weight of everything between us, like the hot, humid air of a Colombian summer.

"Yeah," she whispered. "Maybe you're right. I hope you are."

In that moment, I saw a glimpse of the future I longed for. A future where Renata and I could be together, free from the shadows that haunted us. And I vowed to myself that no matter what, no matter who stood in our way, I would make that happen.

I WAKE BESIDE RENATA, moonlight spilling through the curtains. Last night, she gave me a sharp look when it was mentioned we would be sharing the guest room. After what happened between us, it felt natural to me, but for her... I'm not sure. She's still guarded, still wary, and for good reason.

I had expected her to protest, but she didn't. She climbed into bed, put her head on the pillow, and by the time I joined her, she was fast asleep.

Now she stirs and leans toward me, her small foot brushing against my leg and her hand resting on my abs. Her warmth seeps into me, and I hold her there, my hand on the small of her back, savoring the rare moment of peace. She isn't awake yet. When she is, I doubt she'll be this cozy.

Renata is going to be my wife.

I'll wake beside her every day.

If only I could trust her...

You know I didn't, she had said. But talk is cheap, and loyalty is proven.

If she wants to show that she didn't betray us, that what she says is true, and her brother took her to Colombia to threaten her or to instill fear into us, she'll start by marrying me.

I'll watch how she responds to Carlos's retribution.

I'm expecting a swift, merciless response from him if he is indeed alive and as predictable as I suspect.

I'm lost in a world all my own when I realize her eyes are open. Instead of leaping away from me or cowering in fear, she lies quietly beside me.

Maybe she wasn't as immune to what happened between us as she'd like me to think she was.

I take in her caramel-colored cheeks and warm brown eyes, framed with long, thick black lashes and bold, striking brows. Her lips are turned down in a hint of a pout. I want to kiss them, lick them, bite them, and make them part in a scream while I savor the taste of her.

I swallow, hard as fuck already, and reach my hand to brush my thumb along the scar on her right cheek. She flinches away from me, but I don't let her.

My voice is rough and husky in the early morning, tempered with the effort of maintaining control. "Who gave you this scar?"

Always fucking maintain control.

The corner of her lips quirks up in a sad smile. "You have to ask? My brother, of course. Who else?"

I blow out a breath. "Your brother's evil."

She swallows and nods, then says in a little voice, as if trying to convince herself more than me, "He wasn't always that way. There was a time when he was my protector. There was a time when we were allies, Ollie."

She runs her thumb along my lower abdomen, her touch stirring an awareness in me. I can't believe that she'll be mine. I hardly know what to do with myself.

I shake my head. "I don't care that he used to be good to you. What matters is how he treats you now. You know I'll —if he were alive, I'd have to kill him."

Her eyes flash at me in the darkness. "If I didn't get to him first."

When she turns from me, a shadow of pain crosses her face. "Does your arm hurt?"

"Like a son of a bitch," she says. "But that's not it. I just hate what has to happen with my brother."

There are a lot of things that fucking suck about what's happened to both of us, what has to happen still. If it were me, I'd want to shoot myself before I killed one of my brothers, no matter how badly they betrayed me.

I'm glad I don't have to make that decision.

I tuck a stray strand of hair behind her ear.

"What makes you happy, Renata?"

She thinks for a moment before replying, thoughtful as if she's sifting through thoughts and memories to get to something happy. I expect it will take her a while to respond, but she has a ready answer.

"Puppies," she says, her voice lightening. "Farmers' markets, especially if they have food. And I don't just mean vegetables and fruit, but hot food that you can eat, like Mexican street corn, walking tacos and those fried things on sticks. Ocean views. Sleeping in." Her voice lowers, becoming husky and sensual. "Sex."

I smile, my heart warming at her honesty. I will give her all of that, though sex seems like the best place to start.

I roll her gently onto her back, leaning over her. "I don't have puppies, farmers' markets aren't open yet, and we're wide awake. Sex it is, then," I whisper, my lips brushing against hers.

She smiles—a genuine smile that reaches her eyes and pulls me closer. I marvel at how our bodies fit together perfectly, her warmth enveloping me. Her nipples peak, and her eyes go half-lidded with desire. She wasn't lying—her body responds like we were made for each other. She rolls her hips and lifts her face to kiss me. I kiss her softly, savoring every moment, every taste. I wonder if she remembers what I do—those stolen moments together before we were enemies. Back when we were just doing all we'd ever known.

Her hands roam over my shoulders, her touch sending shivers down my spine. When she bends to kiss my jaw, I press myself down on her.

She kisses down my neck, her breathing heavy with each kiss. She arches beneath me, her body responding to my touch. I take my time, wanting this moment to be sweet and perfect, just like her. My movements are slow and deliberate, sensations heightened by the intimacy of the moonlight on us. We're only human, but the first cast of moonlight will turn us into wolves. I know this by now.

I hold my breath as I slide inside her. I exhale when I fill her. Connected. Fused. Finding solace in each other against the chaos of our lives. In this moment, nothing else matters. Just us, our shared breath, the quiet of two people who will become one. She shudders beneath me when I thrust, her hips meeting mine. I savor her moans. I build a rhythm that's slow, wanting to take my time, but my need for her escalates. I thrust harder. She takes me.

I bend down and take her lips with mine as I come inside her. She cries into my mouth. I bite her lip and relish all of it —the taste of her, the way she shudders beneath me, the way my hot seed spills into her, pleasure ricocheting through every inch of me. I feel the echo of her ecstasy thrum through my veins.

I collapse beside her, my fingers trailing languidly through the silken waves of her hair. The warmth of her breath mingles with mine as I cradle the back of her head, guiding her to rest on my shoulder.

It's happening. I can feel it, gravity pulling me closer to her with each heartbeat.

I'm falling for her, just like my brothers did for their wives.

Hell, it's not *happening*. I'm already there. I can't imagine a world without Renata at the absolute center of my universe.

A small part of me wants to hold onto control, to hold onto everything I've painstakingly built. I have to stay in control.

Someone has to protect us.

CHAPTER TEN

Renata

I REALLY SHOULDN'T BE FALLING in love with Ollie Romanov, or, more accurately...falling in love with him all over again.

But I guess, in a certain way, this is probably for the best. Deep down, I always knew it was inevitable.

We're going to be married, so we might as well like each other.

Still, I feel awkward and shy when I wake up next to him. It was different in the middle of the night when moonlight illuminated his features and mine. What happens at midnight doesn't count at daybreak, right? Late night conversations, confidences—all of it looks different when put under the bright lights of the early morning. I'm not sure what else to do except move forward with our plans.

If I don't want to fall in love, we have to stop having sex. Every time he's near me, he finds more cracks in my defenses, slipping through without me even noticing. I can't risk being vulnerable like that.

But how can I stop it? He's going to be *my husband*.

Ollie's sitting up in bed, staring at me with a look on his face I can't quite decipher. I roll over onto my side as if somehow putting a few feet between us will actually save me. I'm no fool though—I know it won't.

"Good morning."

There's a swift knock at the door, followed by a deep, gruff voice. "I have what you ordered, sir."

Ollie sits up in bed, frowning, every single cell of his being on alert. I'm instantly on guard myself.

He leaps out of bed, wearing nothing but a pair of boxers, and marches over to the door. "Stay there," he snaps at me.

My God, he's scared of everything. We're in his family's house, for God's sake.

"Who is it?" he snaps.

I don't recognize the Russian name.

Ollie curses. "I told you not until *after* the wedding," he says. "Take it back."

Take what back?

I hear a little squeak and a bark. I stare, my mouth agape. Was that...? *No.*

What?

Ollie spins around and looks at me, pointing an irate finger in my direction. "I am opening this door. Pull that fucking blanket up over you."

I look down at myself on instinct. I forgot I'm naked.

"Jesus. Calm the hell down, dude." He glares at me, and my butt clenches. Still, I want to see what's on the other side of the door, so I don't give him shit and instead, do exactly what he tells me.

He opens the door, and all of a sudden, a little fluffy white ball comes running into the room and leaps onto the bed. "Off the bed!" he snaps in a growl. But it's too late. I have a wriggling, adorable little ball of fluff licking my face and wagging his tail so hard his entire body is shaking. "Oh my God, you got me a puppy?"

He stands at the foot of the bed, watching us with that brooding scowl of his. "You like him?" There's something softer behind the question, something he's not ready to show.

I can't stop laughing as I try—and fail—to dodge the puppy's barrage of kisses. His wriggling joy reminds me of something soft and pure I didn't know I still had in me.

I feel like I'm going to cry. "Like him? He's perfect. Oh my God, he's awesome." He remembered that I wasn't allowed to have a dog when I was little. I always wanted one. My throat feels tight. Maybe Ollie doesn't hate me, but even if he does... this sweet little angel won't. I bury my face in his tiny, wriggling body.

"He can't stay in the bed, and he has to be trained in a dog obedience school," he rumbles. "And if he has accidents—"

He rises up on his hind legs and licks Ollie's hand. He pauses, mid-rant and frowns.

"He wasn't supposed to come now," he says, glaring at the door. The big guard looks sheepish and shrugs. "I wanted him to be a wedding present." He looks up at the guard, then shakes his head. "Jesus. Get the hell out of here," he snaps, putting himself between me and the guard so he doesn't see my bare shoulder.

"Do you want me to take the puppy away until later, sir?"

"Yes," he snaps at the same time I yell, "No! Take the puppy? What are you gonna do with him?" I snatch him to my chest, and I swear he almost purrs like a cat. I can't help it. I start talking in a little baby voice. "He knows his mama. Don't you, sweetie? The sweetest thing I ever saw. I love you." And he licks at my face as Ollie curses in Russian.

"Leave him for now and get the fuck out of here," he snaps. The door slams shut behind him.

Ha! Score.

"I can't believe you got me a puppy," I say to him. "I thought you hated me."

He blows out a breath and shakes his head, his eyes flickering with something unreadable. "I never hated you. Not once. I was pissed at you when I thought you betrayed us, but now... I'm not so sure about that." He looks away as if he said more than he intended to. There's a weight in his voice, as if those words have been waiting a long time to be spoken.

"I am not kidding, Renata. I don't like dogs. I got it for you so he could protect you." He rolls his eyes. "After he's trained and grows up. I got him as a puppy so we could train him right away. But listen to me. The dog's not sleeping in our bed," he says, trying to sound firm, but there's a slight crack in his voice. "You can bond with him or whatever, just not here. Got it?"

"Where are you going to put him?" I say in a little voice. "He's just a wittle baby."

"He's not a *baby*. He's a dog. A cur. An animal," he says. "Jesus, this was a fucking bad idea."

"Don't you want me to like you? We're going to be married, after all. It wouldn't hurt if we didn't feel like strangers forever. It might be nice if I don't short-sheet the bed or try to stab you in your sleep." I shrug innocently, then look away from him, realizing those threats are on wildly different planets. One suitable for a summer camp, and the other suitable for women like me.

But I'm not the one who kills people. That's his job.

I think briefly of Carlos and swallow hard.

"I don't give a shit if you like me," he says, but when he looks away, my intuition snaps into place. I stifle a smile. Unfortunately for him, I know a lie when I hear one, and he just lied to me.

"Why do you have that self-satisfied smug look on your face?" he says, shaking his head. Wouldn't he like to know?

"Oh, it's nothing," I say, scratching the little baby's ears.

"Jesus," he mutters under his breath and stomps off to the bathroom, mumbling a stream of grumpy Russian.

The puppy turns to me and nestles his sweet head into my arm. He sighs contentedly as if he wants to fall asleep. This little one has two modes—on and off. I nuzzle him and swallow hard, my eyes blurry. I love him already.

I want to tell somebody. A sister, a friend. But I have neither. My heart hurts.

The puppy whimpers at me and laps at my face, but this time, he's licking away tears. I bury my face in his fur and allow myself this momentary pleasure. I have someone to love. Someone to love me.

Why did he get me a dog?

I remember telling him last night... I liked farmers' markets, puppies, ocean views, and sex.

He comes out of the bathroom, already dressed, his hair slicked back and put together. "We have a wedding to plan. Someone's gonna watch this dog. And we're gonna get shit done. Got it?"

"Well, that's easy for you to say. I have nothing to wear."

There's another knock at the door.

This time, he doesn't look surprised.

"That's Isabella. She got in last night, and she's brought clothes for you." My heart stops in my chest. I am naked in Ollie's bed, and I do not want to see my ex-best friend. Plus, I'm pissed at her. To think that she actually believed I would betray her...

I clutch the puppy in a blanket to my chest while Ollie opens the door. It's not just Isabella, but Isabella and, shocker, her husband Lev beside her. They step into the room.

She gives me a long, withering glance. There was a time when she would've winked at me or done some type of conspiratorial whisper so that I would know she knew I had spent the night with Ollie. Now, I feel like she's judging me like I'm some kind of a whore, and it makes me feel sick to my stomach.

"You got her a dog?" Isabella says with a frown to Ollie. I want to shake her. This is the girl I grew up with, who shared secrets and hopes, who taught me how to skip rocks and pick a lock. This was my best friend, closer to me than any sister, the woman I looked to when the chips were down, who came to *me* when she needed help. I was the one who taught her how to read her brother and know he was lying, how to make herself small and hold her breath when she needed to hide.

I've lived two lives; my first was glued to Isabella's side... and now she's acting as if she doesn't even know me.

I don't speak and let her talk to Ollie. It doesn't matter. How could it? I'm nothing to her.

"It's a guard dog," Ollie retorts.

"A guard dog? I can fit in my handbag!" Isabella snaps at him.

Ollie growls, and Lev steps into the room, holding his hands up to her.

"If he wants to get her a guard dog, he can get her a guard dog. Leave it."

"He was supposed to be a wedding present. Don't get any ideas. This dog is going to grow up to be the most vicious dog you've ever met."

"Sure," Isabella says, placing a large bag down by the bed. "I'll believe it when I see it." She hands me the bag of clothes. "Here. These are for you. I don't wear them anymore. They should fit you, but may be a bit... tight," she says, her tone cold and emotionless.

Oh, the bitch, making an inside dig at my weight. I'm curvier than she is, and she can fuck right off. I want to throw the bag of clothes right back at her. I don't want her fucking hand-me-downs, but most of all, I don't want her disdain. I want to shake her. I'm not a betrayer. I'm not who they think I am. But time will prove this to be true. I have to remember that.

When she places her hand on her abdomen and her face contorts in pain, I forget why I'm mad at her. My heart rate spikes. Lev is beside her instantly, his hand on her back, his other hand on her shoulder.

"What's the matter?" Ollie says.

"Just a contraction," Isabella says. "Whatever. It happens sometimes to women."

"You've got months left," he says, frowning.

"Right. It doesn't mean labor; it just happens, alright?"

"Make sure you're properly hydrated," I say to her. "Braxton Hicks can happen because of dehydration, especially this early in your pregnancy. How far along are you, anyway?" Where the hell did that come from? I'm not in the business of giving a shit about her right now.

She spins around on her heel. "I'm not taking advice from you. Get the hell out of bed and get dressed. We have a wedding to plan," she says. "And since when are you some expert on pregnancy and babies?"

"Maybe when you were traveling the world and sweet-talking your way into the good graces of the Romanovs, I was learning midwifery. But you wouldn't know that, would you?" I grit my teeth. "There are a lot of things you don't know about me, Isabella."

It isn't quite fair. I didn't tell Isabella because she had big plans to overthrow her brother. She wanted to make herself the leader of her family's cartel, and she fucking did it.

I might be a little salty because of the way she's treated me. But, I thought out of everyone here... at least she would know I was telling the truth. I never dreamed she'd believe the lies about me. If your best friend doesn't believe that you're telling the truth, how is someone who is your enemy supposed to?

"What she's saying makes sense, Isabella," Lev says. "You know you don't drink enough water when you travel. Let's go get you some, and then I want you to rest."

Isabella glares at me, but there's a look in her eyes I've seen before. She's hurt. I look away from her, not wanting to meet her gaze.

That makes two of us.

When the door shuts behind them, I turn to Ollie. "Do me a favor and don't open that door again until I actually have some clothes on."

The little fur-ball in my lap sniffs and acts as if he's going to pee. Oh God. Ollie swears and grabs at him, but he wriggles out of his grasp and promptly pees on the floor.

I cover my mouth with my hand to stifle a laugh, and he narrows his eyes at me. I bite my cheek, so I don't laugh out loud.

"Jesus," Ollie says, swearing again under his breath in Russian and advancing on him. He looks murderous.

"Leave him alone!" I leap from the bed and put myself between the two of them. "He's only a baby and has to learn!"

He picks me up bodily and plunks me down behind him, and in two huge strides, reaches the puppy. He picks him up in one hand and holds him up to his nose. "*Neyt*. Do not do that again. Let's go. You will learn to go *outside*." He opens the door and orders over his shoulder, "Look through the clothing and lay it all on the bed. I'll tell you what to wear." I open my mouth to respond when the door slams shut behind them.

Why do I fall for the overbearing sort?

I shrug. Maybe he'll make a good father. He can be stern but protective, and—*no*! Oh my God. I can't start thinking like that. Not yet. He could get in a wild rage and drown the little pup, for all I know.

Ollie Romanov is not a good man.

If I were a betting woman, I'd bet good money that this little puppy is going to have him wrapped around his little finger in no time.

If only I could find a way to wrap Ollie around my finger as easily as that puppy will.

With a sigh, I open the bag and rifle through the clothing.

I'll tell you what to wear?

I wonder if this is a battle I should fight. I can't let every breath out of my mouth and every conversation between the two of us be a fight, so I figure now is probably as good a time as any to actually go along with him. If I'm honest... if I liked him, I would think it was kind of hot that he wanted to pick out what I was going to wear.

I take the bag of clothes, grab the end of it, and shake them all onto the bed. "Here you go, boss." I give the door the middle finger.

"What was that?" Ollie asks, opening the door. The look in his eyes makes me suspect he knew I just flipped him off, but there's no way.

"What? Here are the clothes. You said you wanted to pick them out or whatever. Where's the puppy?"

"In good hands. Now go get dressed." He frowns. "And decide what to name that little mutt."

I shut and lock the door behind me, brace myself on the sink, and stare at myself in the mirror. The swelling in my arm has gone down; that's good. One good thing, anyway.

I'll hear from Carlos soon; I know I will. My brother will contact me, especially since I'm getting married. He probably already knows. I wonder how he'll get in touch with me... He doesn't have my cell phone number because somewhere between being hauled to Colombia and dragged back to New York, I lost it.

Not that any of that ever stopped him before.

I sigh.

There are dark circles under my eyes, and my hair is a wild, tangled mess, but other than that, I haven't really changed much. I'm still me and damn proud of that. I've been dragged from one place to another, manhandled and hurt, accused and belittled, but can still hold my head high.

No one will take my identity away from me. None of them will.

I only wish the Romanovs knew the truth. I hate the injustice of it all. I clench my hands into fists, my fingernails biting into my palms.

I have to stay the course.

I have to seek justice and not manage to get me—or, worse, Ollie—killed in the process.

CHAPTER ELEVEN

Ollie

"RENATA DEFENDED ME," Polina snaps, her fingers absently stroking the mutt, but her eyes are fire. "How could you forget that?"

"Really, son," my mother says sadly, the weight of disappointment in her words as she shakes her head. "Polina's right. Renata saved the day."

Why do the women in my life think they can see right through me, like I'm guilty of some unspoken crime for daring to be loyal to my family? My brothers didn't face this shit.

I scrub a hand across my eyes and pinch the bridge of my nose.

"I got her a *puppy*," I mutter in my own defense, like it's an offering that might fix everything.

"To watch her, and half a minute ago, you looked like you were going to throttle the poor wittle thing," Polina croons.

Jesus.

"She defended you?" Viktor asks, lumbering up beside us. My brothers are in and out today while everyone gets ready for the wedding. "How did I miss that?"

"You were too preoccupied with Lydia and whatever newlywed mischief you were up to," Polina says with a smile and eye roll. "Renata was eating dinner with us and overheard two of our guests plotting to blackmail me. They were college friends of mine, apparently somehow associated with one of Mikhail's informants."

"She was amazing," Mom says, her eyes wide and excited. With her sophisticated silver hair pulled into a tight bun, she is the picture of grace and elegance, but she gets a wistful, almost childlike look in her eyes sometimes. "She sees right through lies," Mom says, almost in awe. "It's a rare gift. Like she holds truth itself in her hands. What I wouldn't have given to have *that* talent when you kids were younger."

She'll always know when I'm telling her the truth. I'm not sure how I feel about that. Not that I plan on lying to her, but ignorance isn't always a bad thing.

"Really?" Viktor asks, giving me a smile. "Our girls are so much alike, aren't they?"

I grunt in reply. His wife's 'talent' is that she likes to set things on fire, so I'm not sure I agree they're anything like each other.

"Ollie," my mother says gently. "Don't let the present situation sway you from what you know to be true, what you remember.

Don't you remember? You investigated what she'd overheard, and it aligned with what she said. You were moved by her loyalty and her ability to uncover the truth, weren't you?"

I was. I softened toward her and actually felt something like trust beginning to form.

"And don't forget when that guy Mikhail knew was framed," Polina says. The little pup is fast asleep in her arms. "Do we have a name?" she whispers.

"No," I snap, turning away.

"Mmm," Polina continues. "Our family's reputation was at stake, as we were guilty by association when what's-his-name was framed for theft, but Renata overheard the accusations and told Ollie it was a lie."

"Oooh," my mother says. "It's almost supernatural."

I turn away and exhale. "Yeah. She knew there were discrepancies in the accusations. I hired a private investigator who confirmed what she said."

Mom shakes her head. "And now you all are disbelieving that she was taken against her will. You maintain that despite the fact that she put her *life* on the line for you, simply by virtue of betraying the cartel and her brother, she turned tail and ran back to him?"

"We have video evidence," I say, but even to me, it sounds hollow.

"Of what?" Polina scoffs. "Her running away? You have no idea who threatened her. You have no idea what they made her do. So what if she ran away? That's hardly condemning evidence."

Oh, but it is.

"I didn't come here for relationship advice," I say through clenched teeth. "I need shit for the dog, and I need to make sure the wedding's all set."

Polina sighs and rocks the dog like he's a baby.

Jesus.

"Yeah," she says softly. "Wedding's all set, brother. No worries there. And Auntie Polina will take care of the doggie."

"Thanks," I mutter.

"But as far as relationship advice?" she says with determination. "*That* is free of charge."

With her nose in the air, she turns away.

God.

We need to get her married off sooner rather than later.

"I have to head back to Renata. We'll catch up later."

I don't miss the way both of them laugh behind my back.

They can take this all lightly if they want to.

I don't have that privilege.

There was a reason we were attacked. There was a reason she was in Colombia.

My family will stay safe no matter what.

"So she can tell when people are lying?" Viktor asks, scratching his chin. "Can you get her to question herself?"

I give him a withering look. "What the hell is that supposed to mean?"

Viktor leans in closer, his expression serious. "If she starts doubting her own abilities, it could throw her off balance. Make her more manageable."

"What the fuck are you even talking about, Viktor?" I shake my head, my frustration at everyone and everything boiling over. "This isn't some game. She's not some pawn we can manipulate or fuck around with. She's going to be my *wife*."

My wife.

He shrugs, unaffected. "Desperate times call for desperate measures. We might need to use every advantage we can."

I glare at him. "No."

I don't even know how that would work, but I want no part of it.

"Aw, Ollie's grumpy again," Polina says. "Here, Ollie, hold a sleeping puppy. I promise it's the cure for what ails you."

Christ.

I have the cure for what ails me, and she's upstairs laying clothes out, waiting for my next command.

I turn on my heel and walk away before I lose my cool and say something I regret. As I head back to Renata, the weight of responsibility presses down on me. I have to protect my family, no matter the cost, even if that means making impossible choices that might tear me in two.

CHAPTER TWELVE

Renata

EVERY SECOND THAT passes is like a ticking time bomb. Every heartbeat that passes brings us closer to destruction.

God. Carlos is on the move. It sickens me to know I'm going to hear from him and terrifies me that I haven't yet.

I have to get married. That's the next step forward.

I find some toiletries and quickly wash my face, brush my teeth, and run my fingers through my hair. I hear the door open. When I go to exit the bathroom, Ollie storms in, looking murderous. Fury burns in his eyes like a storm about to break.

I face him head on. "Someone storm the castle? Attack the moat?" I tip my head to the side. "Has your armor rusted?"

"I told you I didn't want the dog on our bed."

I have to admit, there's something about clean, freshly shaved legs and minty breath that perks me up a little bit, so much so that I almost forgot that I have a steely-faced future husband right in front of me. But whatever would've disturbed me quickly evaporates when I see my fluffy little fur-ball. He's wagging his tail and licking Ollie's hand. Before he catches me looking at him, the tension between his brows softens just a bit. We'll soften him yet.

"Well, Polina watched him, and then he fell asleep. Also, we need a name."

He shrugs and mutters with a curl of his lip, "So *dog* isn't original enough?"

"How about... Princeton? I like Princeton."

He wrinkles his nose. "Sounds like he needs a stroller and a diamond collar."

"I can arrange that."

He grunts, turning away from me as he walks to the dresser and rifles through the clothes. "Yeah, somehow, I find that very easy to believe. Polina's got a dog sitter and bought a bunch of shit for him."

Aww.

"It's time to go. You'll wear a dress I pick out and nothing underneath."

My belly flips, but I play it off with a toss of my head. "Oh, how original," I snap, which earns me a hard smack to the ass.

"Haven't gotten to the original part yet, Renata," he says with a growl. "I have another delivery of sorts that's on its way." Turning me to face him, he brushes his fingers over my chin. "Be patient, little Renata."

I should be offended. It should feel demeaning, but I remember the man behind the fury—the one who saw me, not just the danger that presses in on us. I remember how he would occasionally let his guard down and talk to me, person to person.

I remember all of it. Sometimes, I wish that I didn't.

I lift the sleek, sleeveless dress he hands me and step into it. My breasts fill it out well as I smooth it down and slide on a pair of flats. The fabric is forgiving. It lifts and tucks in all the right places. "Nice choice."

I walk back to the bathroom and do a quick braid in my hair, bringing the thick plait to hang over my shoulder. I snap on gold hoops, a gold necklace, and a little bracelet. I'm pretty much feeling like myself already, even though I would really appreciate shopping for myself instead of relying on the charity of someone who hates me.

My stomach growls with hunger.

"We're going out to breakfast. I want to test something," he says.

I'm usually more confident than I feel right now, but my nerves are on edge. I'm not sure if it's because I'm about to have breakfast with a family that thinks I betrayed them or because I'm afraid my brother is going to find me. And if Carlos comes for me? For us? He's chaos and has no mercy.

I release a ragged breath.

We arrive at a restaurant near the beach, and Ollie takes us immediately to the back, where there's a private room behind glass doors. My stomach leaps into my throat when I see that everyone is there before us—Mikhail and Aria, his other brother Aleksandr and his wife Harper, all of the brothers and their wives, and even some of the children. My God. I don't know what I'm going to do next. I must look like a deer caught in headlights because before we enter, Ollie leans in and captures my gaze. "Nothing matters except that you are mine," he tells me. "It doesn't matter what you did, it doesn't matter who you were. You'll be taking vows to me. You'll be my wife. You might think you don't belong, but you do. Right here. With me."

His vote of confidence does, in fact, give me a small measure of relief. I swallow and nod. "Yeah, of course," I tell him. "Are you going to tell me what you're testing?"

"You're a smart girl. What do you think?"

I frown. "Whether or not my brother found me." A sudden realization dawns on me. "Why I have this cut on my arm that's still hurting."

Oh God. What did my brother do?

"Precisely." He leans in and kisses my cheek, but he's only trying to get to my ear so he can whisper to me. "You can keep whatever's in your arm until tomorrow because I want whoever's watching to see everything. Then, on our wedding night, I'm taking that out of there, and we're escaping where nobody knows where we are. Do you understand me?"

Does he think there's a tracker in my arm?

My heart thunders in my chest. How exactly does he plan on taking it out of me? And where exactly is he going to take me?

I nod and swallow hard. "I understand."

"Good," he says with a smirk. "Go to the ladies' room and wait for me there."

What the actual fuck is he planning on doing? "Excuse me?"

He smiles, but the smile doesn't quite reach his eyes. "You heard me, wife. You've been around my family long enough to know what I expect of you, haven't you?" He leans in and captures my gaze with his.

"Is that right, sir?" I ask him, fire in my eyes. He excites me and infuriates me. "Do you do everything your family tells you? Or is that just for me?"

He cups my jaw in his large, warm palm, and his eyes hold mine. "I'm an old-fashioned man, Renata. My wife does what she's told. You know what it means if you don't."

The vision of him overpowering me, my wrists trapped in his, my eyes locked in his, makes my pulse race. I swallow and nod.

"I do."

The tension between us has shifted again, palpable and electric. His protective instincts have always been intense, but now, there's something in his eyes that makes my heart race with fear, excitement, and anticipation. A shiver runs down my spine when his hand comes to my back.

"What are you going to do?" I ask, my voice a whisper.

"Trust me," he replies, his eyes dark with a mix of desire and determination. "Now go."

I nod, my pulse racing as I move toward the bathroom. Closing the door behind me, I stand in front of the mirror, my breath shallow. He enters behind me, carrying something in his hand.

I look down. It's a silk blindfold. "Ollie. *Here?*"

Obviously *here*.

"Turn around," his voice a command that leaves no room for disobedience. My hands trembling, I face the mirror. I watch his reflection as he stretches the silk between his fingers. He steps behind me, his body pressed against mine as he ties it over my eyes. I'm immediately plunged into darkness, acutely aware of his heat behind me, his breath on my cheek. The faint scent of lavender and vanilla fills the air. Somewhere in the distance, I hear laughter and the sound of running water. "Can you see anything?" he asks, his breath in my ear.

"No," I whisper, heightened senses taking over.

"Good girl," he murmurs, his hands sliding down my arms.

My pulse races, my grip on the cold sink the only thing keeping me from falling completely under his control.

"Hold still," he whispers. "Don't you dare disobey me. Not here. Not now."

My thoughts are a tempest.

I'm old-fashioned.

My wife will obey me.

You know what happens.

Good girl.

Little Renata.

I grip the sink as his hands roam over my body. He lifts the hem of my dress, fingers brushing against my thighs. Pleasure surges through me. He takes his time, his touch disarming, tender, and teasing, building me to a fevered pitch.

I remember last night in vivid detail. Ollie Romanov will take control of me in more ways than one.

I hate and love that he does. "You're so beautiful," he whispers in my ear, his voice reverent. "And so strong. You're going to be mine, Renata, and you're never going to lose who you are. Do you understand me?"

No. I don't understand that at all. How the hell is that gonna work? I shake my head, biting my lips as his hands move higher, caressing my hips, my body arching into his fingers as they move over my bare skin. "Stand still," he growls in my ear, his breath hot against my neck.

His family is right outside the door. My brother is somewhere out there, too, his eyes always on me. Anybody could come in here at any time. He wants me to surrender, and he's pushing me to the brink.

Obeying, my body trembles with a mixture of desire and need. When I feel his hands on my hips again, my heart races. My pulse skyrockets when he presses his lips to my shoulder, his kisses slow and deliberate, a stark contrast to the urgency I feel inside. Why is he being so slow and deliberate?

Uuuuggggh.

He's the quiet one, the patient one who's learned to wait for what he wants.

Lucky me.

"Ollie," I moan, my voice shaky.

"Patience," he whispers, his hands moving to the front of me. Slowly, he trails his fingers up my stomach, brushing against my breasts before moving to unbutton me. The fabric falls away, leaving me exposed. He trails his fingers up my stomach, brushing against my breasts before moving the fabric away. "Hold on," he commands. "Did I give you permission to move?"

My breathing hitches as I feel him drop to his knees. What is he...? Oh my God. I grip the sink so tightly I think it's going to snap. His hands trace the curve of my back, his touch reverent and possessive. When he spreads my legs slightly, his fingers graze the sensitive skin of my inner thighs, and a wave of pleasure consumes me. All he's done is touch me. "Oh my God," I gasp. "What are you—"

"No talking," he whispers. "If you disobey me, I'm going to bring you to the edge of release and then leave you right here. Is that what you want? When I get you alone, I'll whip your pussy and bring you to the edge over and over again. Tell me you understand. Say 'yes, sir' or 'no, sir.'"

"Yes, sir," I whisper, my mouth dry. What is he doing to me? I don't call any man "*sir*." What the hell is this? Is he—oh God. When I feel his breath against my most intimate parts, it's tantalizing, so hot I stifle a scream. His tongue flicks out, teasing me. My grip on the sink tightens. He moans as he grips my hips to keep me steady.

I'm overwhelmed by the sensation, the touch and flick of his tongue sending me closer to the edge. Tension coils inside me, and I bite my lip to keep from speaking.

Just when I think I can't take anymore, he pulls away. I whimper at the loss, but his fingers are quick to guide me up, turning me to face him. He removes the blindfold, and I blink in the light, adjusting to it. My eyes meet his. "Did you enjoy that?" he asks, his voice rough with desire.

"Yes," I breathe out. "I thought you said you were going to punish me if I disobeyed. That you were going to leave me there?"

His lips curve into a dark smile. "Naughty girl. Did you think I was going to let you come in the bathroom? With my family right outside that door?"

"But you said—"

"I'm not done with you, Renata. You filthy, beautiful little slut," he says in a low voice that makes my nerves shiver. "Get dressed and get back out there." He straightens himself, adjusts his raging hard-on, and flicks his hair in the mirror. He turns me around and slaps my ass hard. "Now get out there. And the next time I tell you to come to me, you will *obey* me."

He has me in his control, and I've allowed this to happen. God.

I walk back to the table, all my effort poured into maintaining my composure.

I can do this. Oh God. My legs are shaking, and my breathing's ragged.

Isabella looks perfect, *of course,* her hair all neatly done. She's hidden her tiny little baby belly, but she's barely got any. She sits ramrod straight, her hands in her lap, and doesn't meet my eyes. A pang of sadness hits my chest.

"As of this afternoon, I'm looping you into biometric feedback," Aleks says with a grim smile. "Welcome to the family," he says gruffly. "You're one of us."

"Biometric what?" I ask.

Ollie speaks up behind me. "One of Aleksandr's jobs is to check and track the biometric feedback of all of us at all times. It's how we know where everybody is and if they're alright. He's done it forever. Consider it a compliment."

Polina eyes me weirdly, and that hurts my heart because she was always the friendliest to me, at least back when I was here before.

"Do we have eyes on him?" Ollie says, handing me a menu. I don't need anyone to tell me that he's talking about my brother. That much is clear.

"No. Remember how easily he faked his death," Mikhail says. "Even his closest rivals thought he was dead."

"Are we still sure he isn't?" Ollie says.

I bite my lip, unsure of what I can say that won't sign my own death sentence. As soon as my brother finds out I'm getting married to one of them, he'll come after me.

"Now, children," Ekaterina Romanova says with a smile. "We're not talking anymore about Carlos Carerra, the cartel, or anything that doesn't have to do with the wedding," Ollie's mother says. "I've heard you like a good meal, Renata. Do you have any preference on your dress?"

Thank God.

I never thought about things like this. While I love clothes, and I love getting dressed, I just shrug my shoulders. "Well, I... I'm not sure this is an occasion to celebrate," I say. The room goes silent.

Mikhail narrows his eyes at me. "This will be something that unites us, Renata," he says softly. "You should think about that."

Ollie clutches his cup of coffee. The waitress comes over, and I smile sweetly. "I'll take the French toast and a side of bacon," I order. "This one over here might need a little something sweet for his coffee. Just to sweeten it up a tad. Sugar?" I shrug. Ollie shakes his head at me, a warning, I guess. He told me to behave myself, but I don't fucking care.

"I heard you like shopping," Polina says. "I wish we had time." She's trying, but everything is strained here between us.

If I tell them anything about my brother, he will find out, and there will be retribution. I remember his warning to me before I left. It's absolutely killing me to keep the secret from all of them, but I don't know what else I could possibly do.

I barely taste anything, the tension hanging in the air thick with the presence of the Romanov family. Conversations swirl around me, but I stay silent, trying to absorb everything but actually absorbing nothing. When the family begins to discuss wedding plans, I assume it has something to do with me and do my best to pay attention.

"So, Renata," Harper begins, her tone kind but authoritative. Harper is Aleksandr's wife, and I don't know much about her. We didn't interact much before when I was here, as she was always busy. They have children, and I am told that Harper shoots a gun better than any of the men here. Interesting to note. I do know that before she came here, she was an influencer, knowledgeable about hair, makeup, and clothes. Polina once mentioned this to me.

Harper blushes. "It was just something I did, and I don't anymore, but I'll always be interested in things like this. What kind of dress do you have in mind for your wedding?"

I shrug. "A white one, I guess? Something traditional."

"Sleeveless, lace, fitted, what do you think?" Harper asks, her eyes lighting up as she lists different styles. I don't know what she's talking about as she mentions things like *sheath* and *bodycon* and *A-line*.

I glance around the table, feeling the weight of everyone's eyes on me. This isn't me. I love clothes, and I love dressing up, but the thought of choosing a wedding dress for something like this feels surreal. "I'm not sure," I admit. "I love elegant and simple designs."

Ollie clenches his jaw. "We'll talk, Harper." His eyes meet mine. "I'll choose what she wears."

My body tenses. Back in the room, when he chose my clothes, it felt like he actually cared about how I looked. This feels more like a power move, but I'm caught right in the middle of a "pick your battles" type of situation.

I manage a small smile. "Sounds like a good plan."

"Always a classic choice," Harper says. "Maybe we can visit some boutiques later today."

Ollie shakes his head. "Absolutely not."

Everyone's silent at the table for a brief moment, and finally, Harper's husband, Aleksandr, intervenes. He's a tall man with dark eyes and sharp features, the one who is apparently reading my biometrics. Can he tell when I'm pissed off? Turned on? Probably. Ugh.

"Ollie's right. It's way too dangerous. We know there are eyes on you. It's why we're here, isn't it?" Aleksandr smiles, but the smile doesn't reach his eyes. I suppose he's right. I look over my shoulder, half expecting a crazed maniac wielding a gun behind me.

Of course, there's no one actually here. Not where I can see them, anyway. I know they're here. Carlos told me he would be.

Polina chimes in, her eyes still wary. "Do you have any preference on what we eat?"

I perk up slightly at the mention of food. "I love all sorts of foods. Maybe some traditional dishes from Colombia."

"I don't want anything from Colombia," Isabella says. "Nothing that nods to Carlos. I love Colombian food, but right now, I want nothing to do with my homeland." Isabella gives me a strange look, playing with the food on her plate but not actually eating it.

"It's her wedding," Ollie insists, sitting up straighter. Lev growls under his breath, but Ollie is undeterred. "She can decide what she fucking wants."

"Oh yeah?" Isabella asks, her eyes flashing. "What if she—"

"I want dessert," I say suddenly, interrupting. "I like dessert. I want dessert."

"Since when? You're always watching your carbs," Isabella says.

"The old me did," I say with a shrug. "But the new me doesn't mind fattening up."

Ollie's lips curve into a lewd smile. My cheeks flame.

Lydia, Viktor's wife, grins at me. "We had a great selection of cakes at our wedding, and there's a local place that can provide them for us. No time for anything custom, but they have good stock. We can buy them out."

"Done," Ollie says. "Thank you, Lydia."

"I'm more concerned with who's going to be there. I don't care what we eat, or what kind of music we have, or the venue. It matters who is there. It matters who knows that we're getting married."

I know what he's saying is true, but there's only one person who really needs to see that I'm getting married, and he already knows we will.

As the conversation continues, I contribute where I can, but I'm still guarded. Despite the efforts of the women to include me, part of me is constantly glancing around, expecting Carlos to appear out of the woodwork. Ollie hates me. Would he really protect me?

After we split up to handle different tasks, Harper and Polina walk over with their phones, showing me various gowns. I just shrug, and Ollie has a conversation with them. "That one," he says in a low voice. "Can you get that one?"

"We may not be able to get that exact one, but we can get one like it. What do you think?" Polina asks, her eyes sparking.

"I told you I was picking, Polina. Why are you doing this?" Ollie leans in, his voice a rumble. "You know you're next."

His already pale sister blanches. "Don't be an asshole," she whispers. "You know you were always my favorite. Don't do this now."

"Then don't fucking interfere," he snaps. "I told you I'm picking her dress. And she will like it. If you can't handle that, get the hell away from her."

Oh, I will get to this asshole if it's the last thing I do. You can't tell off a man of the Bratva or shake him until his teeth rattle or slap his perfect face. But you can get under his skin and *persuade* him. It's times like this when I wish I'd had a mother growing up, a woman who could've shown me the methods of female persuasion.

"It's beautiful," I interject. "Thank you, Polina."

She narrows her eyes at him, though she's talking to me. "We'll have it here within the hour, and we'll try different sizes. There's no time for adjustments, so we will find one that works."

Ollie turns to talk to Aleksandr, effectively dismissing any dress conversation.

One of the waiters comes up to me, discretely pushing a folded piece of paper into my hand.

I unfold the paper in my palm, distracted by talk of the wedding.

When I open it, I immediately recognize Carlos's handwriting.

> *I'm watching. Don't fuck me over. Remember your place. You think you can run away and marry into that family? I know who you are, and I know where you came from. I'm watching. Don't forget your loyalty.*

My hand shakes as if I'm holding something on fire. I take a breath, trying to steady myself.

"I have to use the restroom," I say, rushing away from the table. But of course, Ollie is glued to my side. He snatches the paper from my hand.

"Of course he's here, the fucking coward. Doesn't have the balls to show his face to me, does he? Who gave this to you?"

"The waiter. He just rushed up to me. He was a younger guy. White, brown hair."

Ollie scans the restaurant and walks straight to the desk. "Which waiter came into this room?" he asks.

"Sir, the wait staff serving your room is all female."

Of course. Someone's in disguise.

To his credit, Ollie doesn't seem very ruffled. He takes me by the hand and walks to the door. As we head back to the car, I can't shake the feeling of dread settling in my stomach, Carlos's threat echoing in my mind. This is far from over. But for now, I have to keep up the façade and pretend that everything is just fine.

When we get to the door, he reaches for me, wraps his fingers around the back of my neck, and squeezes. My heart hammers in my chest as his mouth descends on mine.

His kiss steals my breath—and for that fleeting moment, nothing else matters. Part of me hates that he does this to me. He doesn't love me.

When he pulls away, his eyes flare with something I can't quite identify.

"Let him see that, Renata."

The door shuts behind us.

CHAPTER THIRTEEN

Ollie

OUR HOME BUZZES WITH EXCITEMENT, cameras flashing. Staff walk about quickly, readying everything and everyone for the big event. If this were thirty years ago, we'd have newspaper staff with wide, flashing bulbs and microphones shoved under our noses. Instead, we've got well-dressed influencers with impeccable hair and perfectly white teeth snapping photos and taking selfies on our lawn.

This is what we want. What we need. The more attention we get, the better.

I hate every second of this show, every empty smile and flashing camera.

Renata stands radiant, her lace gown clinging to her every curve, a queen in her own right, commanding the room without a word. Her dark skin contrasts with the stark white of the gown, lending an exotic air to her beauty. A sparkling tiara twinkles under the overhead lighting, like an elegant halo crowning her head. She smiles for the photographers, her makeup perfect thanks to Harper, hiding the exhaustion and stress of the past few days gracefully.

I stand next to her, pride swelling in my chest, even as I grit my teeth. We wanted this wedding to be a public spectacle, to draw the attention of dignitaries and leaders from everywhere. We scrutinized every detail, every move watched, and intentionally put out feelers for everyone, but we did it quickly.

It worked. So many people are here, I can't name them all. Social media is buzzing with the news, again thanks to Harper.

Renata's personal guard, a new guy, leans in close to adjust her train. Heat pulses in my veins.

"Get your fucking hands off of her before I break them. Don't touch her."

He has the audacity to give me a dirty look. Pursing his lips, he mutters something under his breath to Renata. She pales.

"Want to repeat that again in front of me?" I ask him.

"Ollie," she says. "It's nothing. Don't cause a scene. If we didn't have a billion people in front of us with cameras, I'd slap him myself."

I reach for the guard and grab him by the collar. "What the fuck did you just say to her?"

"Ugh, predictable," Renata mumbles under her breath, but her voice trembles and her eyes are wide.

I don't give a shit.

I shake him. "Tell me what you said before I cut your fucking tongue out and make that the *last* thing you ever said."

"I told her to enjoy it while it lasts," he grits out.

"Watch your fucking mouth," I growl, my voice low and dangerous. I shake him. "Show some respect for my wife. You're dismissed as her guard. Report to Mikhail immediately."

I shove him toward the door, take his picture, and text it to Mikhail.

> If he comes near my wife again, I'll kill him

> My wife already, eh?

I text him back and tell him what happened.

My hand's fucking shaking. I hate that I have to behave in front of the cameras.

Renata places a calming hand on my arm. "It's okay, he doesn't matter, Ollie. He's a stupid boy for crying out loud."

"It does matter. You're going to be my wife in minutes. And they will all show you respect."

The guard turns to me.

"She betrayed you. She betrayed all of us," the guard says. I swivel and strike. My fists move before I think, bone meeting bone, the sound of breaking flesh music to my fucking ears. I caught him off guard, so he doesn't get a chance to block my blows. He falls to the ground.

"Get the fuck out of here. If I ever see you again, I'll kill you."

He scrambles to his feet and starts to run away.

"What the hell is going on here?" Mikhail says, coming around the corner.

I fill him in. Mikhail looks at the retreating back of the guard and makes his own call.

"Shake him down at the gate. I need to see him before he goes," he says quietly into the phone. He slides his phone in his pocket and turns to Renata with an apologetic look.

"I'm sorry about that. It won't happen again."

Renata shrugs but can't hide the slight quiver of her jaw. "If I cared what any of you thought about me, I wouldn't be here."

I reach for her and cup her jaw, running my thumb along her cheek, leaving a streak of blood in its wake. *Shit.* I'll need Harper to fix that. It feels oddly symbolic.

"Are you okay?" I ask her.

She stares me in the eyes, not flinching or pulling away. My hand still vibrates from hitting the bastard. She nods and swallows.

It's going to take some time for her to trust me, for her to know not to fear every touch of mine.

"Are you sure? I'm sorry."

"I've always wanted a hot, jacked bad boy to defend my honor," she says with a hint of a smile and dripping sarcasm.

"Really, Ollie, I'm fine. If something like that is going to ruffle me, I don't belong in this family."

She isn't wrong.

Wait. Did she just call me hot? I can't help but give her a self-satisfied smirk.

The ceremony is brief. Utilitarian. I hope for something meaningful when the older orthodox priest Mikhail arranged to marry us talks about love and marriage and commitment, but truthfully... I don't. All I'm doing is scanning the crowd, looking for any sign of disturbance. I half expect Carlos to come marching in with a machine gun, sending people running everywhere. But he doesn't, and they don't. I'm so distracted, but the ceremony marches on.

Until we get to our vows.

"Take this woman..." The priest's voice is warm, reverent. His bushy gray beard reminds me of a painting of Moses I once saw in Italy.

I swallow hard and meet Renata's eyes. "I do," I say softly when the time is right. Her eyes widen as if surprised. I can't help it. I feel it, too, as if the brief vow in the end is more than words but an incantation that stirs something magical.

"Renata," the priest begins. His voice carries the weight of tradition and authority. Our guests fall into a hushed silence. I cup her hands with mine. Her pouty lips part slightly as she draws in a breath.

"Are you coming here of your own free will and accord?" he asks, holding her gaze. What the fuck? Did he add that? I give him a sharp look, and the crowd behind us gives a collective gasp. I can feel Mikhail getting to his feet, and someone racks the slide of their gun. Mom speaks in a hushed, vehement whisper as if that will stop any of my brothers.

But Renata only looks at me, holding my gaze with her chin thrust in the air. "I am," she says.

He continues.

"Do you take this man to be your lawfully wedded husband, to have and to hold, from this day forward, for better or for worse, for richer or for poorer, in sickness and in health until death do you part?"

Her gaze locks onto mine, and in that moment, the world fades. The seconds stretch into what feels like hours as the world grows so small, it's just the two of us in that brief stretch of time.

"I do," she finally says, her voice steady and clear. The words resonate, filling the space between us.

As he continues, binding our vows, I hold her hand, and our eyes lock.

She's mine, now and forever.

The ceremony passes quickly, followed by the festivities I don't fucking care about. I want her alone.

Finally, much later at night, when the guests leave and the grand hall is silent, I take her by the hand and lead her away to the garden. I want to savor my bride, wrapped in white, a vision of beauty and strength. Mine to have. Mine to protect. Mine to hold.

Mine.

Moonlight casts a silver glow over the hedges and blooming flowers.

"It feels almost enchanted here, doesn't it?"

I can't help but smile and shrug a shoulder. "Yeah." I'm not the poetic words kind of guy, but she's right. There's something about the garden after a ceremony, filtered with moonlight and dusk, that feels as if magic is about to happen.

"I half expect a fairy to land on one of the flowers," she whispers.

She shivers when the wind brushes her bare shoulders. I shrug out of my jacket instinctively and wrap it around her arms.

"Nice," she says with a teasing glint in her eyes. "Will you pay for dinner and hold the door open for me too?"

I grunt. "Obviously. Anywhere you want to go now that the wedding's over?" I ask her.

"Wow," she says with a smirk. "Is this just an illusion of choice, or are you actually asking me?"

I give her a sheepish smile and shrug my shoulders. "Illusion."

She laughs out loud. "That's what I thought," she says. "Well, pretending for a moment it's actually a choice, I would like to go somewhere far away from all of this," she says, gesturing to our surroundings. "Somewhere safe though." She looks up at the sky and sighs. "Do you think it will ever end? The constant danger, the fear?"

"Fear?" I repeat. "I'm not afraid. Are you?"

She tips her head to the side and gives me a curious look. "Of course. I feel him everywhere. As if Carlos is lurking in every shadow, ready to strike. Do you mean to tell me you don't feel fear?"

I stifle a growl. "I wish Carlos would jump out from behind something. I'd love a chance to spill his blood on my family's property and wring an apology out of him."

Her eyes widen slightly, but she only swallows and nods.

Accepting me. Accepting *us*. I put my arm around her shoulder and draw her closer.

"I do fear some things, but not Carlos or his posse. Mostly, I just feel anger. I'm counting down the minutes until I get Carlos in front of me. First, I'll make him pay for giving you that scar. Then, beat him to death so you know without a doubt he will never hurt you again. I relish the day I get to feel his pulse leave his body."

That smile plays on her lips, and her eyes look a little guarded. "In truth, Ollie, I know you could. And that kind of terrifies me a little bit."

"It's not about could, Renata, but when." I tighten my arm on her shoulder.

She's quiet for long moments. "Then what do you fear?"

"I was afraid when you were gone. I was afraid I'd never get you back."

She looks away again, her eyes sad. For the first time since I've had her back, I want to make her happy. I don't like seeing sadness in her eyes.

"I don't know how any of this will end," I tell her, but I make her a vow there and then. "I'll burn the world to the ground to protect you. Nothing will stop me from keeping you safe, I promise you that."

She turns to face me, her expression determined. "I'm not going to let my family control my life, Ollie. I won't let my fears control my life. I won't let any of them break me."

I cup her face in my hands, unable to stop myself. My touch is gentle as I hold her gaze. "I know, Renata. But it's my job to protect you now."

"It's our job to protect each other." She smiles sadly, her eyes shining with tears she won't shed. "We have to fight back. And not every method of protection means a fist."

"Yeah." I nod. My mother protected me from my father, even though he outweighed her in power and rank by a landslide.

"I won't live in fear," I whisper. "We have to fight back. And the first way we do that is by making sure you don't have a tracker in you."

Her eyes widen. "Oh, God," she whispers. "You do think it's a tracker."

I nod. "I waited until the wedding, but it's time. I'm getting that fucking thing out of you now, no matter how much it hurts. You're strong. You'll be fine."

"Oh my God," she repeats in a heated whisper. She pulls out from under my arm and claws at her skin. "I was afraid of that, but the thought—of that *in* me--Get it out! I want it out! How do we remove it?"

That's my girl.

Pride tightens my chest. "It will hurt. Flesh repairs quickly. By now, the skin has grown around it."

"It hasn't been that long," she says softly, unable to hide her grimace.

"Long enough. First, I have to contact Aleks. Let's get upstairs."

"Do it," she says, her tone vehement. "I won't be a pawn in his game anymore. Please, Ollie."

I nod and make the call as we walk swiftly to my room. On the landing, he picks up.

"Ollie? You alright?"

"I think Renata has a tracking device in her arm. I want to check, and if my instinct is right, I need to take it out immediately."

"Jesus. You think they did it when they attacked and cut her arm?"

"Yeah." I open the door. Large vases of white and red roses sit on every flat surface. On the small table in the entrance sits a bottle of champagne nestled in an ice bucket and a silver platter of chocolate-dipped strawberries.

We'll get to that. I point to the armchair for her to sit. She obeys, enveloped in a cloud of satin and lace.

I cover the speaker. "Take it off," I whisper. I take my hand off. "Go on," I tell Aleks.

"Alright, so first we have to make sure that's exactly what you're dealing with." In front of me, Renata unfastens button after button, slowly undressing. I help her tug off the miles of fabric until she's standing in front of me wearing a matching white satin bra and panties.

I'm instantly hard. I grit my teeth and concentrate. "Alright. Tell me how I find it?"

"I have an app that can detect a signal from subcutaneous tracking devices. You'll have to put me on speaker. You'll see me airdrop an app. Install it. That will give me permission."

I see a red flash and a prompt. I hit the button.

"Got it. You're in. Now, hold your phone near the wound on her arm."

God, it's amazing what he can do. This modern technology shit.

I hold the phone close to her bare arm as Aleks does his thing.

"Give me a second. I'm setting it up it now. This is going to scan for any radio frequencies nearby. If it is a tracker, it will ping."

I watch the screen nervously, not sure why. And then I realize if it shows that there is a tracker, *I'm* going to get the fucking thing out of her. I could have one of my brothers do it, but no one's fucking touching her.

The app shows a progress bar as it scans. Renata is breathing quickly, but she stares bravely at the screen right along with me.

A loud beep coincides with a display signal.

"Bingo," Aleks says. "There it is. The signal is strong. Definitely a fucking tracker. Jesus. You were right, Ollie. Renata, you might be amazing at detecting the truth, but this fucker's got excellent instincts. Listen to him."

"Alright, alright. How do I get this fucker out?"

As Aleks instructs, Renata watches me. I brush my free hand across the apple of her cheek. "Are you alright?"

"Never better," she says with a smile.

"Ollie, are you listening? There should be a small bump just below the surface, probably next to her bicep. Feel for it. It's going to be tender. The tracker will probably be about a centimeter long, just under the skin. Once you see it, you're going to have to slice through her skin and use sterilized tweezers to pull it out. It's the only way." He pauses. "Do you want me to come and do this?"

Heat flares across my chest. "No, asshole. If you touch her, I'll kill you, and we need you." I'm breathing heavily. She places a gentle hand on my arm, and I draw in a breath. "I mean, no, thank you, I've got this."

He chuckles on the other end of the line. "Tell me when you've got it."

"Alright. I'll get one of our first aid kids, then let's do this."

Our first aid kits are not your normal run-of-the-mill bandages and alcohol swabs. We keep every room in this house well stocked.

The room is dimly lit, shadows dancing across the walls from moonlight outside the window. But I feel a sense of urgency as I spread out medical supplies on the coffee table and take out the tools that I need.

"Come here," I tell her, pulling out a desk chair. "Sit on my lap."

She walks over to me, a bit reserved, but takes a deep breath and sits on my lap. I inhale and gently remove the bandage from her arm, then feel the tender skin like Aleks instructed. She hisses in a breath and grits her teeth but holds still. Wordlessly, I bend and kiss her shoulder.

"I'm sorry it's going to hurt. But I have to make sure it's there."

"I know," she says quietly. "Do it. I want it fucking *out.*"

My fingers shake a bit and finally brush over a small, hard lump just under her skin, making her wince.

"I think I found it. Jesus," I say, feeling a wave of nausea at the hard bump under her skin. "Feels weird."

"You got it?" Aleks says on the other side.

"Yeah."

"Good. Next, take the scalpel. Make sure it's sterilized first. There should be alcohol swaps in the kit."

My hands continue to tremble a little as I rummage through the first aid kit and take out little white squares of gauze and the sharp scalpel.

"Not something you see in everybody's first aid kit, now, is it?" Renata says with a tight laugh. "This is the mobster special edition."

I snort and shake my head.

While I disinfect the scalpel, she rummages through. "Bandages, gauze, tape, scissors. Pretty standard there." Her eyebrows raise when she pulls out a tourniquet and burn dressings. "Wow. Broad spectrum antibiotics, antiseptic, and a bullet removal kit. *Duct tape?*" Her eyes meet mine. "Are you guys preparing to go to war?"

"Always."

I shrug. "I've seen a lot. I make sure we're all well-equipped."

"Interesting," she says, reaching her fingers for a small leather pouch. She opens it up. "Do all of the kits have these too?"

She takes out a series of fake IDs, a passport, a portable fingerprint kit, a burner phone, some makeup, and basic prosthetics we could use for a disguise if needed. Colored contact lenses, a lock picking tool, and several massive rolls of $100 bills.

She stifles a little gasp when she finds a small vile of sedatives, cyanide capsules, and even a tranquilizer gun. "Holy *shit*, Ollie. What else do you have in here? This is not just a first aid kit. This is a survival kit. We could be bombed, attacked, and still manage to get into every country in the world."

I shrug. "What can I say? Always be prepared."

"Indeed," she says, pulling out a few meal replacement bars, more cash in various currencies, and a few prepaid credit cards.

"Are you guys still there? Or are you bonding and shit?" Aleks snaps.

"Sterilized scalpel at the ready, fucker. Let's go."

Renata braces, her muscles tense.

"You're going to have to make a small incision, just enough to reach the tracker."

She shakes harder and looks away.

"Aleks, hold on a second."

I rummage through the kit and pull out a nip of vodka. "Drink it."

She pops the top off and gulps, comes up sputtering, and tosses the empty bottle onto the floor. "Fucking do it before I pass out."

"Hold onto me. Squeeze if you have to, as hard as you want."

She nods.

I lift the scalpel, draw in a breath, and, in one steady move, make a small, straight cut. She hisses as the blade slices through her skin. Blood wells up, and I quickly dab it with a piece of gauze.

I prod the sliced skin aside. "There it is. I see it."

"I think I'm gonna throw up," Renata says. I reach for the ice bucket and empty it onto the floor. She holds it up to her mouth and dry heaves.

Aleks is giving me instructions on the other line. "Use the tweezers. Be gentle, it's probably started clotting to the tissues, you'll need to be careful not to cause more damage when you remove it."

I grasp the tracker with tweezers, keeping my hand steady with everything I've got. It's slippery, and I almost drop it, but finally, it's free, the fucking tracker clasped between the bloody tweezers.

"Got it."

Renata heaves.

"Good job. Now disinfect and bandage the wound, and destroy that damn thing."

Yeah, I have no intention of destroying it.

I bandage her wound, thankfully small and easy to fix. When I'm done, I can't help but bend and kiss her bandaged arm. I take the bucket from her and place it beside the discarded champagne and ice on the floor.

This all feels strangely symbolic as if taking that tracker out removed something wedged between us.

"Did you take care of that tracker yet?" Aleks asks.

"Yeah about that, I want you to put this thing into a drone and fly it to the most inconvenient places you possibly can, like over huge bodies of water or something."

Aleks chuckles darkly, and Renata smiles at me.

"I am absolutely on it. Now go get ready; it's picture time."

I hang up the phone and take a moment to hold her tighter on my lap. I hug her to me, careful not to touch the tender spot on her bandaged arm or the fading bruises on her abdomen.

I hate that she's been hurt, that I let it happen. I'll never harm her again. She's a victim in this bullshit, and I'm going to burn the fucking world until everyone and anything that will hurt her is annihilated.

She's mine.

With the tracker gone, we are ready to go. Wordlessly, we get ready, careful to get her back into her dress so we can take our poses for social media. We take pictures at all the iconic landmarks, our defiant smiles daring anyone to come after us.

In the garden, Renata turns to me, grinning.

"Come out, come out, wherever you are," she taunts and gives me a broad wink. "I'm not afraid."

She is though. I know she is. I see it in the way she bites her lips and twists her hair, the way she looks over her shoulder.

I vowed I will take care of her, and I never say anything I don't mean.

I watch over her with almost fierce protectiveness, ready to shield her from any threat.

"You're mine, Renata," I whisper in her ear when the last photo is taken and we're finally alone again. "And I'll do anything and everything to protect you."

"Anything?" she asks, her gaze holding a world of hurt.

I kiss her forehead. "*Anything.*"

CHAPTER FOURTEEN

Three weeks ago...

WAKING FELT *like slipping between worlds—the dream still clinging to me like a shadow. I had been held in isolation by the Romanovs for several days, Ollie, my primary captor. He would come in and bring me food, and at first, he'd leave silently. I was told that this was always his way: silence and aloofness.*

"I speak only when it's necessary," he finally said to me one day when I questioned him.

But I suspected beneath that calm exterior was a man capable of doing terrible things.

And honestly? I found it kind of hot.

Being near him felt like standing on the edge of oblivion— one step would send me hurtling into the abyss. But goddamn, I craved the fall.

I reveled in the heart-pounding moments of fear. It felt like a sort of anticipation.

One night, in the middle of the night, I got up to use the bathroom and realized Ollie wasn't sitting in his usual place.

In the Romanov family estate, it was almost a maze, and they'd recently granted me some freedom to explore. I planned on using that to my full advantage.

I wanted to find Ollie.

I walked down the hallway toward a sliver of yellow light spilling from a door that stood slightly ajar.

My instincts said I shouldn't be here. That I should be hiding, or at the very least, I should be in bed. But I felt drawn to that doorway like a moth to a flame.

I wanted to see Ollie. In the short time I'd been a prisoner of the Romanovs, I'd begun to crave his presence.

The harsh sound of a Russian accent made a shiver skate down my spine. I paused in the doorway, my breath catching as I took in the scene. Ollie was there, standing over a man tied to a chair, his voice low and menacing. The man's face was a mask of fear. Ollie stood, bare-chested and slick with sweat, like a warrior on an ancient battlefield, ruthless and unyielding. My God, he was so sexy. The sight of him, so powerful, so commanding, stirred something primal in me. I finally understood why my cousin once confided in me that the best way to get turned on was by watching a man fight.

I knew he was aware of my presence because of the way he tilted his chin in my direction before he went right back to work. He continued to ask questions, none that I could *understand because everything was in Russian, but his voice was calm and void of all emotion.*

I watched as the man spat something out in Russian and turned his head away. Ollie growled back in Russian, stepped forward, and fisted the man's hair. I swallowed a gasp, forcing myself to watch in silence. To not look away.

In one swift movement, Ollie elbowed him in the neck. The man's screams echoed in the room, but Ollie showed no signs of remorse. He wrapped his hands around his neck, and the man turned purple as Ollie barked out instructions in his ear.

Something had threatened his safety... or the safety of someone in his family. His calm was terrifying, a storm just beneath the surface as he delivered blow after blow, unshaken by the raw violence.

He spoke in calm, measured Russian tones, and the man nodded, pleading.

I took a step into the room.

When Ollie turned to me, the hardness in his face melted away, replaced by a softness that was almost impossible to believe. How could this be the same person? I wondered if I imagined it. Was I so desperate for love and attention that at the slightest hint of interest and I'd fall?

A small smile actually played on his lips as he approached me. He reached down, took his T-shirt draped over a chair, and wiped his hand before he touched me. Approaching me, he gently placed his hand on the side of my cheek, perhaps his favorite way to touch me, before he bent and kissed my forehead.

"I'm sorry you had to see that," he said, peering into my eyes. It was a complete transformation—from ruthless interrogator to gentle protector. "Are you all right, Renata? Did something scare you? Do you feel well?" His hand brushed my forehead with a tenderness that felt almost out of place after what I'd just seen.

I swallowed hard and shook my head, not even sure which question I answered.

I'd seen vicious brutality in my life. My own brother had grown to be a man devoid of emotion, but in all my life, no one had ever touched me with such tenderness or looked in my eyes as if he would move a mountain with his own bare hands to make me happy.

I wondered what crime the man had committed to earn such punishment.

That night, as I watched him shift from ruthless to gentle, something inside me broke—and I think I fell in love. I mumbled something about my stomach being uneasy, which wasn't a lie. He frowned and nodded, holding my gaze as if I were the only person in the world and he wasn't still covered in the blood of another man.

"Back to bed," he ordered, his voice gentle but leaving no room for disobedience. A man of few words, I'd quickly learned Ollie always meant what he said. "I'll get you something to make you feel better." He turned me around toward the door. "Go, now, Renata."

"Thank you," I whispered. My eyes flickered at the man in the chair. Ollie didn't know that I could detect lies. Could he use my help now?

Something told me to wait until the time was right.

I went back to bed and lay down. I tried to summon some vestige of humanity, some horror for what I've seen. I wanted to be horrified. I wanted to feel normal, but all I could remember was that tender look in his eyes.

I WAKE, my half-dream slipping away, and there he is—a shadow by the window, watching over me. The soft glow of moonlight in front of him bathes him in a gentle golden hue, casting dancing shadows on the walls. Bare-chested, he's wearing nothing but a pair of boxers and holds a bottle of beer in one hand.

I blink in surprise and look down. I'm still in the white satin panties and bra, the dress over a chair. I don't even remember taking it off. I must've fallen asleep.

"Ollie?"

He turns to me. I'm unable to see his eyes as he's shadowed in darkness.

"What time is it?" I ask.

Shrugging, he puts the bottle to his lips and finishes it. I'm mesmerized by the way he swallows. There's something irascibly masculine about the way a man swallows with his head tipped back, a brief glimpse of his vulnerability.

"Don't know," he says when he's finished. "Don't care."

I look down again as if to remind myself I'm nearly naked. "Did you take my wedding dress off?"

"Yeah. You were asleep, and I didn't want to wake you. Not after that ordeal."

My arm throbs beneath the bandage. I stare at it and breathe a sigh of relief. It's gone. The fucking tracker's gone, and, by now, likely as far away from here as he could get it.

"Eh. Thanks, but I've been through worse than that," I say with a laugh.

He's instantly sober. "I know."

The scent of roses hangs in the air, mingling with the hint of his cologne. I swallow. "I thought... doesn't the Bratva have rules about consummating a marriage?"

"Mmm," he says. "They do." He moves toward me with predatory grace, each step deliberate. As he nears me, I can finally see his eyes, as green as enchanted jade. "You're so beautiful."

A shiver of anticipation ripples through me as he draws closer. When he reaches me, he sits on the end of the bed. "You made me so proud today."

I tip my head to the side just as his hand cups my jaw. "Did I? When?"

"When you took your vows. And when you didn't flinch when I took that fucking tracker out of your arm." His voice lowers. "When you let me take care of you." As he speaks, he traces a finger down my neck, over my collarbone, to the slim strap of my bra. With deliberate care, his touch glides over my skin, sliding the bra off my shoulders like he's unveiling me. It falls half off, cupping the lower part of my breasts.

My heart pounds in my chest. I'm nearly naked before my ruthless husband.

"Thank you," I whisper. "Ollie?"

"Mmm?" he says, staring at my bare skin just before he slowly, deliberately, reaches to my back and unclasps my bra. It falls to the bed, baring my breasts to him. I look at them as if seeing them for the first time. They're full, with large, dusky pink nipples that harden just from the intensity of his gaze and his nearness.

"Yes?" He bends his mouth to my breast and kisses the underside. My breath hitches.

"Do you believe me now?"

"I do," he says with conviction. My eyes flutter closed as relief washes through me. He said *I do* earlier, too, and I feel in that moment there are no two words sweeter in all of English.

He believes me.

It doesn't matter if his family doesn't. It doesn't matter if Carlos is after us and will attempt to destroy us. None of that concerns me now. All that matters is that Ollie believes me. We're married. We're a unit, a team, and no one will tear us apart.

"You have no power to lie, Renata. It's not who you are."

I exhale. "There were times when I wished that I could."

"Yeah," he says, kissing higher up my breast. Anticipation makes my pulse race. "Lying comes in useful, doesn't it?"

He leans in, his lips brushing mine. My chest rises to meet him.

I'm the one who deepens this kiss. I reach for him, drawing him closer to me as his hands roam over my body, leaving a wake of fire in his path. I can feel the urgency of his need in his touch and in the way he kisses me. He moves fully onto the bed, and our bodies press against each other, heat building between us with each passing moment.

His lips trace a path of kisses down my neck, over my shoulders, across my chest, each touch sending waves of pleasure through me. The way he touches me feels reverent, and my heart swells with something like love.

Can I love a man like him?

Could I love anyone less than him?

We move together on the bed, our bodies pressed against each other. The heat between us builds with every second that passes. As we sink deeper into the softness of our shared bed, his movements grow more urgent, his kisses darker. More demanding. I meet him with equal fervor, our bodies moving in perfect harmony. The world outside the two of us ceases to exist. The world could burn to the ground around us, and we wouldn't notice.

Every kiss makes my need for him more urgent, heat thrumming through my veins like molten lava.

I want him. I need him.

He rolls onto his back and lifts me over him, so my legs straddle his. I'm so turned on, my thighs are slick with arousal. He glides me onto him and groans when he finds my wetness. "Jesus, woman," he says in a heated whisper. "You're fucking soaked."

"Mmm." I nod, moving my hips to meet his first thrust. My head falls back as my body meets his. It feels so damn good to be connected to him, and for the first time, it feels like... we're one. United.

"You're shaking," he whispers. He places his hand on my shoulder, tracing comforting circles with his thumb. My body quakes gently. I am. I'm as nervous as a virgin.

It feels like the first time, and in a way... it is.

Our first time as husband and wife.

He cups both my shoulders with his large, warm hands, glinting jade holding my gaze. And once again... there's only the two of us. The world falls away like the cracked pieces of a broken shell, leaving new life in its wake.

Dear God, he's enormous and so fucking eager for me. I lick my lips as his thick, hot cock stretches me, fills me, *igniting* me. My mouth is dry, and my clit throbs as the walls of my pussy clench around him.

Right now, in this moment, words aren't needed; our bodies are saying all that we need to.

I'm sorry.

Forgive me.

We can do this.

I love you.

We draw in synchronized breath, a shared rhythm of desire

and intimacy. The rapid beating of my heart seems to echo unspoken words between us.

As he thrusts deeper, our movements become a silent oath of forgiveness and understanding.

I cling to him, my nails digging into his shoulders, drawing him closer. I need him to feel every inch of me while I feel every inch of him. His hands, strong and steady, grip my hips, guiding me closer. Grounding me.

His lips find mine. We breathe into each other. He's salty and sweet. My breasts swing freely in front of him. Our tongues touch as he grips my nipples and rakes his fingernails over the hardened buds.

As the climax builds, the intensity of our connection overwhelms me.

I cry out his name, a plea and a prayer, as he responds with a guttural groan that vibrates through every cell of my body. As one, we shatter.

He holds me to his chest, our bodies entwined, our hearts beating as one. His lips press to my forehead. I close my eyes, not surprised to find my cheeks are wet.

"I love you, Renata."

"I love you too," I whisper back. We've buried a world of hurt with our vows and honesty.

For now, I let myself feel this. Breathe in hope and exhale fear.

Both of us know the treacherous road before us is filled with snipers and landmines, but together... maybe, just maybe, we're invincible.

CHAPTER FIFTEEN

Ollie

"NOTHING. He's vanished off the face of the earth," Aleks says.

I shake my head. He should know better. Enemies don't just vanish into thin air. They hide, waiting to strike. We're not the kind of people with luck like that. We're the kind of people who make good fortune, not fall into it.

I'll have my revenge when I see Carlos Carerra's lifeless body buried six feet under.

"He had contacts, Ollie. Associates. And the buzz from all of them is that he's gone completely dark."

I shake my head and look through the sliver of an open door where Renata's taking a shower. I can hear her beautiful, resonant voice as she sings. From here, I catch a glimpse of her curves, her head tilted back, hair cascading like dark silk. Every inch of her pulls me closer. I'm hard as a fucking rock.

I try to focus, but she's everywhere—her scent, her voice, her goddamn addictive body—making it impossible to think straight.

"...and they said when he does, they'll let me know."

I rub my forehead with my fingers and concentrate. "When he does what?"

Aleks pauses. "Did you miss that whole thing? Jesus. I've never in my entire life seen you not pay attention or lose focus. All it took was a woman, huh?"

"Shut up," I growl.

"No," he retorts, not bothering to hide his glee. "You're whipped. You, Ollie Romanov, the original stoic himself on record for saying he'd *never let a woman lead him around by his balls,* who turned his nose up at all of us when we got married, have gone and done it."

"No, I haven't. Shut the fuck up."

"Ollie?" I turn to see Renata standing in the doorway, wrapped in nothing but a tiny towel, her skin glistening with water, the towel just above the vee between her thighs. I'm tempted to take her, right here.

I swallow hard and reach out to her wordlessly. I love the way she fits in my arms, nestling right in like she was created to be here.

"...and that's all I know."

I kiss Renata's forehead and swallow my damn pride because, for once, Aleks is right.

I *am* whipped.

Fucking hell.

"Say that again. Renata needed me."

I clench my jaw and ignore his *whoop* on the other line. Self-satisfied prick.

"Are you listening this time? Or has your wife turned your head again?"

Turned my head. She's turned my whole fucking self—mind, body, and soul—toward her. I hold her to me and press my finger to her lips. This is important. I need to hear.

Her tongue flicks against my finger, and my control snaps, desire roaring to life.

Aleks talks to me as if I'm five years old. "Carlos Carerra. The bad guy. Remember him? He's got a dirty cop he confides in. Lucky for us, Carlos fucked over said cop, who's now chomping at the bit to screw *him* over. When he contacts him, we'll know. Did you get that, or do I need to repeat it?"

"Fuck you. I got it. Keep me in the loop."

I hang the phone up to the sound of his chuckle and throw it on the bed.

Renata's hair hangs about her face in untamed waves, droplets pinging her beautiful dark skin. I bend and lick them off her, one by one.

"I decided on a name for the puppy," she says cheerfully.

I stifle a groan. "I don't give a fuck about the puppy."

"Ollie," Renata says with a strained giggle. "We can't just call him *puppy*."

"Why not?" I kiss the underside of her jaw and tug the towel free. She places both hands on my shoulders to brace herself and folds herself into my embrace.

"Because he needs a name," she says staunchly. "And I have one. Also, when do I get him back from Polina?"

I look at the time on my watch. "You'll see him in a bit, but we're traveling today, and I don't want to take him with us until he's well-trained."

"Aww, Ollie." She pouts, and I almost cave.

"Your safety's more important right now. We'll come back, and soon, but until then, I've got a trainer working with him." I kiss her cheek. "What's his name?"

She pulls back a little to hold my gaze. "Arthur!" she proclaims with a note of triumph in her voice.

"Arthur," I repeat, rolling it over in my mind. "That's nerdy as fuck. Why Arthur?"

I hold her in front of me, her bare, still-damp body leaning back so she can have this very serious conversation.

"*You* know. Like King Arthur and the Knights of the Round Table? The name carries a sense of *nobility* and *strength*. He was just a boy who came from humble beginnings but became a great leader. It's a strong, regal name, and that puppy is destined for *greatness*."

Just a boy who came from humble beginnings...

I lean forward and kiss her. "I love it. It's perfect."

She tips her head to the side. My cock presses against her naked body, and I want her... right here, right now.

"What is it?" she asks. When she concentrates, she gets this adorable little furrow between her brows.

I shrug. I don't always like talking.

"You can't always revert to silence, Ollie."

"Why not? It's served me well. It keeps people thinking." I kiss her again, deeper this time, tasting her, claiming her with every stroke of my tongue.

"Don't distract me with sex," she groans out.

"I will absolutely distract you with sex."

"But we don't have time."

"Time? Who's keeping track of time?"

"*Me,*" she responds. "Isabella said I should join the girls for self-defense classes today, and I want to."

This time, I don't respond because I'm warring between what I want and what she wants. This is new to me, thinking about another person. I'm black and white, as predictable as the sunrise, and I want to keep her trust.

"I want to be the one who teaches you."

I kiss her again. With her wet hair in my fingers, I tangle and tug until her mouth parts further. I bite her lip and taste mint.

We pull away. "Ollie," she says gently. "I need to make peace with Isabella. It's the only way we can truly unite this family. You and I both know how much better off our family will be if we're allies, not enemies."

I think it over while I kiss the soft fullness of each breast, one at a time. "True."

There's a sharp knock at the door. I adjust my cock and nod toward the bathroom. "Get your robe on. That will be Polina with... Arthur. How about *King* Arthur? I like that."

"Ooooh," she says. I let her go with reluctance. "King Arthur is perfect."

The door shuts with a click. Half a minute later, I've got a wriggling, squirming, *way* over excited puppy licking my face.

Khristos.

Polina covers her mouth with her hand and giggles. "He likes you."

I grunt and hold the pup in front of me. "Listen up, King Arthur. You're not allowed in here until you know where to do your business. You'll learn to obey, and soon." I take him by the scruff of the neck and give him a little shake. "Understand?"

He predictably licks my hand.

"You clearly instilled the fear of God in him," Renata says approvingly behind me.

"Morning, sunshine," Polina says. "Are you joining us for practice?"

Renata looks at me, and I give her a reluctant nod. "This one time, and only because of what you said you needed to do."

She grins at me and takes off the robe, revealing workout clothes underneath. I was totally played. I narrow my eyes at her but can't resist that shit-eating grin she gives me.

"You and King Arthur can bond, and I'll be back in a bit," she says, heading for the door.

"We'll join you." Polina snaps a leash on the pup and pats his fuzzy little head. I put him on the floor, and he trots beside us with an almost majestic air as if he knows he's been crowned royalty.

I hold his leash firmly by my side. "Heel, boy." When he gives me a lopsided grin, I frown at him. "Behave. This is not fun and games. You are supposed to be protecting her." I point to Renata. "You get that?"

He wriggles his little butt and barks, though it sounds a little more like a squeak than anything.

We've got some work to do.

When we reach the training room, Isabella stands in front of the girls wearing a tight tube top and workout shorts. She's starting to show and isn't afraid to flaunt it.

When Isabella married Lev, she said the women in our family needed self-defense classes. She wasn't wrong. We're a newer group, under new leadership, with my brother taking the reins in the wake of my father's death. We've focused our energies on protecting our family and putting down solid roots. Teaching the women self-defense was not a priority, but it has been helpful.

Renata hangs back. It's unlike her to be shy.

"Go on," I urge her. When she gives me a quick glance, I reassure her. "You belong there, Renata. Go." I give her a hint of a nudge in that direction.

She takes a deep breath, steadying herself as she faces the mirror in the training room. Isabella knows she's there but, at first, doesn't acknowledge her.

The afternoon sun filters through the high windows, casting a warm glow on the exercise mats spread across the floor. I stand in the doorway with the pup, who's fallen asleep against my foot, snoring softly. I lean back farther so I can watch in quiet, folding my arms across my chest. Watching.

I want her fully capable of defending herself, but she's right —she and Isabella need this. Their combined forces will be so much more powerful. Renata adjusts her stance, mirroring Isabella's actions.

"Relax your shoulders," Isabella snaps. "You're too tense."

Renata exhales, following her advice.

"Not like that." Isabella's voice is sharper now, and I can see Renata stiffen from here.

"Like this?" Renata adjusts again, but it's evident she's frustrated.

Isabella steps closer, her eyes hard on Renata as the other women here—Aleksandr's Harper, Mikhail's Aria, and Polina—continue the drill. "You have to be precise. Control your breathing. Don't just follow my movements like a robot. Understand them. Make them *yours*."

Renata's face flushes. I know her well enough to know she's

fighting both embarrassment and anger. "I'm *trying*, Isabella."

"Try harder," Isabella retorts, her tone unyielding. "Do you think an enemy will wait for you to get it right? You think half-assing it will cut it?"

Renata's fists clench. "Of course not. I'm not stupid."

"Then show me!" Isabella's voice rises as she shoves Renata's shoulder. "Prove it!"

I clench my own fists but hold myself back.

Something snaps in Renata. "Enough!" she yells. "I'm not half-assing anything." She shoves Isabella back with a force that seems to surprise them both.

For a moment, they stand still, staring at each other before they both spring into action. There's precision in Renata's strikes, a power that catches Isabella off guard. She's forced to defend herself vigorously.

"There you go," she says with reluctant pride as they continue to spar. "That's it, Renata. You're *fierce*. I know where you come from. I know who you are. Fucking *prove it*."

They move as one, sparring, blow after blow, following until Isabella calls for a halt, her palm in the air. Both of the women are heaving from the exhaustion, their hair wild and untamed. Renata's clings to her damp neck.

"Better," Isabella says. "Control your emotions when you fight. Anger can be powerful, but it can be your downfall if you don't pace yourself."

Renata nods, more subdued. "I get it."

"You're getting the hang of this."

"Thanks," Renata says softly. "It's been a while since I've felt this... powerful."

Isabella's expression softens. She lays an absentminded hand on the gentle swell of her belly. "You've always been powerful. Capable. Strong. You need to remember not to bow under the weight of adversity. Lean into it. Make its energy your own."

Renata stares at her friend. "Thank you. I'll remember that."

Isabella holds Renata's gaze for a long moment and finally nods.

"You did well. I'm proud of you." She turns away and helps Polina with her stance.

I beckon to Renata. "Come here."

She gives one last look toward Isabella, who turns and nods, dismissing her. They're moving forward.

When Renata reaches for me, I place a gentle finger under her chin, capturing her gaze with mine. "I allowed that because you two needed to reconnect. But from now on? I'm the one who teaches you self-defense. I wanted you to make your peace, but I'm a jealous man, Renata. I don't share. What's mine stays mine, and no one else gets a claim on you."

Her eyes twinkle mischievously, but she only nods.

"Say goodbye to King Arthur for a bit. We're going out."

"Out where?"

I blow out a breath and look around me, half expecting the motherfucker to materialize out of thin air.

"Away from here. I want to test a theory."

Turning to face her, I pull her closer to me.

"What theory is that?"

"That he's watching. Waiting. If I can..." I reach for the back of her head and cup her to me. "I'll draw him out, like a poison that needs to be purged. I won't stop until he's eliminated, once and for all."

My lips meet hers. I remain alert but can feel her sinking into me when I pull her closer to me and tip her head back, one hand at the back of her neck, the other cupping her perfect round ass.

Carlos who?

When we pull away, she's breathing heavily. I hold her to me protectively with one arm, and with the other, I flip the bird to the wide open air around us. Carlos Carerra can kiss my ass.

"Well then." She gives me a curious look. "Just in case?"

"Just in case." I take her hand and lead her to a car that waits, purring, at the curb. "Let's go, Renata."

I've lived like a nomad for years. Once Carlos is buried, we'll put down roots and settle down with King Arthur, preferably in a place that has a farmers' market and a change of seasons. I don't really care where, as long as she's with me.

I want to give her everything she needs, and it begins right here. Right now. We're putting everything behind us and forging on.

She goes with me without protest.

Maybe it's because she finally worked things out with Bella. Or perhaps she feels what I do, that whisper of promise and a hope of good things to come.

I feel lighter than I have in years. Hopeful. Renata is mine, and the world is our oyster.

If only... if only it could last.

CHAPTER SIXTEEN

Renata

I SIT NEXT TO OLLIE. He's driving and has been in silence for over an hour. There's no denying he's the quiet sort and only talks when he feels he needs to.

Right now, he doesn't need to. It's not the brooding silence my father would lapse into once in a while, the type designed to make you feel guilty like you did something wrong and afraid of what he'd do next.

No. Ollie is as different from my father as humanly possible. His silence isn't oppressive like my father's was. It's steady, commanding, as if he holds all the power in those unsaid words. It's quiet authority, making his silence feel powerful instead of passive aggressive.

He's as different from *everyone* as he could be.

I'm learning to lean into the quiet and silence and to appreciate when he does talk. He only speaks when he has something to say.

"Where are we now?" I ask, a little confused with the readings on GPS. Ollie said it's unreliable here.

"We're in the upper part of New York State," he says quietly. "There's no sign that anyone's followed us. Aleks reports the drone carrying your tracker is having an excellent honeymoon in Puerto Rico." I stifle a snort. The ruse will be short-lived, and when Carlos finds out we deceived him, he'll lose his fucking mind. But I'm enjoying this while it lasts.

"He could be gone," I say quietly. "He could still be tracking the drone."

Ollie sobers, his eyes on the road ahead of us. "Is that what you think?"

I look out the window. I swallow hard and respond cryptically. "If Carlos is still alive, which you maintain he is... I don't think he's caught on yet. I think Carlos is waiting, like a predator, waiting for the perfect moment. Waiting until the time is right before he strikes—" I swallow, nod, and continue. "Yeah. That sounds more his speed." I lick my lips. "I mean, if he were here..."

What will he do when he finds the two of us? He knows Ollie means something to me. He knows he's my husband.

My gut says retribution will be swift and merciless.

If it were just me, I'd be fucked. Thankfully, I'm not the only one here, the only one defending myself.

The Romanovs can hold their own.

I look out the window and twist a strand of hair. I nibble my lip thoughtfully. I have questions about him, about who he is. His motivations. I've seen him do terrible, cruel things, and yet...

"Ollie?"

"Mmm?" He taps the steering wheel as if lost in a world of his own. And maybe he is.

"Do you, like... ever have any regrets for... hurting people?"

He doesn't really show any signs that my question disturbs him or fear of answering honestly. That's not who he is.

I inspect an unruly cuticle and pick at it, suddenly nervous.

Finally, he shrugs a shoulder. "I'm not the family assassin, Renata."

"I know, but... well. You've murdered people."

He clenches his teeth. "Yeah. Truthfully?" He lets out a breath.

"Yeah. I wouldn't ask otherwise." My heart beats faster. Do I want to know the answer to this question?

His voice is cold and ruthless when he finally answers. "My only regret is not making some suffer longer before I ended it."

Oh God. My breath catches, but I force myself to stay composed, to not flinch or show discomfort. What do I say to that? What *can* I say?

Is he wrong?

Am I?

I've seen what people are capable of. I suppose if I were the average girl next door, I could have ended up with an average man. Maybe we'd meet at a bar. Is that how people still do things? We could be having conversations about grilling the perfect steak, discussing the best way to invest our money, or debating who to vote for in the next election.

But that life is a distant dream now. Ollie isn't a next-door neighbor kind of guy. I can't ask him to go for a walk on the beach or take me to a cozy dinner without considering the potential dangers.

He's the man that walks through fire and expects you to follow.

His voice breaks through my thoughts, softer now, almost reflective. Another woman might mistake his tone as casual. "How did you get that scar, Renata?"

He's watching me, really watching, and for a second, I feel exposed and vulnerable in a way I'm not used to. Answering him as his wife won't be the same as answering him before.

The memory of that night flashes before me, the pain unbidden—the fear and blood. I swallow hard, tracing the scar. How should I tell him? Is there anything he already knows?

Driven by a need to survive, to protect myself from threats that constantly loom over me, I've had to be strong. To push through. But there's a part of me, deep inside, that still craves trust and acceptance. A part that regrets the things I've done, the people I've hurt. A part of me that wonders if I'd only done things right by my family, would they have kept me as their own?

But Ollie... maybe he doesn't need redemption the way I do. He's fully submerged in the darkness as if it's part of his identity. And maybe that's what is so unnerving and fascinating about him.

I take a deep breath and look ahead of me.

"There was a time when Carlos was protective and caring, but then he became obsessed with power and control. As he climbed the ranks in the cartel, he became best friends with Javier Morales. I wanted a way out. To him, looking for a way out was the ultimate form of betrayal."

Ollie nods and barely reacts, but his jaw is clenched, and we're driving faster now. The other cars outside our windows fly by. My belly drops as the needle on the speedometer creeps up.

"I discovered he'd been manipulating me. He wanted me to marry into another family. He had a good friend who was obsessed with me. An older guy. He set us up on a date, and at first, things were fine..."

I look out the window. I will never forget what it felt like to be that small and powerless, to know the only weapon I had was my body.

"His friend tried to seduce me. I wouldn't let him. I left and ignored his calls. He was creepy as fuck." I shiver at the memory of his oily voice and loose skin, the way he smelled like expensive cologne and cigars. "Then Carlos called me to him and announced that he'd arranged for my engagement."

I laugh bitterly. "If I knew then what I know now... anyway, I told him no. We got into a huge fight during dinner. He threw his plate at me, and it shattered on my face. Isabella was the one who brought me to the hospital. She had a friend there who wouldn't talk."

Ollie's grip on the steering wheel tightens. I can't look at how fast he's going. I reach a hand to his arm. "Please, Ollie. Driving faster won't make this go away. Please, slow down."

He lets out a long breath and begins to slow down. "Sorry. I didn't realize I was doing that."

"I know."

We sit in silence for a moment. He reaches his hand to my leg and strokes his thumb along the bare skin.

"My brother didn't mean to hurt me. He saw the next step forward for our family and was taking the brunt of my father's rage."

"That doesn't fucking matter," Ollie mutters.

I sigh. "But it does. I'm not saying it was right, but he told me later that he was trying to protect me, and marrying into this other man's family was the best choice."

"The damage was done, though, Renata. He hurt you. He scarred you."

"I know," I say softly. I swipe at my cheeks, remembering how it was after that night. "After that, he didn't trust himself not to hurt me, so he disappeared. There was a rift between us, a constant reminder of how far he had fallen."

"Renata."

"Yes?"

"Is there still a part of you that believes Carlos can be redeemed?"

I turn my head and don't answer right away.

"Yeah. I still remember what he was like as a boy. How he took care of me. It's... complicated. He might be a monster in your eyes, but he's still my brother."

"I know."

"The brother I loved is still in there somewhere, Ollie. I know he is."

The view outside our window has changed. The houses are farther apart now, and there's more green between them. Wide fences mark property, and in the distance, the sloping mountains beckon with scattered clouds.

"Renata—"

"I know he is. Imagine if one of *your* brothers turned his back on you. Hurt *you*. You'd want him back, too, wouldn't you?"

"First, the answer is... if any one of my brothers turned their back on my family, he'd be exiled. We aren't united by blood, Renata. We were all adopted by my parents, our family forged on loyalty and love."

"Really?"

"Really."

"Second." His voice takes on a darker, more serious edge. "I don't appreciate being interrupted. I give you space to talk without interruption."

I feel small and chastened. "Sorry about that."

His voice is a low, soft command. "Interrupt me again, and you'll find yourself over my knee before you realize what's happening. Clear?"

My pulse races. I swallow and nod. "Mhm. Got it." I look down at my hands and place one on top of his, my voice a low purr. "Yes, sir."

His low growl of approval is all the answer I need. He may give me shit about my own kinks, but my husband is kinky as fuck, too.

"Your brother is our enemy. The brother you knew is gone, and if history is any indication, he will never return."

I nod. It doesn't hurt as much as I expected it would because he's not telling me anything I don't already know deep down in my heart.

"Renata," he says softly. "You have a family now. A family that will protect you, cherish you, and fight for you no matter what. You're a Romanov now, and we will prove our loyalty to you."

I watch the fading sun outside our window, and my heart swells. He's right. The brother I knew is gone. The man who took his place is no friend of mine. But the Romanovs are my family now, and with them, I'll find the strength, loyalty, and love I've been searching for.

"Are you hungry?"

I sigh. "Always."

He squeezes my knee. "Good. There's a little diner ahead. No one's followed us. Aleks is watching."

I smile. "Oooh. I've always wanted to go to a diner."

"I'm guessing you don't have them in Colombia?"

"No. I mean, in some larger cities, you can find American-themed restaurants, but they're unusual. We prefer our own food."

He gives me a rare smile. "Then you're in for a treat."

"Yeah?"

"Something uniquely American I go for every time I come back to America. I crave a good ol' American breakfast. Bacon and eggs, those little fried potatoes. Toast with these little pats of jelly."

"They sell breakfast?"

"Yes, every kind of breakfast you can imagine. Of the American variety, anyway. And sandwiches for lunch, all the sandwiches."

"Burgers? I love an American burger."

"With fries? You got it."

Now I'm starving. "Can I get an ice-cold Diet Coke on the side?"

"Of course." He opens his door and comes to my side. We're the only ones here, and for once, it's nice to see that Ollie is almost... *relaxed.* Carlos is momentarily distracted; his family's got us on their radar. We've got this.

A neon sign flickers above the small diner like a beacon of light in an otherwise desolate place. It looks like it's straight out of an American movie from the fifties, and my heart soars. We're honeymooning! Me and my badass, grumpy husband.

He opens the door, and I'm immediately presented with a large glass display case of assorted pies and pastries. "I'm *starving*."

The bell on the door jingles as we walk in, the scent of warm coffee and fried food greeting us. The only person here is an older woman with graying hair and glasses wearing a frilly apron. She's holding her phone at arm's distance, pecking at something on the screen, her tongue sticking out of her mouth.

"Welcome," she says warmly, placing her phone in her apron pocket.

Her eyes go wide as saucers when he enters behind me. I look over my shoulder and try to see him the way she does—scary, badass, and dangerous. "Have a seat. You have your choice of the place. Anywhere you like, hon." I can tell this isn't something she offers just anyone, as only the first four tables are set. There are benefits to being with Ollie.

I draw closer to him. I fully intend on *enjoying* said benefits.

He leads us to a booth near the back, away from the windows and close to the kitchen. Of course he needs to be able to have a good vantage point.

I can't help but notice the way the red vinyl squeaks under Ollie's weight. I fit here just fine, but even though Ollie isn't quite as enormous as the others in his family, he still dwarfs this place. The table between us is small. When our knees brush under it, it sends a spark of something down my spine I can't ignore. He picks up the sticky menu, scanning it with a look of utter concentration.

I stifle a giggle.

"What's so funny?" he asks, his eyes flicking up to meet mine.

"Nothing, just... I've seen you take down a man twice your size without flinching, and here you are, staring down this little menu like it's a life-or-death decision..."

"Food *is* a life-or-death decision, Renata," he says seriously, though his lips twitch.

"Is that so?" I say. There's a lightness in my chest I haven't felt in so long, it almost scares me. It feels dangerous and wonderful. "What might you recommend for someone who could be looking at her last meal?"

His eyes narrow playfully. It's a welcome change from his usual stern demeanor. "The bacon cheeseburger followed by apple pie with a scoop of vanilla ice cream. Anything else is just playing with fire. Too risky."

I frown and shake my head with mock seriousness. "Definitely not the avocado toast and lemon meringue, then?"

His eyes go wide in mock horror. "Have you listened to a thing I said?"

The waitress sidles up to us, pad in hand. "We're out of lemon meringue."

My instincts flare, and I stare at her, surprised. She's lying. Over pie? I bet if my hot-as-hell husband asked for it, she'd miraculously find some.

Hmph.

"Coffee?" she asks Ollie. "I'll make a fresh pot, sir."

Jesus. *Gag me.* I want to ask if she'd still be hot for him if she saw how easily those hands of his can wrap around a traitor's neck. I've seen that in person, thank you very much, and can say with confidence it takes a special kind of person to learn to appreciate the nuances of brutality.

He shakes his head. "No, thank you, but my wife might want some." He quirks a brow to me.

I shake my head.

My wife.

I'm not used to that. I swear the waitress's face falls. "Ma'am?"

I shake my head. Ollie orders for both of us, which both annoys and pleases me. My chest tightens when he orders, "An ice-cold Diet Coke, extra ice with a wedge of lime, please." Just how I like it.

There's a hardness to him, yes, but there's something more, something almost vulnerable in the way he quietly entwines his fingers with mine, tracing the oval shape of each nail with the pad of his thumb. I don't miss the way his gaze flits to the door, windows, and restroom every now and again.

"Do you need to check in with Aleks?"

"Yeah." He slides his finger over the screen of his phone and shrugs. "No updates."

I'm not sure if that's a good thing or a bad thing. It's easier to keep your eyes on a moving target.

"Thank you," I finally say.

"For what?"

For protecting me. For listening when I need to talk. For being a rock-hard fortress that won't let me down.

I shrug. "For ordering for me."

"You like everything," he says with a wistful look in his eyes. "You make it easy."

"I make what easy?" I ask, my heart beating faster. I'm not sure why. I swallow hard.

"Everything."

My heart seizes. I hold his gaze as I lean across the table. I want to kiss him.

"Me?" I whisper. "You sure you're not talking about someone else?"

"No one else, Renata. Just you."

Leaning forward, he holds my gaze. He's utterly concentrated on my lips as if they hold magic. I swallow hard, the air between us charged with something electric. Magical. I'm not sure if it's that we're married now, we've escaped our hunters, or that we're alone in this strange, timeless place in the middle of nowhere, but it feels like everything else fades away, and it's... just us.

I lean in. I want to kiss him. I want to ask about his past and talk about the future. I want to hear him bless me with the rare gift of his words because right now, we're in this strange bubble of newness and quiet.

I'm breathing heavily. His eyes have darkened, framed with thick brows, his lips downcast, making me quake with something that feels like fear mingled with need.

Two platters clang on the table in front of us. "Anything else I can get you, honey?" She seems oblivious to the spell she just broke.

"No, thank you," Ollie says, his hands pulling away from mine as he straightens.

"Enjoy, sugar," she says with a wink to him.

"I will," I say sharply. She turns away in a huff.

"Behave yourself, Renata," he says in that chiding way that makes my nipples furl.

"She's flirting with you."

He only shakes his head. "Eat, baby." He lifts his burger and takes a huge bite.

I dig into mine with gusto until I've left just enough room for pie. He eats all of his, then pulls my plate over to his side when I'm finished and eats every last crumb.

She brings over a plate of warmed apple pie topped with a generous dollop of vanilla ice cream and two spoons. I take a big bite. It's spicy and sweet, the ice cream rich and creamy. "Mmm."

He leaves the last bite for me. "Ladies first." I smile and scoop it up.

"Thank you." I'm quiet for a moment. "Ollie, is there ever any going back?"

"Going back to what," he asks, playing with the salt and pepper shakers in front of us as if they're chess pieces.

"Back to life before... all of this. Back to normalcy."

He casually shrugs a shoulder. "There has never been normalcy for me. My mother wasn't always a single mom. Eventually, she became a drug addict who slept with rich men to pay our rent. She overdosed and froze to death on the streets of Moscow when I was still young. That's when the Romanovs found me."

My heart aches. "I didn't know that."

He shrugs. "It's irrelevant."

It isn't though. But I don't say that out loud.

"My father scrapped together a family that needed him. It's one of the best ways to ensure loyalty, isn't it? Take ten dogs that are starving to death and feed them. Take ten that have regular meals and a roof over their heads. Which will be the most loyal?"

"Is loyal the right word?" I ask thoughtfully, sipping my Diet Coke. The ice clinks against the glass as it hits my lips. Wordlessly, he gestures for a refill. "Desperate, maybe. Grateful, yes. But loyalty isn't born of having a need met—it's born out of a sense of trust, of knowing that someone will be there for you, no matter what. True loyalty comes from a bond, not from filling an empty stomach."

He pauses, his expression unreadable, and traces a pattern in the condensation on his glass. I watch the blunt tip of his finger. Why does everything he does feel so utterly, irascibly masculine?

"Maybe you're right," he finally says, his tone softening. "But in a world like ours, desperation and fear are all you need to keep people in line."

I nod slowly, knowing he's right but wishing it weren't so dire, so bleak.

"Is that really how you feel about loyalty, Renata?"

I hold his gaze and nod.

"That true loyalty comes from a bond? From a sense of trust?"

"I do."

His green eyes hold mine for a beat too long, making me squirm under the heat of his gaze. "I'll keep that in mind," he says softly as the waitress presses a green-and-white bill onto the table.

Ollie stands, tosses five $100 bills on the table, and reaches for my hand. It's warm and firm around mine, and I take a sense of comfort in holding it.

I stare. "That's a lot of money," I whisper.

"Good," he whispers back. "Maybe she'll buy a dildo with a Russian accent."

I squeal and clap my hand over my mouth. "Clearly, you and I do not shop in the same stores."

He grins, making my heart turn over in my chest. I feel like I win a small victory whenever I can make him smile. The edges of his eyes soften just a touch.

As we head toward the door, I can't help but glance back at the tables where the waitress stands, her mouth agape.

The night arrived while we were inside, the air cool and refreshing after the warmth of the diner. Ollie still holds my hand and gives it a gentle squeeze.

"You know," he says, sobering. "What you said in there about loyalty and trust... it's rare in our world."

I nod. "I know."

My God, do I know.

"It's something worth protecting, isn't it?"

"Yes," he says as we reach the car. He does his obligatory scan of the car, our surroundings and checks in with Aleks, but we're still in the clear. Our honeymoon gift.

"It is," he says softly, opening the door for me. "Something worth protecting. And something worth fighting for."

The door shuts with a click.

He slides into the driver's seat, and the engine roars to life with a low, rumbling growl. Something has me on edge, but I can't quite place it. Maybe I'm not used to being protected and safe. I've spent too long fighting for survival to trust when things are good.

Are they good?

This is no joy ride; I know that. Ollie's testing to see if Carlos has discovered us.

"Can I drive?" I ask before we leave.

He growls and gives me a sidelong glance.

"I know, I know. You like to be in the driver's seat. You like to be in control. Well, maybe I do too."

He frowns as he thinks this over, fingering his keys before he finally blows out a breath and hands them to me.

"Go on. Be careful, Renata. This engine's powerful." I stroke his thigh and wink at him. "I think I know how to handle powerful things, don't you agree?"

We drive in quiet, my eyes focused on the road. As I round a bend, the headlights catch something in the distance—a dark figure standing in the middle of the road. I gasp and slow.

"Ollie—"

"I see it," he says quietly, his voice low, something in it sending a chill down my spine.

"Keep driving straight at it, Renata," he says in a quiet command.

I accelerate. My heart pounds. I stifle a whimper as we approach, the figure looming closer. I whisper a strangled prayer as I drive closer. "*¡Ay, Dios mío, protégeme de todos mis enemigos!*"

"Should I—*Oh God*—what am I—"

"Don't swerve. Drive straight at it," he orders, his voice a dark promise of danger, pulling me deeper into his world. His grip on my thigh tightens.

I feel like I'm going to be sick. Bile burns the back of my throat.

"When I tell you to swerve, *do it.*" The little hairs at the back of my neck stand up. I'm not sure if I'm more afraid of him or whatever's in front of us.

Just as I'm about to crash right into whatever it is, he shouts, "Move!"

I yank the wheel, swerving sharply, tires screeching as we narrowly avoid the shadowy form.

"Park!"

I slam on the brakes, and he opens the door and vaults into the dark night. My heart pounds, adrenaline coursing through me as I look back.

I'm alright. We're alive. I didn't hit anything, and... no one's there.

He runs into the night, but it's only him. Whoever or whatever was there left as quickly as it came.

"What the hell was that?" I ask when he comes back to the car. "I saw someone there!"

"Someone or something," he says with a nod. "Yeah. Have you ever used a gun?"

I gawk at him. I'm still panting, still trying to slow the rapid beating of my heart and remember how to breathe again.

"Your silence is answer enough for me. You keep driving. I'll keep watch."

It feels oddly symbolic. Will our whole life together be like this?

CHAPTER SEVENTEEN

Ollie

WE SAT ALONE *in the garden. I had managed to convince Mikhail to give us a little space. The air was cool, the scent of blooming flowers fragrant in the air. We walked in silence as if each lost in our own thoughts.*

"Tell me about you, Ollie. You've asked me about me, and I feel like you already know me. But I don't know much about you."

No one ever asked me that before.

I never wanted to tell anyone. I didn't think anyone would ever care enough to ask.

My family knew, all my brothers, of course, but it wasn't something we ever talked about.

I looked at her, and for some reason, felt I could trust her. I shrugged. "There's not much to tell."

"I find that hard to believe," Renata said sweetly. "I know you've been through a lot, and I think a part of you is actually really good."

I laughed, not sure how to take that. "Uh, thanks?"

"You know what I mean," she said quietly.

I did know.

"All right, I'll tell you about me if you really want to hear it." I ran a hand through my hair. How was it that I could face an enemy or a whole room full of enemies and not feel as nervous as I did now? I hated this. But there was something about her...

I took a deep breath, my eyes focusing on the distance as I began to talk. "When I was a kid, my father was involved in a bunch of shady shit. I wasn't aware yet. I was just a kid, and I didn't realize who my father was or what he was doing. My parents would always fight at night, and I didn't know about what until that day his enemies came."

She listened intently, her eyes reflecting her emotions. She didn't move, sitting as still as a statue as I continued.

"So my father's enemies came for him one day," I tell her softly, even though my voice is still tight with emotion. "They broke into our home. My father didn't survive that day. His enemies made sure of it, and I was just a boy. Powerless."

"Ollie," she whispered, tears filling her eyes.

"I hid," I said in a whisper. "My mother and I hid and watched as they tortured and killed my father. I was just a kid, but even now, I'll never forgive myself for hiding. For *not stepping out and doing something—anything to stop them."*

She reached for my hand. "You couldn't have stopped it, Ollie. You were just a boy, and no one could expect you to face that kind of danger alone. Your mother was probably only trying to save you."

I shrugged. "I don't know. It doesn't make it any easier. I think she wanted him dead. He was terrible to her. I still wish I could've done something. If I could go back in time..."

We stood in the garden, the shared confession hanging in the air between us.

WE'RE ten minutes out from a small motel in the northernmost corner of upstate New York. It's midnight, and Yelp assures me this place gets less than stellar reviews, but that's not my priority. I'm less concerned about the condition of the place and more about its strategic location. The run-down motel sits on a rise, giving me a perfect vantage point—a place where I can see any threat long before it sees us.

"Oh my, honeymoon central, you've outdone yourself with this place Mr. Romanov," Renata says sarcastically with a smile. "Hopefully the coffee's good at least."

I glance at the map again, confirming the terrain. If we're lucky, this motel will give us the upper hand, making sure I can see any enemies before they see us. Aleks assured me no one's followed us, but after the strange incident with the cloaked figure, I don't trust anyone or anything.

No more strangely cloaked figures appear in the middle of nowhere. Renata has an endless list of who or what it might have been.

"Misplaced scarecrow, that's it," she says as she puts the car in park. I grunt in response. Maybe it was, maybe it wasn't.

I doubt it.

"You asked God to protect you from your enemies back there."

"Did I?" She squints adorably, screwing up her face as if trying to remember. Moonlight illuminates the silvery length of her scar running down her cheek. I reach my hand out to touch her, and this time, she doesn't flinch. This time, she places her hand atop mine.

My heart swells.

"What did I say?"

I repeat in a high-pitched voice. "*¡Ay, Dios mío, protégeme de todos mis enemigos!*"

She playfully punches my arm. "My father used to say that. I didn't even realize that I did it. Where did you learn Spanish? You speak it beautifully."

I shrug. "It's one of my many talents."

I see no evidence of anyone following us, so I carry our bags to the main desk and head inside. A scrawny teen with a scraggly beard sits at the main desk. It's an older place but clean, with only one car in the main parking lot.

The teen behind the desk barely glances up as I approach, his attention glued to his phone screen.

I drop the bags on the counter, getting his attention. His eyes widen slightly as he takes in my size. Renata lingers just behind me, assessing the situation.

"I need a room." My voice is flat, leaving no room for an argument.

The kid fumbles with the computer and frowns as he taps the keys. "Uh, yeah. I might have one or two available." He raises a brow. "One queen or two doubles."

I lean in closer. "My wife and I would like a queen. No kings?"

"We don't have kings here."

The kid's eyes flicker nervously to Renata before quickly returning to the screen. Renata clears her throat and catches my attention. She tilts her head slightly, her eyes narrowing as she shakes her head at me.

"Are you sure about that?" she asks, her voice molten honey as she laces her hands around my arm. "I thought I read on the online that you had king-sized beds." She leans in closer. "My husband barely fits on a queen himself, never mind when I join him."

"Right, uh, we might, but I think we're out..." he stammers.

I turn my arm over, showcasing Bratva ink. "You sure about that?" I ask calmly, belying the threat. This asshole's used to throwing his weight around and bullying people just for the hell of it.

"I, uh... let me check again. I might have one more..."

I lean in slightly, looming over him. "Good idea," I murmur.

With shaking hands, he finally produces a key. "Here you go. Room 214, the one with a kitchenette."

He pushes the key toward us.

"Free continental breakfast in the main lobby in the morning. Enjoy your stay."

He gets up and flees the desk.

"Thank you," Renata calls out to his retreating back.

We make our way to our room. "Why did he lie to us? That's strange," she says, shaking her head. "He was hiding something."

"I'm not really that strange. A kid like him is probably on a drug dealer's payroll and instructed to keep the larger rooms open for deals and other 'activities'. We'll have to keep an eye out."

She sniffs. "Yeah. It seems like that's sort of the order of the day, isn't it?" We stop outside the room with the number 214 emblazoned on the door.

"Mmm," I tell her. I lean over and kiss her forehead. "I chose this place for its vantage point. I've got this. I'll keep watch. No one's getting past me."

I open the door, pleased to find it simple and aged but impeccably clean. "This will do," I say with a shrug, tossing our bags down.

"Little seven-year-old me would've thought she died and went to *heaven,*" Renata says with a smile, inspecting the bathroom. "There are even little bottles of shampoo and conditioner in here. I thought only *super-rich* people got to stay places. My father simply didn't trust anyone enough to go to a motel."

I grunt. I know the feeling.

I pull out my phone, checking to see if there are any updates from Aleks. Nothing new.

Just as I'm about to put my phone away, a message pops up from Polina. I open it to find a whole stream of pictures of Renata's puppy attacking a stuffed tiger, rolling in the grass, and curled up, sleeping in a little dog bed.

"What's got that smile on your face?" Renata asks curiously. Am I smiling? "I'm scared to find out. Could be anything from a stupid meme to the death of an enemy." She's stepping out of her clothes, momentarily distracting me. I reach for her and cup her ass, drawing her close to me while I show her the phone.

"King Arthur in all his kingly glory!" she says with a grin. "Aw, wook at dat sweet wittle face. I can't wait to see him again." Her eyes are bright with affection, a glimpse of the innocence I'm fighting to protect.

I toss the phone aside and pull her onto my lap. "We will. It's good to see you smiling. I want to make you happy."

She straddles my lap and frames my face with her small, delicate hands. "What makes *you* happy, Ollie?"

I blow out a breath. "You. Here. Safe."

Her heart-shaped face tips to the side. "Do old motel rooms make you happy, *Ollie?*"

I kiss her fingertips. "I treasure moments like this—quiet, safe, knowing no one can touch us here."

"Are they rare in your world?" She holds my gaze with hers.

I swallow and nod. "Yeah, baby."

One thing I love about her is the way she can seemingly hold two emotions at the same time. Right now, she's looking at me with both understanding and sadness in her eyes. "It's my world too. I get it."

Her fingers trail down the side of my neck. I stifle a groan, my cock rock hard beneath her ass. She obviously notes this with a teasing smile and she grinds her ass seductively on my lap.

"Behave," I grunt and slap her ass. That doesn't help my erection. She bites her lip and leans in, brushing her lips against mine in a kiss that quickly deepens. My hunger for her grows with every layer we strip back, the need building for too long. I lose myself to her, wrapped up in the sweet taste of her, the delicate scent of floral laced with citrus, the warmth of her hot pussy separated from me by a thin layer of fabric.

When she pulls back just enough to breathe, she smiles at me. "No."

A mischievous glint lights her eyes when I fist her hair. "Did you just say no to me?" My heart beats faster.

She licks her lips. "You heard me." She lifts my arm, kisses my bicep, then extricates herself like a magician. She giggles as if she got away with something, a teasing glint in her eyes as if she's daring me to chase her—as if I can't reach her in two steps and won't spank her pretty little ass raw for her troubles.

The large window has thin curtains that don't quite close all the way. Moonlight filters through.

"Don't you fucking dare, Renata."

Outside, the world is quiet and dark, but behind her, there's a parking lot and a distant road.

"Dare what?" she asks with wide-eyed innocence. "*This?*"

She stands by the partially open window and tugs off her top. Anyone outside would get a full view of her naked back and bra strap. Her silhouette framed by moonlight, bold and unafraid, like she's daring the world to watch her. I watch as her fingers trail over the white-edged underside of her bra.

"Renata," I say warningly. Her gaze never leaves mine as I stand and unfasten my belt. She takes off the rest of her clothes before I can reach her, and they fall to the floor in a heap.

Her body is all curves and shadows and calls to me like a beacon. She knows exactly what she's doing, pushing me, testing the boundaries I've drawn. She slowly draws the curtains back, fully exposing her naked flesh to the world beyond the room.

She's crossed a line.

She gives me a sly smile, daring me to do something about it.

Turning away from the window, she arches her back as if offering herself to me. The sight of her exposed like this sends a rush of heat through me. My belt slides through its loops with a hiss, and her gaze flickers to it, a spark of anticipation in her eyes mixed with fear.

"I've been *way* too lenient with you," I scold, doubling the belt over in my hand. "What makes you think you can behave like this and get away with it? Obviously, I haven't done my duty as your husband."

She bites her lip, her eyes burning with desire, and doesn't answer, but the challenge in her gaze is clear. I close the small space between us, grip her wrist, and yank her back from the window. She gasps as I bend her over my knee and pin her down. My hand flattens on the small of her back, easily keeping her in place. Fire thrums through my veins.

"You've pushed me too far this time, and now you're going to see what happens when you cross a line I set for you, Renata."

She glances over her shoulder, her eyes dark with anticipation, her lips curled in a *come-hither* smile. "Ohh, I'm so *scared.*"

I narrow my eyes at her, lift my knee to give me better access, and relish the way her hands flail out in front of her to brace herself on thin air before I snap the folded belt across her ass. My cock aches at the way she squeals and tries to squirm out of my grip, but I hold fast. I do it again, harder this time, loving the way her body tenses and she moans.

"You crave this, don't you? Being over my knee, knowing you're mine to control and punish." My breath is hot against her ear.

"I love it when you take control," she whispers, her body softening against me. I bring down the belt again, a sharp crack that makes her gasp, her fingers digging into me. The sound echoes in the small room. I flick the belt again and again, hard enough to redden her pretty ass but holding myself back with effort.

When her ass is seared a pretty cherry red, and she's panting heavily, slick cream coating her inner thighs, I slide the belt between her legs. "Mmm. Beautiful. I love the way you look when I punish you."

I ease the belt to her clit and tap. She squeals and wriggles. "Are you going to be a good girl?" I ask, tapping her pussy again, harder this time. Her back arches, and I swear she's on the edge of climax.

"Yes," she gasps.

"That's what I want to hear. Touch yourself, angel. Stroke your clit."

She reaches for her pussy and quickly finds her folds. She strokes upward, moaning when she finds her swollen clit. I hold her against my knee, drop my belt, and cup her hot ass with my hand. "You're wet, Renata. Did your spanking turn you on?"

"Oh God, *yes*," she moans out, her hand moving faster between her legs.

"Good girl. I want you to crave my discipline. Touch yourself. Keep going. Don't you dare fucking stop." I slap the underside of her thigh. Her hips buck, and she whimpers with need. I hold her against me and lift my belt. "If you stop, I'll spank you raw and leave you wanting. Don't push me, woman."

"I'm not—going—to—*stop*." She moans.

"Good girl," I say approvingly. I give her another sharp smack. "I'm gonna have my work cut out for me keeping you in line, aren't I?" I strap her again. She moans again, blissed out, hardly able to respond.

"Yes," she breathes in a whisper.

She strokes with frantic movements, now on the cusp of release.

"Don't you dare fucking come. You must beg me first."

"Please!" she says in an impassioned whisper. "*Please*, Ollie. I need to come. I'm going to come."

"No, you're not, you haven't proven your loyalty to me yet. Keep touching yourself and don't stop."

I strap her ass hard again with my belt. The way it stings and her perfectly plump ass jiggles make me so fucking hard I can't help but bend and bite the pink imprint it leaves behind. She writhes almost uncontrollably under me, torn between obeying me and just ending the torture I'm imposing on her.

"Oh god, Ollie, no. Please baby. I can't hold it. Let me come, please. You can't do this to me. Arghhh. Jesus Christ, fuck, shit, ahhh... Ollie, *please... please, please let me come.*"

She screams, and I slap ass yet again. "Not. Yet. I need to know in my bones you are mine and will do whatever I tell you regardless of how much you must suffer. Show me that all of you belongs to me, Renata."

"I'll do whatever you say, I'll give you everything, I'll never disobey you... oh my god, please I'm begging you... let me *come, please!*" she pants uncontrollably, body shaking, a fierce moan building deep in her chest as spasms begin to overtake her completely.

"Come for me. Come for me now, baby."

Renata arches her back and comes so hard her whole body shakes and spasms as if she's being electrocuted. It takes all of my strength to hold her down as I shove my fingers deep into her core and pump, my hand sopping wet. The walls of her pussy clench around me, crushing my fingers with her eager spasms. She's still coming a full minute later as she screams my name in ecstasy over and over again.

CHAPTER EIGHTEEN

Renata

I'M BLIND, gasping for breath, every cell in my body on fire when he braces himself above me. I'm dimly aware of him shedding his clothes. The ache for his weight on me is unbearable, a need that consumes every cell of my body. When he joins me, his skin flush against mine, our bodies pressed into the bed, I exhale in contentment.

He claims me in a single, brutal thrust, so intense the world spins. I gasp for breath when his big, rough hand wraps around my neck and squeezes. My pulse races, blood pounding through my veins as he pumps into me. A second orgasm eclipses the first. I'm lost to him, gasping out incoherent pleas and whimpers, my voice cracking under the weight of my need.

"Take me. Take all of me," he breathes into my ear. "I want you to know you're mine."

Another hard thrust before he pulls himself nearly fully out. I arch my hips, trying to meet his thrusts, whimpering at the loss of his heat, craving the fullness and completion of him inside me when he glides back in to complete me. My pussy clenches, and another spasm of pleasure consumes me.

"Ollie," I gasp. My face is too hot, his hand just tight enough. My vision grows hazy as my body's consumed with another orgasm on the heels of the last. I've lost count.

He shoves his cock into me, lowers himself down, and kisses me when I'm still coming. His tongue meets mine. I whimper and claw at him, my fingers scraping along his back tats. His hand tangles in my hair, and as I gasp for air, I revel in the perfect blend of pain and pleasure, each tug sending shockwaves through me.

"Look at me! Keep your eyes on mine. Do not look away, Renata."

I lick my lips and ride out my pleasure as he rocks his hips with mine. His hot seed spills inside of me. His deep, satisfied growl reverberates through me, so primal and masculine I can't help but moan in response. He slams into me again, his eyes boring into mine like flames of green fire. I watch him chase his pleasure with mine and trail my hand down the side of his arm. He's beaded with perspiration but barely winded.

As he lies beside me, still pulsing inside me, I relish the heat of his claim, the way his release marks me as his, binding us together in the most intimate of ways.

I roll over as he quietly gets up and walks to the bathroom

and reach for his balled-up tee. It's warm and smells like mountain air and alpha male. Like him.

I curl up in a ball, blissfully content, my body flushed and numb with a pleasure I've never felt before.

"I don't know if I need a joint, a bar of chocolate, or a bath," I murmur, my voice gravelly. "I can't move."

"Maybe a nap before I order some food and fuck you again." He lazily saunters over the bed and lies down next to me.

I crawl up on his chest and smile, my eyes closed, breathing him in. My body feels light, but my eyes are so heavy. I fall into a deep sleep.

When I wake, Ollie's sitting in a corner of the room. The view is hazy, and I blink my eyes. The shades are drawn and in the distance, I hear the rhythmic thudding of footsteps on the pavement, someone jogging outside. It must be very early in the morning, a dim light seeps through the curtains.

Ollie holds a tablet in his hand. He's slightly turned from me, bare-chested, wearing a pair of boxer briefs. I gaze at the deep marks I left on his back, vivid reminders, as if I've branded him with every desperate touch.

I lie in bed, not daring to make a sound. I want to observe him like this, silent and thoughtful.

His fingers flick over the screen of the tablet. I squint my eyes so I can see more clearly. I'm suddenly very wide awake when I realize he's watching recorded footage... of him.

I don't know who the man is, but he works for my brother. They were tight when they were younger. The man kneels on the pavement, the night dark, while he pleads in Spanish for his life. Ollie's voice is cold and calculating as he questions him.

"Where is she?"

It takes me a moment in my sleepy haze to realize the *she* is me. I watch in horror as the man continues to plead for his life. Someone mutters in Spanish—the person making the recording.

I close my eyes. I don't want to see this. I don't want to hear. It's so low it's like background noise, but anyone would recognize the desperation as he begs for his life.

I open my eyes just as Ollie puts a gun to the man's head and pulls the trigger. I can't completely stifle my gasp. Ollie turns quickly to see me watching him. Our eyes meet.

"I'm sorry I woke you," he says with genuine warmth, his eyes lighting up. He places the tablet on the table and walks over to me. I flinch when he reaches to touch me.

A deep furrow knits his brows. "What is it, Renata? Why are you looking at me like I'm going to hurt you?"

My heart races, and my stomach aches. How could I have been raised in this life and still, even now, be consumed with revulsion at violence?

When I don't answer, he strokes thick, rough fingers through my hair. He hasn't shaved in a few days, his jaw covered in rough stubble. As he drags his hand down to my shoulders, he frowns, touching me with such tenderness it's as if he's memorizing the way I look and feel.

"Everything I do, I do to ensure your safety, *meelaya*."

Sweetheart.

His touch is gentle, his voice soft, as he pulls me into an embrace, his touch reassuring.

"You'll hold our children with the same hands you use to hurt people."

"Yes," he says quietly and offers nothing else. Agreement. No explanation and no lies.

"What if I don't like that?"

"Like what, Renata?"

His heart beats under my cheek.

"This lifestyle. What if I want to... to leave it behind us? Have a life that is normal and pedestrian."

A beat passes before he shakes his head. "*Nyet.* You say this now, Renata. You've got a tender heart. You're sensitive. I knew this when I first met you." He smiles sadly. "Why do you think I bought you a puppy? But you and I both know there is no escape from what's before us. Not for me. Not for you."

He's right; I know he is. I could pack up and leave. Run away. But my brother is alive, and he'll stop at nothing until he finds me. Everything we are, everything we own, is tied up in the Romanov family line and the Los Sangre Dorada. We'd be penniless and friendless with targets on our backs.

But we'd be free.

"Let's talk no more of this," he says, bending to kiss my forehead. It doesn't feel as tender as it did before. "Are you hungry?"

The apple pie I ate at the diner seems like ages ago. "I'm starving. But I'm not so sure this is the kind of place that has room service."

He shrugs. "We don't need room service, and we will skip the continental breakfast. There are four different places nearby that offer delivery, I can order whatever you want with the touch of a button."

Oh, right.

I sit up. "Sounds great."

I walk to the bathroom and clean up. The shower is larger than I expect, and the little bottles of toiletries, while not expensive, smell faintly of lemon. I take my time washing up, and by the time I join him, wrapped in a white towel, he's got several cardboard containers on the bed.

We sit cross-legged on the bed, inspecting each one. Turns out ordering breakfast takeout doesn't hold a candle to actually going out to a diner, but you can't eat in a restaurant half-naked, so it's a good trade-off. The eggs are a bit cold and the toast soggy, but there's a warm muffin studded with plump blueberries topped with thick sugar.

I take a bite. "Mmm. This is delicious. Do you want it?" I ask.

He shakes his head and eats the cold eggs. "You eat it. I'm fine with the eggs."

"You do the high protein thing for your manly physique?" I ask, smirking.

He winks. "It works."

I slather butter on the muffin. "Yes, it does. Do you know how to cook?"

He nods. "I do. I travel a lot, so it helps to know how. You?"

I pick a blueberry out of the muffin. It's plump and sweet, and still warm. I notice idly that my finger's stained with berry juice. Silently, he reaches for my hand and licks the juice off the tip. My heartbeat races. Why does everything he does to me turn me on?

"Yeah," I say, yanking my hand back so I can concentrate on filling my belly and not worrying about sex distracting us. "I had to learn to cook as a matter of survival. My father was absent more than he was present. My brother used to cook for me when he was younger."

I remember sitting at the kitchen table, swinging my legs because I was too short to reach the floor. "Carlos learned how to make huevos pericos, a kind of scrambled eggs with tomato and onion, and arepas with cheese."

But that was when I was little, it feels like a full lifetime ago.

Ollie's eyes darken. He doesn't like when I talk about Carlos fondly. How can I help it? He was good to me back then.

"I want to tell you what happened, but you don't seem to like when I talk about Carlos."

He shakes his head. "You should be able to tell me anything. I'm your husband. And what I think about Carlos is irrelevant."

"It isn't, though, Ollie," I say pleadingly. I place my hand on his arm. I love the warm, reassuring feel of his muscles when he looks at me.

"I just don't want you softening toward him. It won't do, Renata. You must be ruthless, fearless, and as impassive as you can to keep yourself and the people you love safe."

And right there and then, whether he wanted to admit it or not, he just gave me a little glimpse into what it means to be him, didn't he?

Maybe we both don't have to be that way.

"When we were kids, Carlos was different. He was my older brother, but I always felt like I was his protector. He was different... in not a *good* way."

I pause, trying to figure out how to continue.

"I understand," he says. "We all came from fucked up backgrounds, didn't we?"

I nod and swallow. We did. We have.

"He was always so angry and controlling, like a mini version of my father. I didn't realize how bad it was until... until the day he hurt another child. Badly."

Ollie's jaw tightens. "What happened?"

"Carlos got into a fight with a neighbor's child over something stupid. He pushed him down the stairs. I watched. I tried to stop him, but I couldn't. He knew exactly what he was doing." I shake my head. I can still hear the boy's cries for help, still feel myself grasping for thin air too late. "The boy was in the hospital for weeks. He broke his back."

"Jesus," Ollie mutters.

"My father covered it up, of course," I say, unable to hide the bitterness from my voice. "He paid off the family, bribed the local law enforcement and his men made the press stay quiet. But I never forgot. That day I knew what he was capable of."

Ollie nods quietly. "I understand."

"But he never raised a hand to *me*. Everyone treated me very well in school, and if they even hinted at any less, all that had to happen was someone reminding them who my brother was, and it stopped. He was gentle with me. Protective."

Just like Ollie.

In sharing this story with him, I realize why I fear Ollie's dark side so much.

At some point, will Ollie turn on me too? I've seen how obsession and protection can morph into something dangerous.

"I get it," Ollie says gently. "I've seen things in my brothers and my father that were similar."

I don't know about his father, but I know that at least his brothers didn't turn on him.

"It was hard," I tell him, shaking my head as if somehow the gesture will make it go away. "Still is. I've always felt responsible somehow, like it was my fault he is the way he is. As if I could have done something, anything to stop him."

"You were just a child," he says gently. "It wasn't your fault."

I shake my head and sigh. "But so was he."

"I know. Thank you for telling me though. It helps me to understand what we're dealing with here."

I nod, feeling a strange sense of relief at having shared this with him. "There's more. I want you to know that Carlos has a motive. This isn't just about power or control but about revenge. His worst actions have always been fueled by revenge."

"Revenge for what?" Ollie asks, his eyes narrowed.

"For everything. For the way my father treated him. The way the world treated him. He blames everyone and everything for his problems, and he wants to make everyone pay. He takes no accountability for his choices, it's always someone else's fault."

Ollie's expression darkens. "We need to be more careful, then. He won't stop. Not until he gets what he wants."

I nod. "One hundred percent. And we can't let him win. Just like that little boy who was feared and unstoppable—we have to intervene. We have to stop him."

"We'll stop him together, Renata." Ollie squeezes my shoulder. "I know that it hurts. Remembering how he was. I've gone through something similar."

I nod. I want to ask him for more details, to elaborate, but something tells me to stop. I think I've had too much sharing of dark past details for today.

"Polina sent me more pictures." He takes out the iPad. I blow out a breath, thankful for the change of subject. I don't know if I'll ever be able to see him using that damn thing without remembering what I just saw. But when the screen fills with pictures of my sweet pup, I smile. "When will we go back?" I ask quietly.

"As soon as I'm confident your brother isn't following us." How can he be really, truly confident? I saw that shadowed figure in the road last night.

Maybe it was a coincidence.

But maybe it wasn't.

We finish our breakfast in silence. I suppose I'm going to have to get used to eating in silence, for Ollie is a man of few words. We clean up, and he leans across the bed to me, kissing me.

"You taste like blueberry muffins."

I smile and shrug. "Beats huevos pericos, I can guarantee you."

My heart flips in my chest when he smiles. It's so rare, it feels like unearthing a precious gem. I have to admit, I still fear him—a lot, but still, a part of me wishes I could just make him feel at ease for once. I wish I had the power to magically make the tension around his eyes soften and do something to help him truly *sleep* at night instead of catnap like he typically does.

"Look," he says, pointing to the iPad he's put by the window. It's an ocean landscape, complete with the sound of crashing waves. "I found a farmers' market here in town today, too. Did I miss anything?" He pulls me to him and holds me. "You said you like puppies, farmers' markets, ocean views, sleeping in, and what was that other thing... oh yes, *sex*."

He remembered. I swallow the lump in my throat.

"You get a gold star," I say with a pang. I want this to last. I want to hold onto this moment, but I know I can't. I remember trying to catch fish with Isabella with our bare hands, how they were slippery and wet and would slide right through our fingers. We'd think we actually caught one, only to groan as it slithered away. This feels vaguely the same.

"I know I've asked you this before, but what truly makes *you* happy, Ollie? I want you to be completely honest with me" I pull away and place my hands on his shoulders, holding his gaze with mine.

For a moment, he's so serious I don't think he's going to respond. I'm getting used to his quiet ways, but it still unnerves me a little. "It's not that complicated," he says in a low voice. "I like knowing that the people I love are safe."

I wait for him to continue, but when he doesn't, I can only nod in understanding. "That's it?"

He holds me, pressing his hand to the back of my head and tucking me close. Our hearts beat in sync. "That's it."

Am I one of "the people he loves?" The thought surfaces, but I'm too afraid to ask. I know I overthink things, and I know that a part of me fears that is exactly what I want.

I make no sense even to myself. I know we said the words, but I want him to *truly* love me. Who wouldn't?

I'm also not so sure what it will *mean* to be loved by Ollie. Will I be smothered? Chained?

Will I have any memory of where I begin and he ends?

Is this what I want?

We linger for a moment until the world outside starts to seep back in. I think we'll have to be mindful of this. It's easy to forget it isn't just the two of us sometimes.

Ollie's phone on the table buzzes, breaking the silence. I remember in vivid detail what I saw on the iPad. I can still conjure up the cold, distant sound of his voice. The man's pleas for mercy. The boom of the gunshot and the thud of the man's dead body hitting the ground.

Does Ollie have a conscience at all?

"Go get dressed," he says in a quiet command.

I pull clothes out of a bag and do what he says, but I don't miss the way his face darkens as he reads a message on his phone.

"What is it?" I ask, already bracing myself for the answer.

Something's gone wrong.

Again.

"Aleks says they've found your brother, he's definitely alive," Ollie replies, his voice now all business. "He isn't anywhere near us yet. We're safe. But he was sighted at The Cove earlier today."

Oh God. It's happening. I knew it would come to this, but it still hits me with the force of a tidal wave. My heart sinks to the floor.

Ollie's face is unreadable as he dresses, shifting seamlessly back into the cold, distant, calculating person I first met.

The difference is so palpable I can't help but wonder if I've imagined any warmth.

"We're heading into town to go to the farmers' market. Your brother can kiss my ass." He tugs on a tee, his muscles tense. "I want to take you before it gets too crowded. Let the men back at The Cove do their job and find him." His green eyes laser in on mine. "Stay close and do what I tell you, Renata. Is that clear?"

I can only nod as I try to push away the anxiety that rises in my chest. I get dressed and put my hair in a messy bun. When I return to him and we leave the room, he acts as if I'm a witness in a relocation program or something, holding me behind him while he scouts ahead of us. I don't bother to remind him that Aleks just told us moments ago no one's found us here. It's just as well, he wouldn't listen to me if I did.

Normally, the vibrant energy of a farmers market would lift my spirits, but today, it feels like a distraction, nothing short of a temporary escape from the storm that's brewing.

In the distance, someone plays a guitar, her soulful voice both beautiful and poignant. Ollie holds my hand.

The market stalls overflow with fresh fruits and vegetables, the air thick with the smell of ripe tomatoes and vendors showcasing their daily specials. Children dart between the stalls, and a sweet black puppy on a leash barks playfully between them.

We pass a stall selling freshly roasted coffee. I buy us both a cup as Ollie takes the opportunity to scan the crowd with practiced precision. His expression is, as always, tense and alert. One of the children runs from another and nearly knocks into me.

"Easy," Ollie says, steadying the boy with two hands on either side of him. "You almost ran into my wife."

The boy blanches and nods. I look in surprise at Ollie and try to see what the boy sees—a man twice his size wearing a leather jacket, covered in tattoos, with dark-green eyes that have no boundaries.

No wonder I'm having second thoughts.

"Do you want anything?" I ask. Perhaps a chocolate chip cookie will sweeten him up and soften the edges.

Perhaps not.

He shrugs. "Whatever you're having. Mexican street corn?"

"No! Where?"

He jerks his chin at a vendor three stalls down.

"*Sí.*" *Elote* is one of my all-time favorite foods.

The plump woman with a kind smile running the stall hands me two paper boats filled with grilled corn slathered in mayonnaise, chili powder, cojita cheese, lime juice and cilantro.

He hands her two $100 bills and tells her to keep the change. "No, no, this is too much," she begins, but he only shakes his head and leads me away.

I take a bite. The flavors burst on my tongue. "This is delicious. Do you like it?"

I try to pull him into a conversation, but he only shrugs. "It's fine." I can't help but notice the way his shoulders are slightly hunched, like he's expecting something, or some*one*, to jump out at us.

We weave through the crowd and take our time looking at handmade jewelry, jars of homemade jams and preserves, and smelling baskets of cinnamon and clove potpourri. He buys me a turquoise beaded ring at one of the stalls on the edge of the market, closest to the music. "It's pretty and dainty," he says, sliding it onto my finger. "Like you."

I kiss his stubbled cheek. "Dainty?"

"Mmm."

When we reach the stall with fried dough, my mouth waters. "Care for a taste?" the vendor asks, holding out a sample.

When I reach for it, Ollie shakes his head. "If you want one, he'll make it fresh," he says in my ear.

"Okay." I bite my lip. "Yeah, let's get one." We buy one and share it, but the silence between us feels louder than the bustling market. I try to ignore it, but Ollie's continued distanced demeanor makes my chest feel tight.

Though the market buzzes all around us, it feels as if we're miles away.

"Do you want to go back?" I finally ask. "You need to be in the thick of things, don't you?"

He exhales and shakes his head. "It isn't that, Renata. I trust my brothers. But I don't like waiting for your brother to find us. I thought I'd feel differently about him once we were alone and safe, but the truth is... I feel like we're only post-poning the inevitable."

The inevitable being my brother trying to murder me and my new husband putting a bullet between his eyes. Just like he did to that man on the video.

"I agree," I say. The fried dough sits like a rock in the pit of my stomach. "Let's go home."

CHAPTER NINETEEN

Renata

"IT'S ALRIGHT," I tell Isabella. "You're going to be okay, breathe."

She's experiencing contractions, and it's way, way too fucking early. A few minutes ago, she screamed from the bathroom, telling us she was bleeding heavily. Polina freaked out, her face paling, and she screamed for Lev. I'm standing next to Isabella now, trying to keep my own fear in check.

"Lie down," I tell her softly, guiding her to the couch. "There are plenty of reasons for bleeding, Isabella. Not all of them are dangerous." A woman's body is complex.

My words are steady, but inside, panic claws at my chest, my heartbeat thrumming in time with every second lost. I'm trying to keep calm, but the fear is clawing at me from the inside.

I hear the sound of a door opening, followed by the stomping of heavy feet, and suddenly, the entire male side of the Romanov family is standing in the doorway—or, more accurately, elbowing each other out of the way. Lev bulldozes through the wall of men, eyes wide, wild with fear, and heads straight toward us. His face is pale, his eyes wide with fear as he looks at me. "What happened?" he asks, his voice tight.

I fill him in quickly. "She needs to get to a hospital immediately," I tell him, keeping my voice as calm as possible. "It could be nothing, but we need to make sure."

Someone is on the phone, calling for an ambulance. I hold Isabella's hand tightly. She is such a strong, ruthless woman, but I've never seen her look more afraid than she does right now.

I speak to her in soothing tones, the way I wish someone would if I were in her situation, stroking my thumb across the top of her hand. "Someone get her something to drink," I say aloud.

A moment later, Ekaterina arrives with a glass of juice. She kneels on the floor in front of Isabella and gently presses the juice to her lips. "Here, drink this," she says softly.

She brushes her hand across Isabella's brow, and my heart aches. Ekaterina is everyone's mother. She has seen and endured so much, and yet she still has so much more to give.

The sirens grow louder, their wailing cutting through the tense silence. "Lev, come here and sit beside her," I say, glancing up. "One of you needs to go outside and bring the paramedics in so they know where to find her."

Though my heart hurts for Isabella, I tell myself it's going to be okay. I turn to find Ollie in the wall of men and realize that every one of the men in the room is holding a handgun.

"Put those away," I hiss, staring at them. "You can't have those out now!"

Ollie's gaze meets mine, and a sheepish smile tugs at his lips, as if his instinct to protect was never in doubt. The others follow suit just before the paramedics arrive. "How do you think those are supposed to save her?" I mutter, shaking my head.

"We didn't know why she was screaming," Ollie explains, his voice low. It makes sense—Polina's scream set everyone on edge, and with the looming threat of Carlos, they all came in here ready to kill.

Reality sinks in like ice down my spine—this really is my life now. We have enemies not just in hiding but possibly standing before us with friendly faces.

Take no prisoners. Show no mercy.

Three paramedics, two women and one man, enter the room and quickly assess the situation.

"I studied midwifery in Colombia," I say calmly. "I believe she may have a complication that could explain the bleeding, but we need to be sure. We want to bring her in right away so she doesn't lose any more blood."

One glance from the paramedic, and something feels off. My instincts flare—this isn't right.

Oh God.

Something's wrong. I shake my head, trying to clear it. It's probably just Ollie's suspicious energy rubbing off on me.

"What will you do to treat her?" I ask one of the paramedics.

"We won't treat her, ma'am," he says quietly. "We'll bring her to the hospital where she can be evaluated."

"Have you been working with each other for a long time?" I ask, my eyes narrowing. Ekaterina and Polina look at me sharply. It's not a typical question to ask EMTs, but my instincts are on high alert. Something is wrong here. Something is off.

"Yes," one of them says, just as another says, "No."

The room falls silent. I meet Ollie's eyes and slowly shake my head from side to side.

"Thank you. Could you please give us a minute?" I ask the paramedics, "Please wait in the other room." The paramedics retreat at my request, clearly not wanting to incur the wrath of the Romanov men in the room.

Shit. We need her seen immediately, but I can't send her away with people I can't trust. None of us are capable of helping her though. We don't have the right tools or the right skills. My belly aches.

"Nikko," Mikhail says quietly. "Why don't you go back over the security footage of the ambulance arriving here?"

He turns to Ollie. "Ollie, why don't you go investigate that ambulance."

"We need to get her seen immediately," Lev insists, his voice tense. "What the fuck? You guys are overreacting."

But I meet Ollie's eyes across the room and shake my head again. We aren't overreacting. They're lying.

"What's happening?" Isabella asks, her voice trembling. "What's going on?"

"We just want to make sure you're safe," I say placidly, trying to keep my voice steady." Just trust me."

Maybe Ollie isn't always overreacting. Maybe we really are in grave danger.

I give Isabella a curious look. "What have you eaten or had to drink in the past couple of days?" I ask her.

She lists off a few normal things. "Why?" she asks, fear creeping into her voice. "Do you think I was poisoned?"

"I don't know if I trust anything right now, Isabella," I say quietly. Yes, someone could've given her something that caused cramping and bleeding; it's definitely possible...

Maybe Carlos has found the damn drone and knows he's been fooled.

Maybe this was Carlos's plan all along—make someone sick, call paramedics, infiltrate. How else would they get in here? They can't get into this fortress.

"Everything checks out," Lev says a few minutes later. "There's nothing suspicious out here."

But I don't know... He wants his wife safe, but is he over-looking the obvious? I look at Ollie again.

"Wait until Nikko gets back from checking everything."

"I heard the sirens. Then, for a few seconds, nothing else happened. They didn't come any closer. There was a pause before the paramedics got here," I say softly. "Something could've happened then."

I beckon the paramedics back into the room. I turn to the paramedic standing in front of me, a tall, thin woman with blonde hair in a severe bun. "Is there anything you need to tell us?" I ask, watching her closely.

"No," she says too quickly, her voice strained. "We need to get her to the hospital, ma'am."

Hmm. I can't quite read her. She's iffy.

I turn to the next paramedic, a young man who looks like he's barely holding it together.

"Is something wrong with you?"

His eyes widen. "No, not at all," he stammers.

He's lying. I know the signs immediately. I stand up, feeling as if I'm throwing him under the bus, but I can't ignore what I see. "He's lying," I say softly to Ollie.

Ollie moves like a shadow, silent and deadly, gripping the paramedic's neck with a vice-like force that says more than words ever could. Isabella screams, and Lev rushes to hold her.

Ollie pulls out his knife, and for a moment, I think he's going to slice the man's throat right here. Nobody breathes as Ollie slashes at the man's clothes, tearing off his shirt to reveal a tattoo I recognize all too well.

"Cartel," I say, shaking my head. "Oh my God. *How?*"

Ollie turns to the rest of the paramedics, still holding the one in his grip. "He can't hurt you now. Tell us what's going on."

One of the women nods, her face pale. "You'll find our associate in the passenger seat," she begins in a quiet voice just as Nikko bursts back in. "They have a hostage in the ambulance."

"Can we trust the rest?" Lev asks, his voice tight.

Ollie grips the traitor by the neck. "I have him." He gives him a shake. "Is there anyone else with you?"

"No!" the man cries out, but I can tell he's lying. I feel sick to my stomach as I turn to Ollie. "He's lying."

"Who can we trust here, Renata?" Lev says, his wide eyes locked on me.

"The two women. They're the real paramedics. Go with them, Lev. One of you—Mikhail? Nikko? Somebody go with them."

Ollie is going to interrogate this man, and I need to be here to help him.

I feel like I'm going to be sick.

I can do this. I have to. For Isabella. For Ollie.

For me.

They gather up Isabella, placing her on a stretcher. They take her out to the ambulance, and the cold reality of the danger we're in sends a shiver down my spine.

We can't even call an ambulance and be safe. What are we going to do? How are we going to navigate this?

The ambulance leaves, and the fragmented remains of the Romanov family stand in front of us. Mikhail jerks his chin toward everyone but Ollie. "Get your weapons and come with me," he says, the tone of his voice chilling me to the bone. "Renata, leave us."

The man screams, begging for mercy. I remember the video Ollie played in the hotel room—the tone of the man's voice sounds familiar. It's the desperate pleas of a man who knows he's going to die, and painfully.

"Everybody get the hell out of here, Renata stays," Ollie barks.

Mikhail opens his mouth, but Ollie cuts him off. "She can tell when people lie. It will make things go much quicker." Mikhail's face darkens as he considers Ollie's demand but finally agrees, then steps out of the room.

"Ollie," Ekaterina says quietly, her pretty face pinched as she leaves the room, "Please mind the carpet. It's new, dear."

"Jesus," Ollie mutters. "This is why the other rooms are concrete."

Within moments, it's just the three of us—Ollie, the traitor, and me.

Ollie sent one of his brothers to go get what he needs, and he'll will be back in a moment.

He grabs the man and shoves him face-first against the wall, his hand on his neck. The man's face grows purple, and he smacks with his hands fruitlessly. Ollie is impassive, his face a blank, emotionless mask.

I try to summon a level of anger. This asshole used my best friend to get to Ollie. He was going to kill the man who I love. But even now, while I logically know this to be true, I'm sick to my stomach, knowing what I'm about to witness.

Ollie is my husband. Time and time again, he has brutally hurt people, and I've even seen it. He's murdered. His hands have been stained with blood. Even in Colombia, there were whispers of the lone wolf, the silent one, a man of Russian descent who lived in New York and had come to enact brutal, bloody revenge. He was feared by the biggest, most powerful man I knew in the LSD.

Everybody feared him.

I fear him.

"Stay here," he says as he drags the man to a corner of the room. "You won't leave my side, Renata, but I don't want you to have to witness everything."

I close my eyes and remind myself how quietly and gently he touches me. His hands as soft and tender as could be. What if I were the one who did something to betray him? It wasn't that long ago when he thought I had.

I close my eyes and cover my ears but can't completely block out the sound of the man's cries and Ollie's harsh voice, the blows he delivers. I open my eyes when he drags him back in front of me. Ollie moves with cold precision, drawing the shades. His broad shoulders loom, blocking out the only sliver of light. With ruthless efficiency, he ties the man to a chair, the ropes cutting so deep into his flesh, fresh blood stains them.

His face is bruised and swollen, bleeding from multiple contusions that make it hard to recognize him.

Do I recognize him?

Ollie circles him, calm and methodical.

"Do you know him, Renata?" When his eyes meet mine, I have a terrifying shock of recognition.

"Yes," I whisper. "He went to school with Carlos, but I can't remember his name."

"It doesn't matter what his name is," Ollie says, his eyes narrowing. He remains calm as he traces his thumb along the edge of a huge blade. I try to breathe, reminding myself that this is necessary, that there is no peaceful way forward. But the bile still rises in my throat, a stark reminder of the scene that's about to unfurl before me.

Ollie steps in front of the man and tips his head to the side, inspecting him as if he's a specimen in a biology lab. I've seen that cold gaze in his eyes many times before, the one that chills me to the bone. This is the Ollie they whisper about, the one who enacts revenge without mercy or hesitation.

"Who sent you here?" His voice is low, but the threat unmistakable. The man groans, barely able to lift his head, but Ollie grabs him and forces him to look up.

"Was it Carlos? Tell me."

"I—I don't know anything!" the man sobs.

"Fucking hell, let me be the type who stands up to a fucking interrogation and doesn't shit his pants," Ollie murmurs with disdain. "You're a big, tough guy when you're swaggering down the streets of Colombia, aren't you? But here, when it's just me versus you, you're a child." He shrugs. "My brothers aren't even here."

The man's eyes are wild and desperate. "He knows you betrayed us," he says to me with a sneer. Ollie backhands him so hard that the man's head snaps back, and I feel the crack of his hands in my bones. I flinch.

"Who?"

The man clenches his jaw and doesn't respond, turning away. Ollie's expression doesn't change. With ruthless precision, Ollie's blade flashes in the dim light, cutting through flesh with a swift, practiced strike. No room for mercy. The scream that follows tears through the air.

"The carpet, Ollie," I whisper.

Ollie violently kicks the man's chair to the side as the tiled pathway that leads to the doorway narrowly catches the falling blood.

I have to bite my lip to stop from crying out myself. Is this what I've become? Immune to violence and more concerned with Ekaterina's carpet than a man's life?

"Where is he? What is he planning next?"

"I—I don't know anything!" the man sputters, blood dribbling from the corner of his mouth. His eyes are wild with fear, darting from Ollie to me as if hoping I'll intervene. I look away, unable to meet his gaze because deep down, I know exactly how this is going to end.

"Is he telling the truth, my love?" Ollie asks me.

I have to shake my head. I can't look in the man's eyes. "No, of course not," I whisper.

Ollie's blade moves with surgical precision, cutting into flesh, severing tendons. The man's cries turn into desperate sobs.

"Tell me."

His body jerks against the restraints as if he's trying to escape the agony, but there is no escape from Ollie.

I force myself to watch the way Ollie's hands work—steady, controlled—as if he's done this a thousand times before, and his hands function on sheer muscle memory. The way he twists the knife and lifts it before inserting it again is almost surgically clinical.

This isn't just about getting answers, it's about making sure this man suffers as much as possible in the process.

"Ollie," I whisper. My voice breaks. He doesn't hear me, or maybe he does, and he just doesn't care. He's too far gone, too dedicated to the work in front of him.

The man finally breaks, sobbing out names, places, anything to make it stop. But Ollie doesn't stop. He doesn't even slow down. All I can do is stand and watch, sick to my stomach, as the man I love turns into a monster before my eyes.

I try to close my eyes and block it all out—the sickening noise of flesh being destroyed, the slosh of blood, the man's screams—but I can't. This is who Ollie is. This is the man I love. And no matter how gently he touches me or how soft his caresses, no matter how lightly he whispers my name, this is the side of him that will always haunt me.

He turns to me and must see the nausea or fear because his demeanor softens for a moment. He wipes his hand, the mask slipping enough to let me see the man beneath the killer. "Are you alright, Renata?" His voice is soft, but his eyes are again hardened steel, a reminder that this violence is an irascible part of who he is.

"Yes," I whisper.

His face falls. "I thought you were the only one who could detect lies, but even I know that's not the truth."

I swallow hard. "I'm fine," I insist.

With a look of concern, he wipes his hands on a cloth like one might wipe them after an oil change rather than a man who just tortured someone mercilessly. He reaches his hand to me and places it on my shoulder. To my credit, *this* time, I don't flinch.

"Go sit down, Renata," he says softly. "We're almost finished here."

He holds the man upright in front of him and asks one more question. "Where is Carlos?" Ollie's voice is low, deadly calm, every syllable a promise of pain if the answer doesn't come quickly.

"He's here," the man says in a sob. "He's here. It's too late."

He slumps over in the chair dead. Blood thrums in my ears, and ice pulses in my veins. I stare at Ollie, who pulls out his phone and dials Mikhail. They have a hurried, intense conversation in Russian where Ollie relays all the information he's just extracted from the corpse seated in a chair in the tiled pathway of the room. The carpet is immaculate, not a drop of blood anywhere.

"We have what we need," Mikhail says. "Lock everyone down."

CHAPTER TWENTY

Ollie

HE'S HERE. In America. The Cove. Or worse, right here—in our fucking home.

I stand with my phone still in my hand, the words of the conversation I just had with my brother echoing in my ears.

Lock everyone down.

The order is given. Protocols snap into place like clockwork, but none of it fucking matters because he's already here.

If I know my brother, he's already bringing Isabella back from the hospital with a doctor. But none of this matters because the one thing I've spent years trying to avoid is now staring me in the face: our enemy has come to us. Everything we've done, everything we've trained for, the safety protocols—it's all gone up in fucking flames. He could be in our home, and it could be too late.

I turn to look at the slumped-over body of the man I killed, wishing I had maybe slowed shit down a little. I wanted more details. His last words ring in my head like a death knell.

He's here. It's too late.

And in that moment, I feel dread. The kind of cold, bone-deep fear I've trained myself to push aside—so foreign to me at first, I don't recognize it. But this time, it's different.

This time, I have Renata.

I look at her—her face pale, eyes distant and hollow—and I know I've lost her, piece by piece, with every drop of blood that stains my hands. The horror of what I just did and what she witnessed is written across her features. I should've kept her away from this—from the monster I am—but I didn't. I let her see it all, the blood, the brutality, the fucking darkness that festers inside of me. I let her see it all, and it's not the first time. I can still feel his blood on my hands like a second skin, and a part of me wishes I could feel more than that.

It's all the time I spend dwelling on this shit. We need to move.

"We don't know what he meant," I say, my voice cold, distant, almost disembodies, as if it's coming from an over-head speaker. I want to reach out and pull her close to me and tell her it will be okay, but I can't because I don't believe that anymore. The worst has come to our doorstep—Carlos has found us, and I've exposed Renata to the very thing I swore I'd protect her from.

When her eyes meet mine, I see all of it—the doubt, the fear, the realization that I will never change. She doesn't say anything at first, but she doesn't have to. I can see it in her eyes. She's utterly terrified of me.

"What did that mean?" she says, trying to summon whatever strength she has left, even though she looks as if she wants to collapse. She's been through a lot tonight. First, Isabella's scare. Then, the realization that our house security was penetrated when the paramedics arrived. Witnessing me stab a man and make him bleed out on the floor. She's seen it all.

If anything, it feels like a death by a thousand cuts. She's seen me at my worst, time and time again.

"I don't know." We're silent for long minutes.

The silence between us is suffocating, and all I can think is that I did the exact thing I set out not to do.

I knew better than to fall in love. I knew better than to think I could have this, that I deserved it. Because the second I let my guard down, the worst possible scenario played out. I exposed the only person—the only woman I've ever loved—to the demon that rages inside me. And now, I can't even protect her.

"I'm sorry," I choke out, the words hollow because I don't even know what I'm apologizing for. For falling in love? For failing to protect her? For letting her see the darkness inside me? For not protecting her—from him, from me?

But the words hang in the air—too little, too late, a broken promise. I reach out to her, but she steps back, the distance between us growing. What started as a crack is becoming a chasm. And that's when I know it. The worst possible outcome to this whole situation is staring me in the face.

"Renata," I beg, my voice raw. I don't even know what I'm asking for—forgiveness, a chance, anything that keeps her from slipping away.

"We have to find him," she says in a whisper, her face white as a sheet. Even her lips look pale.

"We will."

"He's here?" she says in a voice so soft I can barely hear her.

"We have to assume that's what he meant. He could've meant The Cove, or he could've just been saying something to terrify us, knowing that he was going to die and wanted to plant fear in us, but we have to assume what he said is true." I close the distance between us and hold her by her shoulders. "Tell the truth. Tell me now. What did he threaten you with?"

She shakes her head. It feels as if Renata is slipping away from me, and I can't do anything to stop it. It's like an endless nightmare, with the woman I love just out of reach, and no matter how hard I try, no matter how fast I run, no matter what I do, I can't hold her, she just keeps slipping through my fingers.

Memories crash over me—every promise I made to keep her safe, every whispered dream of a future together. They feel like lies now. Lies I had to tell myself because I wanted to believe that I could be more than what I am. That I could be a man worthy of her love. But I'm not that man, and I never was, and never will be.

"We'll find him. We have to."

CHAPTER TWENTY-ONE

Renata

I STARE AT OLLIE—MY protector. The monster. My husband.

The tension is so thick it's choking me. He stands over the slumped man, blood on his hands, and yet somehow I'm the one who feels like I'm drowning.

Is he dead? I can't tell. Maybe it doesn't even matter anymore. He was just a tool, punished by the man I married. The man I thought I could love.

He was a means to an end, and Ollie did what he had to—wrung him out until there was nothing left.

The man's screams still echo in my head, each one like a dagger twisting in my gut. Ollie's face is a mask of control—impassive, but there's something in his eyes that looks like a plea. He blinks, and whatever humanity I imagined is gone. The same darkness I've come to expect is in its place, the inhumanity I've tried so hard to ignore.

The unease turns into a cold, hard knot in my belly.

He's here. It's too late.

A chill wraps around my spine, my worry burrowing into my mind, feeding on my deepest fears. "What does it mean?" I ask, but the words taste bitter. I don't even know if I want the answer anymore. What's the point of a next step if every move feels like a death sentence?

Ollie straightens, the lone wolf, the protector who would tear the world apart for me. But even as he promises safety, I wonder. What happens when the threat isn't out *there,* but standing right in front of him?

I've only ever loved three people—Isabella, Carlos, and Ollie. The three most unhinged, ruthless people to ever walk this earth. What does that say about me? Why do I gravitate toward the ones that burn everything they touch?

What in the actual fuck is wrong with me?

"First, we assess who's still here. You. My mother and my sister. Lev and Isabella are at the hospital, and everyone else has gone home. Next, I contact Aleks. We need to find out where he is." He draws me closer to him with one beckoning of his finger. I step closer to him even though I don't want to. The smell of another man's blood still lingers on him.

At my resistance, Ollie's expression shifts, the concern he showed for me moments ago slipping away like clouds through fingers. Maybe it was only an illusion, something I thought I could hold. His eyes are cold, merciless, his posture rigid. The man I love is gone; the cold, calculating murderer now stands before me.

"I need to keep you safe," Ollie orders, his voice cold and devoid of any comfort. There's no tenderness or reassurance, just command. He's not my husband right now but a general issuing orders.

I swallow, trying to steady myself as the reality of what happened settles in. We're not safe. The man who's haunted us has found us, and there's no time to waste. My only salvation is the man who stands before me now.

"You'll do exactly what I say while we make sure everyone is secure," he says harshly. Cold. He speaks to me like I'm one of his soldiers, but I'm not one of his men—I'm his wife, but right now, it doesn't seem as if he cares.

I shake my head. What matters is doing what he tells me and making sure that we stay safe.

"Keep barking orders at me, Ollie," I snap, my voice tense with anger. "Keep whispering sweet nothings in my ear and see how far that gets you."

"Renata," he says in a growl, his patience threadbare. "Behave yourself. Do *not* test me right now."

I grit my teeth because a part of me knows he's right. This is not time or place.

I follow him out of the room, even though I don't really have a choice because he's gripping my arm tightly. My legs are jelly as I will myself to keep going. My mind races, thoughts spinning out of control as I try to process everything. The house that's supposed to feel like a fortress feels like a trap, every creak of the floorboards and whisper of the wind outside making me jump. We gather in a second room, thankfully, because the one beside the living room still holds the body of a man bleeding out... or dead.

Tension is etched on everyone's faces as Ollie stands near the window, his hand hovering near his gun as he scans the grounds outside.

Ekaterina stands close to him, her fingers twisting nervously around the hem of her shirt. "Renata," she says gently, "Are you all right?"

I shake my head and don't answer.

"What's happened?" Polina asks, her face pale.

"We're locking everything down," Ollie snaps, his words clipped and sharp. He's already shifted into commander mode, the warmth he showed me earlier buried under layers of cold calculation. "No one leaves until we know the house is secure. I questioned the man who infiltrated us. He told me that Carlos is here."

"Here?" Polina's voice wavers, her face a mask of barely contained fear. We all feel it—the unspoken terror that Carlos could be in the very walls around us.

Ollie laughs mirthlessly. "Unfortunately, that's as far as we got. Your guess is as good as mine."

Polina and I share a glance.

"I wasn't able to get more information out of him. He could've been referring to New York for all I know." His stance tells me there's no damn way he believes that to be true.

But we all know the greatest threat is if he's in this house.

"Bring it," Polina says as she pulls out a gun.

"Who the fuck gave you that?" Ollie asks.

"You think only the men in this family carry weapons? Where have you been? Oh, right. Moscow. Paris. Colombia. Guess what, brother? While you were globe-trotting, Isabella trained us in self-defense, and Harper recently gave us shooting lessons."

I've heard that Harper is a master with guns, and I love that she's shown them how to use one.

I'm next, girls.

"You know how to use that?" Ollie asks. I cringe.

The sound of outrage from me, his sister, and his mother all at once makes him put up his hands like a little boy. "Okay, okay. I just want to leave with my balls intact, thank you."

"Say something like that again, and I will show you exactly how good I am at using this gun!" Polina says, glaring at him.

"Which part?" he says. "The part about using the gun or my balls being intact?"

"Yes," she says.

"Fine, so you know how to use a gun," he mutters. I'd think he was being a dick if I didn't know he was worried about us. "Mom?" he says.

"I'm not as good as Polina," she says. "But there's no one who can get me in a chokehold that I can't get out of." She smiles sweetly at him.

His eyes widen slightly. She's so badass.

Ollie turns to me. "Renata?"

"I've only just begun lessons, but Isabella tells me I'm a quick study," I say. Somehow, being around his mom and sister reminds me that we are part of something different, something bigger. I get one little glimpse of what it would be like to be truly one with this family.

"We need to lock everything down," Ollie says. "Aleks is going to check for biometric markers. I want a full sweep, inside and out."

He has a hurried conversation on his phone in Russian.

"Are they at the bunker?" Ekaterina asks quietly. Ollie gives her a short nod.

"Is he inside this house?" She doesn't ask how he got here, but *if* he's here. I see the fear in her eyes, in the way Polina clings to her, and I know this isn't the first time they've been in a position like this. The question hangs in the air, the unspoken terror we all feel is undeniable. If he's in this house, we're sitting ducks, and I fucking hate that.

Ollie speaks almost mechanically. "We're going to scan now. For now, everyone stays right in this room. No one goes anywhere alone."

"For how long?" Polina asks.

"As long as it takes," Ollie snaps.

"Relax, Ollie. I know the woman you love is here with us. We all know that. Guess who else knows that?"

He pinches his lips together and doesn't reply.

When Polina turns away from him, tears are shining in her eyes. Ekaterina wraps an arm around her, whispering something in her ear that sounds like Russian, but I can see the fear in her eyes too. It isn't just me anymore—it's all of us, making sure none of us become collateral damage in the twisted game between Carlos and the Romanovs.

A sudden crash outside the room makes me jump, but it's just Aleks returning from his sweep of the house. I have to remind myself to breathe.

"I don't see anything. I checked every room. There's no sign of forced entry and no sign of anybody here but us. If he's here, he's damn good at hiding."

"That's because he's not here," Viktor adds, his tone frustrated. "There's no indication that anyone is in this house. He said that just to scare us."

Ollie doesn't look relieved, as if he doesn't even believe them. His expression remains hard and unreadable. "I'm not convinced. I'm not taking any chances. We stay locked down until I'm certain," Ollie commands, his voice a low growl. He won't' be satisfied until he's torn apart every inch of this house, hunting for shadows.

"What will you do?" Polina asks.

"I've already checked and told you there's no evidence of anybody else in this house. He must be in The Cove. We know this."

"Get in touch with Toschi," Ollie says.

Who is that?

Will it always feel like I only see half of what's going on around me?

"I did," Ollie says. "He's in The Cove, but he hasn't revealed his location to anyone."

"Fine, then. Everyone stays here. We will find him."

"It's like finding a needle in a haystack," Aleks says, obviously frustrated. "Can't you see that?"

"What would you have me do?" Ollie explodes. "You know he's after Renata."

His brothers leave when they realize no one can talk sense to him.

Hours pass, each one feeling more interminable than the last. Polina and Ekaterina try to lighten the mood with small talk, but even they eventually fall silent. It seems pointless to force conversation when we're all here, tense, wondering what the next moment will bring.

Finally, Ollie gives in. "There's no evidence he's here," he says with palpable reluctance. "But I'm not taking any chances."

"Shocker," I mutter under my breath, making Polina smile, though it fades quickly as Ollie's eyes snap to mine. Even now, with all the uncertainty swirling around us—about who I am, who he is—there's a dangerous edge to his gaze that sends a shiver down my spine.

Oh, Ollie.

"Why don't you and Renata go back up to the guest-room," Ekaterina suggests gently. "I promise that Polina and I will stay right here in the house until you give us further instructions."

His jaw clenches, teeth grinding. I can only pity anyone foolish enough to confront him now. He's wound so tight he's like a spring just about to break.

"Fine." He exhales sharply. "Aleks—"

"I'm constantly monitoring biometric feedback in the house," Aleks interjects, his tone clinical. "All of you need rest, food, and water."

Ollie hesitates, then reaches for my hand. I pretend not to see it, stepping ahead of him instead. I don't want to be petty, but I don't want to touch him right now.

I haven't come to terms with the fact that I love him—all of him. The darkness, the brutality, the cold, calculating killer. But how do you reconcile love with fear?

The thought of being alone with him now, facing the coldness in his eyes and the violence I know he's capable of, is too much.

I walk away. He lets me.

"Where are you going?" he demands in a harsh whisper.

"Where you tell me," I snap back, anger flaring. "Do I have any choice in the matter?"

"No, that's not up for discussion. You're staying with me."

"And if I don't want to?" I challenge, watching hurt briefly flicker in his eyes before it's replaced with anger. "Dammit, Renata. Can't you see I'm trying to keep you safe?" His voice lowers to a rough whisper, his frustration obvious. "Why can't you see that?"

"I can, but I'm under no illusion that I'm safe *from* you, Ollie." The words slip out before I can stop them, hanging in the air like a death knell. He recoils as if struck. Maybe I have finally struck a chord in him because for the first time ever I see pain in his eyes, buried beneath layers of anger and cold calculation.

"I don't want to stay here," I whisper, my voice breaking. "Not with you like this."

"Like what?" he asks, his voice a dangerous edge of darkness.

I don't answer.

We walk in silence, and I wonder if he's too far gone—too deeply entrenched in his role as the cold commander to ever turn back.

When we reach the room, he opens the door, steps inside, and yanks me in after him. He slams it shut and presses me against it, capturing my lips in a fierce, desperate kiss. My body betrays me, going boneless as I melt under the heat of his touch, and I hate myself for it.

He kisses me like today is the only day we have to live, like there's no promise of tomorrow. He kisses me as if he's begging for forgiveness for being who he is. He kisses me as if he loves me, and it shatters my heart in two.

"Just because we haven't found any fucking sign of Carlos doesn't mean we're safe," he murmurs against my lips, his voice strained.

"Will we ever be?" I ask, my voice trembling despite my best efforts to keep it steady.

"Of course we will," he says, but I hear the lie beneath the bravado even though I don't want to.

No, we'll never be safe. There will always be something threatening us. We'll always have to be on alert, and I hate it. I want to run. I want to get away from here. And if I didn't think that was the weakest possible response, I would have.

"Renata," he says, his tone softening, becoming tender again. I don't want him to be this way—it's so much harder to resist when he is like this.

Why do I even try to resist him?

I've spent my life protecting myself from vulnerability. I've had to. I would never have gotten this far if I didn't. I don't know how to manage this.

"Talk to me."

"I don't know, Ollie. I'm afraid. And it's not just Carlos."

He closes his eyes and breathes through his nose. "I don't know a way forward. I don't know how to show you not to fear me." He shakes his head. "I can't fucking help who I am."

"I know!" I cry, my voice breaking. "Don't you understand that I know that? But I can't just wave a magic wand and become somebody else."

"Neither can I!" he snaps back.

It's a fair point, and I know it. I try to draw back, to lean into being an adult instead of a headstrong child. "This isn't getting us anywhere."

Finally, he blows out a breath. "Aleks said you all needed food, water, and rest."

"So do *you*."

"I can't sleep, knowing he's out there, knowing he's coming after you!"

I shake my head. "You'll have to. What are you going to do—run on fumes for five days? Ten days? A month, whatever it takes?"

He groans, blowing out another breath in frustration. He walks over to a small refrigerator in the corner of the room that I hadn't noticed before. "We have emergency food reserves in here. Eat."

"Only if you do." If I have to adult, so does he.

He opens it, takes out a meal replacement bar and a bottle of water, and hands them to me, then gets one of each for himself. I'm no fool, so I eat the bar, even though it tastes like sweetened chalk, and I drink the entire bottle of water.

I walk to the bathroom and splash water on my face. I don't know how I can feel as if my insides have been stirred around with a spoon and baked, yet I still look totally fine. If anything, the scar on my face seems more pronounced than before, but that's probably because I need some sleep. The scar feels weirdly like a symbol of our broken relationship.

Ollie is talking on the phone in rapid Russian, probably going over whatever he and his brothers have found.

"How is Isabella? Any update on her?"

He looks at me. "She's all right," he says. "She's still there. She's asking for you."

"Me?"

He shakes his head. "She says there's something she needs to tell you, but she won't say what."

I frown. What would she need to tell me?

"So? Are we going there?" I ask, even though I know that's impossible. "How is she supposed to tell me what I need to know?"

"Of course not. You'll talk on the phone."

Right. If we're sitting ducks, it makes no sense to bring the pregnant one here.

I take the phone and answer the call. "Isabella? Are you all right?"

"I'm fine," Isabella replies, her voice steady but with a hint of weariness. "I had a scare, but nothing serious. Apparently, this can happen sometimes. Lucky me."

"Why are you bleeding? What happened?" I ask, anxiety tightening in my chest.

"They told me the cramping and bleeding are unrelated. Some women just have a heightened sensitivity, which can cause light or even heavy bleeding. They mentioned something about a pregnancy hemorrhage—it's where blood collects between the uterus or something. It sounds terrifying, but they assured me it often resolves on its own and doesn't harm the baby. As for the cramping, it's just dehydration. They gave me fluids through an IV, and I'll be able to come home soon."

Ollie watches me closely, with that intense expression he gets sometimes—his eyes narrowed, arms crossed over his chest. He's perched on the edge of the bed, his brow furrowed, green eyes blazing with intensity.

"I'm so glad to hear that," I say, exhaling with relief. There are so few people I truly care about in this world and knowing at least one of them is safe brings me some measure of comfort. She needs to carry this pregnancy to term safely.

Isabella's tone shifts, becoming more serious. "We need to talk, Renata. And while I trust my husband and yours, what I need to tell you is highly confidential." Her voice lowers. "I sent an encrypted message to your phone. You need to step away from Ollie and listen to it. Do you understand?"

My heart beats faster, and my skin feels prickly. I swallow hard and nod, my voice steady despite the turmoil inside me. "Where's Lev?" I ask, keeping my tone deliberately light.

"Oh, he stepped out to get me something to eat," she says sweetly. "Please confirm you heard what I said."

"I did. I'll be in touch. Thank you so much for letting me know."

I hang up the phone, my heart pounding. I hate lying—it feels wrong, but I need to find out what she sent me. What is this about?

"And?" Ollie's voice cuts through my thoughts.

"She just wanted to talk about, you know, girl stuff," I say, shaking my head. I force a yawn. "I'm exhausted. We were talking about things like hemorrhoids, bleeding, and periods. Do you really want the details?"

Ollie stares at me, unblinking, clearly unconvinced. He doesn't buy it for a second. How am I going to get my phone without him noticing?

I'll have to wait until he's in the shower, distracted, or maybe even awake in the middle of the night. I'll find a way.

My phone sits innocuously in my bag on the bedside table. If the message is encrypted, it means no one else can access it. That's a relief, at least.

On a whim, I decide to head into the bathroom. My headphones are in that bag too...

"I'm going to get ready for bed."

Ollie holds my gaze for a moment longer. "All right," he finally says, his voice a mix of suspicion and concern. "I'm coming with you."

Oh, sweet Jesus.

"Ollie, can't I even go to the *bathroom* alone?"

"Carlos could be in this house, Renata."

"And if he is, I'll scream for you, and you'll come to my rescue. Deal?"

"Fine," he grumbles, "but I'm standing right outside the door if you need me."

I know his concern is genuine, but it's damn near suffocating. And where would Carlos *be*? Aleks already ran a complete security scan and can't find any evidence that someone else is in the house.

I think he's overreacting, as usual.

I grab my bag. He only gives me a curious look, which I ignore. I make a big deal of shutting the bathroom door and rolling my eyes, really just to distract him from what I'm about to do.

I run the water and pull out my toothbrush, making as much noise as I can to mask my real intentions. I unzip my bag, retrieve an earpiece, and slip it into my ear. My hands are shaking as I tap my phone screen. There it is—a text message from Isabella, waiting for me to open it. I press the play button, and the screen prompts me to use my thumbprint to unlock it.

"Everything all right in there?" Ollie's voice is laced with suspicion, even through the door.

"Yes," I reply, forcing a light tone. "My molars look excellent. No signs of tooth decay!" I hope he doesn't notice the slight tremor in my voice. "No villains in the shower, and I don't hear any ticking bombs," I add, hearing a low growl from the other side of the door that nearly makes me smile.

Isabella's voice comes through the earpiece, guarded and rapid.

"I have a man who works for me that has information about Carlos. He's learned that Carlos is working with La Sombra Roja. They've offered him a million dollars for your capture, believing you hold critical information that could either solidify their power or dismantle their operations entirely. They believe you know the Romanov family and the

Carrera cartel's most sensitive secrets, including alliances and details of their financial operations—information that could help them dominate the Colombian underworld."

My pulse quickens as I process her words, but Isabella isn't finished.

Why doesn't she want Ollie to know this?

"However, there's more. This part will impact you greatly. You're supposed to inherit five-hundred million dollars when you turn twenty-five, from your mother's family. La Sombra Roja wants to take you and your money to expand their empire."

My breath catches. This isn't just about family—it's about power. The stakes are far higher than I imagined. Of course, Carlos's vendetta wouldn't have pushed him this far alone.

"Carlos is using this as his ticket back to power. We need to bring him out of hiding now. The longer we wait, the more desperate he'll become. And this is why my message to you is private, Renata. Ollie will *never* let you use yourself as bait, but it's only way to draw Carlos out into the open. We know Carlos is nearby. Get away from Ollie. Use yourself as bait. Bring Ollie with you if you have to, but you must draw Carlos out of hiding."

There's a rush of static, and the recording ends. I stare at my phone, the water still running in the sink. My heart races as I shut off the faucet and shove the phone back into my bag.

I know what I have to do.

CHAPTER TWENTY-TWO

RENATA SLEEPS next to me as peacefully as can be. It feels like she's hiding something, but she's been closed up and walled off from me since she saw me beat the shit out of Carlos's lackey. I make no apologies for who I am, but I need her back. The thought of losing her makes my chest tighten. But how do I keep her close when I'm what she fears most?

It takes me a while to fall asleep because I know Carlos is close. He's not in this room—I'm sure of that much—but he's lurking somewhere, lying in wait, biding his time. I know men like him, and I can feel his presence like a dark cloud hanging over us. Frustration gnaws at me, the urge to bring him out into the open so strong that I even considered setting fire to my own family home just to smoke him out. My thoughts desperate, reckless, but the need to get to him is overwhelming.

I finally sleep fitfully; the only thing soothing my restless mind being the warm body of Renata beside me. But even that comfort is fleeting. Morning comes too soon, and I'm up early, checking in on everyone. My mother is fine, my sister is safe, and my brothers report that nothing's amiss.

I honestly didn't expect anything else. This is how men like him work. He doesn't have the backing of dozens of men, so he has to bide his time and strike hard and fast when you least expect it, like a snake in tall grass.

When is he going to make his move? How much longer do we have to wait?

Renata wakes up next to me, rolling over and propping herself up on her elbow. Her gaze is intense, and there's something in her eyes that makes my gut twist.

I don't care if she's angry with me or upset, I lean over and kiss her cheek before I tuck an errant lock of hair behind her ear. I wish she really knew how much I love her, that she really, *truly* understood.

"No matter what happens, Ollie, I need you to know that I love you. And I need you to trust me."

I reach out and cup her jaw in my hand, forcing her to meet my eyes. "That sounds like something I would say to you. Is there something you need to tell me?"

"No," she says, but she's definitely lying.

"Renata..." I press, my voice low with warning.

She cuts me off, her tone firm. "What did I just tell you? I love you, and you need to trust me. Can you do that or not?"

There's a determination in her voice that gives me pause. I frown as she continues.

"You're not the only one here, Ollie. I had a revelation overnight. I know we've fought. I've struggled with who you are, with who I am. But there's nobody else I'd rather be with. So please, Ollie. Give me this." Her voice drops to a whisper, her eyes pleading.

I think silently for a moment. I know I love her. I love her like a man starving to death loves his next meal, like a drowning man loves air. *I love her.* Of course I do. I'd give my own life for this woman. I brush my thumb along her cheek, tracing the scar that marks her skin. Some might think I'm crazy, but I find it beautiful—unique. It defines who she is. I've never known a more beautiful woman in my life. It's like that scar is the one flaw that sets her apart from all the rest, making her one of a kind.

"I love you. I trust you," I tell her, my voice steady.

She exhales slowly, then whispers, "Give me a weapon, please."

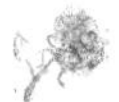

CHAPTER TWENTY-THREE

Renata

I WISH he had more time to show me how to really use it, but we'll have to make do. I can tell he's reserved, but he's trying, and God, if that doesn't mean fucking everything to me right now.

Maybe loving someone doesn't mean perfection or never failing. Maybe it means showing up. Maybe it means learning, time and time again, how to keep going despite not even really knowing the steps to take or the moves to make. Maybe loving someone means not giving up, regardless of the odds you face together.

Thankfully, Ollie nods. He pushes out of bed and walks to the dresser, pulling open the bottom drawer. When I see what he's offering, I gasp but quickly stifle it. *Yes.* Now we're playing with the big guns.

"Take this," he says, handing me a compact, handheld canister that's about the size of a tube of lipstick. "There's a nozzle and safety cap to prevent accidental discharge. You hold it firmly in your hand with your thumb on the safety, point the nozzle directly at your attacker's face, and aim for the eyes. A single burst should be enough to disable. As soon as you pull it, step *back* so you don't inhale the air around it."

"What will it do?"

"It'll cause temporary blindness, difficulty breathing, and intense burning, giving you enough time to get away."

His voice is steady, but I can see the tension in his eyes as he watches me.

I take the bottle, my hand trembling slightly as I place it on the table beside me. "Thank you."

"If you ever need to incapacitate a man, go for the balls," Ollie says, his tone deadly serious.

"Seriously?" I ask, my eyebrows raised in disbelief.

"Seriously," he repeats. "A hard strike with two fingers, a kick—it doesn't take much. Just don't hesitate. That's the key. You'll only have seconds to act, but that's all you'll need to get away." He shakes his head. "Swear to fuck, my balls are aching just from the thought of it."

I snort and shake my head. This is an easy one.

Ollie continues. "If he's standing close to you, balance your stance. The knee strike is one of the most effective ways. Aim for the center of the groin, be quick and forceful, and drive your knee upward. This is something you can do if your attacker is directly in front of you or you're being held or grabbed. If there's more distance, you can aim for a front kick or even pick something up and whack him with it, but make sure your aim is solid."

"Okay, alright, I've got it." I nod, my mouth dry. I have a sudden, sharp headache I know is only stress, but I still feel nauseous.

I nod, trying to absorb everything he's telling me.

"After you hit someone's nuts, he'll double over. It could also make him disorientated or nauseous, but it's a rare guy who will be able to walk for long if you strike him where it hurts."

I nod, feeling a bit more prepared, when he reaches into the drawer again and pulls out a small, slender knife.

"Go for the exposed, soft parts of the body," he says, handing it to me. "And don't hesitate, Renata. Women may not be as strong as a man, but that isn't the point. I just gave you three weapons you can use against an attacker. What makes you most vulnerable is your unwillingness to use them. You *have* to be willing to hurt someone to save yourself. Jab, twist, do whatever the fuck you need to do. This is also useful if you're ever restrained. Got it?"

I nod again, taking the knife and tucking it into my sleeve. I've dressed in form-fitting clothing, something that will allow me to move quickly if I need to. I have a feeling I will.

Ollie turns to me, his expression softening as he looks into my eyes. "I don't know what's going on in your head right now, but I know this—you're a survivor. You're fiercely determined." He pauses, his gaze steady and unwavering. "Your greatest weakness here is remembering who your brother was to you. Know this, Renata—that man no longer exists. That doesn't matter anymore. Hold onto the memory of who he was, but don't delude yourself about who he is now."

His voice grows husky with emotion, and it takes everything in me not to break down. "Sometimes, relationships fade, and people change. We need to remember what we had with them instead of lying to ourselves about the way things are now."

His words cut deep because I know they're true. I've been lying to myself, hoping against hope that my brother isn't the monster I know he's become. A part of me still hopes that Carlos loves me the way I once loved him, but Ollie is right—that's my greatest weakness. If he shows even a hint of caring, if he apologizes, I know I might cave to him.

It's hard to describe the bond between a brother and sister—something no one else can understand. No one knows what I went through growing up like Carlos does. No one knows the threads that wove the fabric of my being the way he does.

I could tell Ollie everything, but he'll never understand the way Carlos would. Flesh of my flesh, blood of my blood... Eventually, I'll have to give myself space to grieve what once was—to mourn the death of the brother I grew up with.

For now, I have to survive.

I stand quietly, going over the instructions he just gave me as I watch Ollie get ready.

I wish for all of this to be over. I'm ready.

So is he.

We head downstairs as if we're in the middle of an active shooting situation, inspecting every crevice, every corner. His guards are stationed at various places—in doorways, by windows. He doesn't trust this situation, and neither do I. Where could Carlos be?

Or maybe we are mistaken?

Did the man Ollie killed lie to us?

I sigh. I know the truth. I know when people lie, and he spoke the truth.

Carlos is here.

Not in New York. Not in The Cove.

Carlos is in this house, and he's here to kill me.

CHAPTER TWENTY-FOUR

Ollie

WHEN WE REACH the dining room, we're alone. There's evidence that my mother and Polina have already had breakfast—my mother's favorite coffee mug sits in the kitchen sink, and Polina's cereal bowl is next to it, with a little milk and spoon sitting in it.

If it were up to me, nobody would be wandering around anywhere. But goddamnit, we need to force Carlos out of hiding.

In silence, I scramble eggs while Renata makes toast. She butters it liberally and slides it onto a plate next to my eggs. When she comes near me, I draw her closer. I hold her. I kiss her temple and breathe her in, and for one stolen moment, we're at peace before we pull away.

I don't know what's going to happen today, but I heard her loud and clear—*I love you, and I need you to trust me.*

Aside from my brothers, I don't trust anyone.

Learning to trust Renata may be the hardest thing I ever do, but I can do it.

"How's Isabella?" I ask, knowing she's not going to tell me shit about Isabella.

"She's fine. She's going home today." She bows her head and looks away for a moment as if steeling herself, gathering her resolve. Her eyes are wide when she looks up at me. "Remember what I said, Ollie," she says quietly, pushing her plate away.

I nod. "I do."

She mouths, *I love you.*

What the fuck?

I stare at her as she shoves her plate away. "I'm done, Ollie. I can't do this anymore. I need space. I feel like I'm suffocating here."

Oh, she does not. She will not fucking—she gets to her feet, and I stare at her, confused and a little suspicious.

"What are you talking about? This isn't the time or place."

"I know! My brother isn't here. You guys have already looked everywhere. Aleks has checked. He's not here because Carlos is dead. I told you he was dead," she says, tossing her head.

What the fuck is she doing? I stare at her, my eyes narrowing.

Rolling her eyes, she continues. "If he actually was here, he wouldn't be hiding like this. That isn't his way. You know that. He'd just confront us."

She pushes away from the table. "You watching my every move is driving me crazy. You even wanted to go to the bathroom with me!"

"Renata," I growl, my hands clenching into fists.

"No, Ollie. I need to get out, to think, to breathe. I can't stay here like this. I didn't even want to marry you, you know that."

I don't think so. My eyes narrow on her. "You're not going anywhere. Not while your brother is still a threat."

She looks desperate and frustrated, and I half wonder if this is an act when she faces me, her eyes blazing. "You don't own me, Ollie Romanov. I am not a prisoner, and I'm not going to sit around and let you control me like this." Her nostrils flare.

Jesus.

Has Renata been in league with Carlos the whole time?

She swears she was taken from us even though every recording we had made it look like she was the one who left on her own. Even her best friend thought she was a traitor.

Has she manipulated us?

Damn. If she's acting, she's a really good actress.

She strides toward the door, her heels clicking on the floor. Is she serious?

"Where the fuck do you think you're going?"

"Out, Ollie. I can't do this anymore. My brother is dead, and you're delusional if you think that we're going to sit around waiting for him to come. I won't play these games anymore."

Her movements are quick and agitated as she heads for the door, grabbing the handle.

I reach her in two quick steps. "You're not going anywhere without me."

"Is that the sum total of our life to you?" She yanks her arm free from my grip, her eyes flashing. "I told you, I'm done with this. If you don't let me go, I will make you." Without warning, she reaches for the small canister in her bag.

I step back, startled. Holy shit. Did she ask for weapons so that she could arm herself against *me*? Did I just fucking walk into a trap?

As Renata marches toward the door, her frustration obvious, something changes. I feel it in my gut. The air feels thicker, and my nerves are on edge. My instincts are ready to snap, and before I can say a word, the door swings open.

And there he is. Carlos Carrera, my archenemy, one of the few men Renata has ever loved, scrawny and mean. He stands in the doorway, his eyes darkening as he stares at her. "Step back, Romanov. One move, and she dies." He shakes his head, a gun trained on Renata. "You didn't listen to me, little sister."

How the hell did he get in here? He must've been hiding in plain sight. My mind races, trying to figure everything out. We're by the porch, near the front—the only place we hadn't checked—the ventilation system that runs through the walls, hidden behind grates and ducts. *Goddamn* it. He's no stranger to evading detection. He must've found a way to block his biometric signature to make sure we didn't pick up his presence here, and he's slight, so it could've worked.

Fucking manipulator. It doesn't matter how he did it—he could've scrambled signals, fed false data, or cloaked himself somehow. He came here for a reason.

Carlos's gaze lingers on her like a predator sizing up prey before an attack. Something's twisted in the way he looks at her, like she's betrayed him, as if their family still claims some kind of ownership over her.

But he's wrong. She owes him nothing.

He snarls at her while my mind races with plans to thwart him. To protect her.

"You weren't supposed to tell lover boy that I was alive."

"I didn't," she says. "I know why you want me, Carlos. Isabella told me everything. You're not going to get your way."

She still clutches the pepper spray. I can tell that she's surprised and definitely afraid but also determined. She is not going to back down in front of her brother.

He blocks the exit while I assess what the fuck to do. Suddenly, strong arms grab me from behind. I fight, but whoever holds me doesn't let go. I look over my shoulder to see a masked man behind me. *Fuck.* Where are my brothers?

Carlos gives me a smile. "Did you really think I'd come alone? Knowing that you'd kill me on sight? I've seen how good you are with a weapon, fucking Romanov."

This is personal. I don't even know why, but this is fucking personal.

"You didn't think you'd get away so easily, did you, Renata?"

Every muscle in my body tenses. "Leave her alone," I warn, even though I know it will do no good. I flex and try with all my might to get away from whoever holds me, but he's got me in a grip so tight I can't budge.

Carlos laughs. "Or what, Ollie? You'll kill me? Just like you killed my men?" His eyes gleam as he looks at me. "Are you protecting my sister? Just so you can fuck her again? So you can take everything that belongs to her? Does she even know why you married her?"

Renata's eyes widen as she looks at me. What the fuck is he talking about?

"Ollie," she whispers.

"Don't let him manipulate you. Don't listen to him."

He takes another step closer to Renata, but she stands her ground and clenches her teeth. "Carlos, it doesn't have to be this way," she begins to plead.

No! If she thinks for one goddamn minute, she can make him listen...

"Don't you fucking touch her," I growl, my voice shaking with rage. Carlos smirks.

Where the hell are my men? Where the hell are my brothers?

"There's something you don't understand, Mr. Romanov," Carlos says with a sickening voice. "Renata has always been mine. Blood is thicker than water, especially for the cartel. Don't you know that?" He shakes his head.

Renata tightens her grip on the canister, her knuckles white. Carlos doesn't know she has it, he hasn't seen it yet. She glances at me, and I give her a silent nod. We are going to have to fight our way out of this together.

"I came here to get you, little sister, because we have everything we need—no one can stop us now. I knew that if I sent you here, I'd be able to find a way in. I also knew that if we trapped you, we'd get critical information about the Romanovs. And we did, didn't we?" he says with a smile. Renata shakes her head as if confused. Has she been working with him all along? "You've made it so easy for me, Renata. Thank you so very much for your cooperation, sister. I'll now take you with me, turn you over to trusted partners, and take my fucking inheritance."

"What inheritance?" she asks, but she's a terrible liar. I don't know what the fuck he's talking about either, but she definitely does.

He reaches for her, and with a scream, she pulls the trigger.

CHAPTER TWENTY-FIVE

Renata

MY HAND TREMBLES. Even now, with everything he's done, with all the lives he's ruined—including mine—I hesitate. I should want to hurt him, but I don't. And that's what I hate most about myself.

The spray goes a mile wide.

Carlos only shakes his head, and then, in two steps, he reaches me. He doesn't hurt me, though, but puts my hands behind my back, almost gently, and pulls a large zip tie from his pocket.

He's planned this. This is exactly what he planned to do all along.

"I told you what would happen, didn't I?" he whispers softly. His voice is cold, and I hate the way my stomach turns just looking at him.

"I told you what I would do," he says, and I can't help it. I see the little boy I knew. I see it in his eyes and the way his mouth twists, as if he's acting, like somebody is pulling the strings on a puppet.

"Who's putting you up to this, Carlos? This wasn't you, this isn't *you!*"

He only stares at me and doesn't move, but his muscles are tense, his eyes alert. He's waiting for his chance.

Ollie won't let him live; he can't. Carlos is dead. I know it. But how can I be the one who pulls the trigger? How will I forgive Ollie if he does?

Carlos continues to lecture as if convincing himself that he's doing the right thing.

"I told you what the consequences would be if you betrayed me. You provided me exactly what I needed, little sister. A way in to the Romanov family. Thank you for that," he says with a smile.

What is he talking about? I feel half-sick.

"I promised you this, didn't I, Renata? You'd watch me destroy everything you love— slowly, painfully—and now look at you. You handed me the perfect opportunity. It's almost like you wanted me to do it."

A blade glints in his hand. He's holding me to him as he addresses Ollie. "I saw what you did, Romanov. Now you can have a taste of your own medicine."

"No!" I scream. Where is everybody? How are we at the Romanov estate, and it's just me and Ollie in a standoff with

Carlos and one of his men? There should be guards, his other brothers, *anybody*.

Carlos advances on Ollie.

I still have the slim knife Ollie gave me tucked in the back of my pants so I could retrieve it if need be. This is my opportunity. My brother doesn't consider me a threat yet.

He will soon enough.

I free the blade from its sheath tucked into my backside with my wrists and slide the slender blade down until it hits my fingers. I try to do it as quietly as I can, all while trying to distract Carlos. "You were never like this!" I scream. "Our father would be disgusted with you!"

I go on about tradition, loyalty, all the while sawing at the zip tie. He fastened it lightly, it's not hard, I just need more time. Out of the corner of his eye, the masked man holding Carlos looks at me. He sees what I'm doing. *Shit*. I wait for him to give me away, but he says nothing. What the hell?

It all happens in seconds. Carlos springs at Ollie as my binds come free. I keep my hands together so he doesn't see that I'm freed and eye my canister where it fell to the floor. Carlos is standing with his back to me. I stand still, pretending that I am still restrained.

"You fucking asshole," Carlos says with fury to Ollie. Ollie's still restrained, so Carlos easily decks him. Ollie's head snaps back, and blood spurts from the corner of his mouth.

No.

I can't take this anymore. I will not see him hurt Ollie.

In one quick movement, I grab the canister from the floor and lunge at him. I push him from behind, and when Carlos twists, I do exactly what Ollie told me to—I kick him between the legs. My foot meets its target with sickening accuracy.

My brother howls, and when he falls to the floor clutching himself, I pull the trigger on the spray. This time, I don't miss.

My belly twists with nausea, but I keep at it. I pull the trigger again and again until my brother is screaming in agony and writhing on the floor, one hand between his legs and the other at his eyes.

"Help me!" he screams at the man holding Ollie, but the masked man does nothing and only watches.

I reach for Ollie as the man holding him lets him go. I stare in shock, ready to defend Ollie, ready to help when all of a sudden, Ollie is standing in front of me smirking. I blink in surprise, but he doesn't hesitate. It's like he knew it was only an act, that the man holding him had no ill intent.

"Get back, Renata!" Ollie orders while he picks up Carlos and slams him against the wall. He hits him with an uppercut that makes Carlos scream. I stand back and watch in horror as the only two men I've ever loved brawl.

I scream as they punch each other, rolling on the floor. Fists fall like anvils, but Carlos is basically blind, so he lashes out like cornered a wild animal.

It's a fight to the death, as if his life depends on it, and it fucking does. I know it does. Ollie punches and kicks, and Carlos claws and screams. Knives flash and slice, blood splatters on the floor. Finally, Ollie kneels on my brother, holds his hands above his head, and exposes his neck.

Carlos blinks, still blinded. "No!" he shouts. "You can kill me, but it doesn't end here."

He turns toward me. "They want you, Renata. They want your money." He shakes his head, and again, I see the boy I grew up with. "I'm sorry, La Sombra Roja... they made me do it, I had no choice." he says to me, shaking his head from side to side.

Tears well in my eyes. "Don't kill him, Ollie. Please don't, please."

I can't help it. But Ollie stares at me and shakes his head before he wraps a rope around Carlos's wrists.

"He hurt you," Ollie says. "An eye for an eye," he growls.

That's when I see the mark Ollie made on my brother's cheek... one that mimics mine. I knew he would get retribution.

I place my hand on my cheek and don't talk. I swallow. I'm battling mixed emotions.

"I don't ever want to see him hurt you again, Renata."

"There has to be another way," I plead, begging for my brother's life. "Please."

Ollie bows his head, frowning at me. "If I let him go—"

I shake my head. "I'm not asking you to let him go, Ollie. No. I'm asking you to find another way. Something. Anything."

Gunshots ring out in the distance. Carlos writhes in Ollie's grip. Ollie moves with the lethal precision of a man who has everything to lose. Every punch is weighted with the raw, violent need to protect *me*—his wife. His world.

"My brothers are coming. You're fucking dead, Carrera. The only reason you're still alive is because I love her." He lifts him by the shirt and shakes him. "Do you understand me?"

My brother nods and turns his head away. "It won't end, Renata. La Sombra Roja want you, they want your inheritance." He pleads with me. "I won't hurt you, Renata. Let me go, and I'll fight for you."

It's the first time in my life I wish I couldn't detect lies. It's the first time in my life I wish for ignorance because my brother is lying.

"Oh, Carlos," I whisper. "You're lying." I shake my head. "He's lying, Ollie." My brother can and will kill me as soon as Ollie lets him up.

"She's *mine*," Ollie growls. He gets to his feet and steps on Carlos, holding him in place with his gun locked on him. Carlos throws his head back and screams like a wolf howling. I shiver.

"Anyone who's listening. Anyone who's watching. You don't get to touch a hair on her head without coming through *me* and every one of my brothers. This is Renata Romanova now. My wife. My whole world. Mine in every way that matters. And if anyone—*anyone*—ever tries to take her from me, they'll meet the same fate."

I stare at him as if I've never seen him before. Raw pain and savage beauty shine on his face. I know in that moment he'd die for me. I've never been loved like this before.

Turning to me, Ollie reaches out a hand, and once more—right in the middle of his savagery—he finds tenderness. He can annihilate all of creation and still always find space for me. It's our theme, what unites us—beauty in the storm. Love in the midst of tragedy. My vicious protector who will never hurt *me*.

Ollie cups my jaw in his hand and nods to Carlos's masked man, only... this isn't one of Carlos's men. He takes off his mask. I don't recognize him, but when he does, I see a flash of a scar on his inner wrist. This was the man who protected me from Carlos in Colombia. I realize with a flood of understanding... he's the Romanov mole. He's one of them.

"Take him," he tells him. "You know what to do."

"Turn her away, Ollie," he says in a low growl. "Get her out of here."

I reach for Ollie as he reaches for me. The doors to the dining room burst open, and Ollie's brothers, Nikko and Viktor, huge and ruthless, barrel through the doors.

"He's in there. Get him," Ollie says. "I don't want his filthy blood on my hands."

He slams the door behind them. I bury my head on Ollie's shoulder and flinch at the sound of gunshots.

CHAPTER TWENTY-SIX

Ollie

I HOLD Renata close to me, unsure of what she's feeling or if she'll ever forgive me for my role in her brother's death. I know how she felt about Carlos in the end, what she hoped for, and how it all crumbled.

We walk into the living room, away from the porch, the kitchen, and the dining room, away from the memory of what happened in our final standoff with her brother. Nikko and Viktor will take care of the details.

My phone rings.

I don't want to talk to anyone right now—I just want to be alone with my wife. But I know I have to answer. My time is no longer my own.

Without even checking the caller ID, I pick up the phone.

"Are you two okay?" Lev's voice is on the other end.

"Yeah. He was here. We've got him." I blow out a breath. "Carlos is gone. Where are you?" I respond, keeping it brief. There will be time for detailed conversations later, but for now, we need to exchange the essentials.

"Jesus. Good though. We're on our way home. Isabella and I will be there soon."

I'm relieved to hear that. There's so much we need to discuss.

A second call comes in on the heels of the first. "What happened?" Mikhail demands in a furious rush of words. There's nothing he despises more than knowing someone he loves was nearly killed. And I can't blame him for that.

I tell him everything, sparing no detail. Throughout the entire conversation with my brothers, I keep Renata on my lap. She doesn't cry, but she buries her head in my chest, her hands tucked up against herself like a small child.

It's only after I hang up that I realize I've been rocking her gently as if driven by instinct.

Mikhail explains that when everything went down, my mother and sister's guards kept them barricaded safely in their bedrooms. Thank God for that. Those guards will be getting a hefty bonus.

Renata and I sit in silence for long minutes. Finally, I ask her, "Are you okay?"

The words are too little, a drop of water in a desert, but she's graceful and classy, as always.

"Surprisingly, yes," she replies. "You know I didn't want to see..." her voice gets a little choked, but she swallows and continues, "*that* happen, but I've been thinking about what you said... about not holding onto who people used to be? And I realize now that my brother wasn't the same person I grew up with anymore. He just wasn't. Whatever." She shakes her head and exhales, her breath warm against my skin.

I gently thread my fingers through her hair, wishing I could soothe her. I wish I could make all the pain disappear for her, but I know it wouldn't help her even if I could. She's mine now, and this is the life we live. This is the life we will always have.

A little ball of white fluff, comes bounding through the door like an animated cotton ball. Renata sits up, and for the first time, a tear falls down her face.

"King Arthur," she whispers. The small dog leaps into her lap, his tiny paws pressing against her chest as he licks her face mercilessly. She holds him close, whispering sweet words in Spanish, calling him her little warrior, her little buddy. I know there will come a day when this little guy actually defends and protects her, but for now, his unwavering, unconditional love brings a smile to her face. This little guy deserves a treat.

"I will always love you for getting me a puppy," she says quietly.

We don't talk about Carlos—not then. We don't need to.

I saw her plead with him, and I even saw his own internal struggle, as if a small part of him wanted to return to what once was. But we both knew he had sold his soul to the devil, and keeping him alive wasn't an option. I hold her to me as she cradles the dog. "I love you, Renata. And I'm so very sorry about your brother."

"Ollie... the fact that you weren't the one who killed him in the end means more to me than you'll ever know."

If I had no other choice, I would have done it, but she doesn't need to know that. Not now.

She looks thoughtful. "That man with the scar on his wrist —he saved me from Carlos back in Colombia."

I nod. "He works for us. He'll be debriefing with my brothers later."

"Jesus. He took the risk of going undercover with *Carlos*?"

"Yup."

"He's got balls of steel," she says with obvious admiration.

I ruffle her hair. "No talking about another man's balls."

"Why is he debriefing with your brothers? Why not you?"

"Because I have another job now." I kiss her cheek. "Making sure you're all right. You've just been through hell."

"I know, but I can't explain it... I just... I feel a strange sense of relief now. I didn't even realize how wound up I was, waiting to see what would happen with my brother. But now that he's gone, I feel relieved. And—"

We both understand that we're not safe, not yet. Carlos revealed he was working with someone else. Whether or not they will now come after us is still uncertain. "It feels like his death marks the end of an era, and now I can finally move on."

"I understand that completely."

I hold her in the quiet, and for long moments, neither of us speaks. So much has happened in such a short time, and we need space to process it all.

"It seems like real love means being willing to sacrifice for the other," Renata says softly. "I will give up my freedom, my independence. All of it. And I know you will protect me. I will protect you, too, and do my best by you."

I kiss her cheek. "I think truly loving each other means accepting the past, giving each other space to heal, and being willing to support one another, no matter what."

Our love has been tested by both our personal demons and the forces outside of us. But what matters now is that we respect each other and are committed to finding solutions, to compromising, to finding peace.

Footsteps sound outside the door. Isabella and Lev have arrived.

CHAPTER TWENTY-SEVEN

"ARE YOU ALL RIGHT?" Isabella asks me.

"I'm fine. So is Ollie. What about you?"

"I'm good," she repeats, brushing it off. She walks into the room and takes a seat across from us. "Ollie, my apologies. I was the one who encouraged Renata to bait Carlos. I knew that you would never allow it, so I made it happen."

He clenches his jaw and glares at her, obviously not super happy about the situation, but what is he going to do about it now?

"Is it always going to be like this? I'm not sure if I'm happy about the fact that you're constantly going to be doing this. Are you going to be interfering all the time between me and my wife?" Ollie asks

"No," she says quietly. "It isn't like that."

These two have always been this way and always will be. He's protective, and she's headstrong.

"Listen. I know you have to get shit done, but I also don't want you going behind my back, Isabella. How would you feel if I did that with your brother? With your husband?"

"If you told me the truth, I would've done my best."

Lev snorts. "You would've allowed Renata to be bait for Carlos?" he says. "Bullshit, Ollie. You would've made her stay right by your side, and the next thing we know, six months from now, Carlos would still be at large."

"Glad one of you can be so lax about all this," Ollie snaps.

Something's shifted in me. His protectiveness and sternness are kind of... cute.

Cute? What's wrong with me?

I take a moment to appreciate how good it is to be held like this. I haven't had many moments in my life where I felt completely safe. I inhale his clean, strong, dependable scent. Lev is right. He would never have allowed me to be hurt by Carlos. And I love that about him.

"You two are the people I love most in this world," I say, and to my credit, my voice doesn't even waver. "You're going to have to bury the hatchet or whatever the fuck you need to do so that you get along. Isabella did what she thought she had to, Ollie. So did I. Going forward, we need to make it a rule that we will be as transparent with each other as possible, and when that's not possible, we trust each other's decisions."

Ollie half smiles. "Sounds about right to me. That's what my brothers and I have to do."

"Exactly."

Isabella and Ollie are still kind of glaring at each other, and it finally dawns on me that maybe they're so at odds with each other *because* they both love me.

She's as concerned about me as he is, and they can't agree on what they need to do. Well, who would've known? I'm a little honored. I've never had this many people love me.

Lev looks at me seriously. It's funny how he isn't related to Ollie by blood, but they look a bit alike. Maybe it's the Russian blood and alpha male thing.

"Renata," Lev says carefully. "We need to discuss what happened with your brother, what we will do with his body, and what happens next. Are you all right with having that discussion now?"

I thought maybe I was, but I feel my eyes widen in horror, my heart pounds, and my palms feel sweaty. I guess my instincts have answered for me. "No, I'm not alright with that," I say honestly. "I would much prefer you guys have that discussion without me. Thank you."

"Of course she's not okay with it!" Ollie snaps at Lev. "What the fuck is the matter with you? That was her brother, you asshole!"

I place a hand on his chest to calm him down. "It's all right," I say. King Arthur looks at me with his little teddy bear face and licks my finger. I scratch his ears, and he lets out a deep sigh, lies down, and promptly falls asleep in my lap. My heartbeat slows. He might be the best gift anyone's ever given me.

"Ollie, it's okay. He asked, and I answered. But thank you."

He finally grunts and nods.

God, I love him so. It's the sort of thought that makes all other thoughts diminish as it takes hold, emblazoned in my mind and heart. *I love him.*

I thought I did before, but now I know love is so much more than a shared connection and attraction.

Maybe love isn't perfect without a struggle, but it grows stronger through adversity, embracing all parts of who we are, from the passionate to the everyday. Maybe weathering troubles only underscores our commitments to each other.

Maybe love is about respecting the other person's differences, loving them, flaws and all.

Maybe love takes time and flourishes as it ages if it's well watered and attended to.

Maybe, just maybe, I'm alright with not having all the answers, not doing everything perfectly. Because I love Ollie Romanov, flawed and human, fierce and devoted, and I know he loves me.

I have seen his transformation, and I am honored to see where we go next. From a ruthless enforcer who kept me prisoner, I watched as he gradually opened up to the possibility of a real connection, real love, of finding a way to balance his dark past with hope for the future. He found a way to break the barriers that held him back and let me in.

When I met him, I was a guarded survivor, resilient, yes, but walled off from anything and everyone around me. I've learned to trust myself, to trust others, to find a sense of peace and acceptance for both of us.

I don't have to be strong and ruthless like Isabella, amazing with a gun like Harper, or a brilliant scientist like Nikko's wife Vera... or any of those things. Maybe I can just be... *me*. Renata Carrera Romanova.

I have a place here too. I belong.

"Mikhail is going to want to talk about everything that happened because we need to act now," Lev insists, talking pragmatically and, thankfully, unaware of the transformation inside me. He and Ollie hold the kind of silent exchange that I don't quite understand.

Lev glares, and Ollie shakes his head. They grunt and gesture, and finally, Lev throws his hands up in the air, and Ollie speaks up. "Listen. Renata has been through enough. We'll make sure that everything is locked down, of course," Ollie says. "But I don't want to put her through this right now. She deserves a break. It's been too much."

"I'm fine," I say quietly, but when Ollie opens his mouth to protest, I shake my head. "I promise," I say softly.

Ollie finally nods, even though his grip tightens a little bit more on me. "All right. Are you hungry? Need water? Something to eat?"

Lev's dark chuckle from across the room catches Ollie's attention.

"Shut up," Ollie snaps.

But Lev shakes his head. "No. I am so not going to fucking shut up. After you lectured every single one of us about not falling in love, about how weak we were because we did it, look at you," Lev continues in a mocking voice. "Can I get you water? Something to eat?"

"Lev, my God, grow up," I snap at him, but I can't help but smile. "I'm fine, but I'm not getting off Ollie's lap no matter what you guys say. So you can tell Mikhail he can just fuck off if that's what he wants to do."

"What was that?" Mikhail asks from the doorway, and I feel like I'm six years old. I bury my face in Ollie's chest.

"Nothing," I say, which makes Ollie chuckle.

"Give her some space. She's under duress," Ollie says quietly. His lips quirk up as he leans in and whispers in my ear. "Behave yourself." My cheeks flame.

Thankfully, Ollie changes the subject. "We all need to chat. Mikhail. What's going on?"

The rest of the guys walk into the room. I guess I'm all brave about telling Mikhail to fuck off unless he's standing right in front of me. This group doesn't take kindly to disrespect, and my husband doesn't either.

Begrudgingly, I'll admit I kind of love that about him.

"Isabella discovered that unbeknownst to her, Renata has a huge inheritance coming to her she didn't know about and a rival cartel, La Sombra Roja, got wind of it," Mikhail says. "Carlos admitted in the end that he was working for them, that they intended on taking Renata for their own so they could claim her inheritance. And—"

"Which is bullshit to me," Ollie says. "She's married."

Isabella interjects. "They are known for being ruthless and disregarding the laws of the land, so to speak."

"Do you have personal experience with them?" I ask her.

"Unfortunately, yes." She swallows hard and looks at Lev before she speaks to Ollie. "You need to keep a close eye on Polina. That will be one of the options left to them, you see. Now that they know Renata is married, they will likely come after Polina. They will stop at nothing. They are ruthless. Evil," she says. "The only reason why we haven't had a flat-out war with them is because my father made a truce years ago. They will consider that void now since my brother is dead."

"But you aligned yourselves with the Romanovs," Ollie says as if that explains everything.

They go on and on, discussing international organized crime syndicate bylaws and rules, regulations, respect and disrespect, and a litany of names of people I don't know and don't care to know. But I only hear one thing...Polina is in danger now.

Will it ever end?

Probably not.

Maybe that's okay.

Maybe these guys form their identity through being enforcers, strong and courageous. And maybe we women were meant to be the counterpart that challenges them. Because when I take a man like Ollie Romanov into my hands, and I know that he's fallen for me and loves me? I feel as if I could rule the world.

"Mom is dying to feed everybody," Lev says.

My stomach growls on cue. "Rivals and threats aside, real food sounds great right now."

"We need to shower," Ollie says. But I know him. He wants to get away. He wants me alone.

"No problem," Mikhail says, obviously forgiving me. "We'll have food sent up to your room. Can you tell me what you want to do next, Ollie? Maybe take her as far away from here as you can? You've been dealing with Carlos now for quite some time. Now that he's gone, you need a reprieve."

"I know," Ollie says quietly. When he looks at me, though, I know exactly how to respond.

"We don't want to travel. You guys have had Ollie going all over the world, and he hasn't been able to put down roots. He's the only one who hasn't. He may be too selfless to admit it, but he's ready to settle down. With *me*."

Ollie bends and kisses my forehead. "Thank you. We'll stay here until we find a place of our own. This is where we belong," Ollie says.

"Mom is gonna like that immensely," Lev says with a smile. I smile myself. So will I.

Polina takes King Arthur, and we walk up to the bedroom. I take a long, hot shower while Ollie fields a few more calls, and just when I'm rinsing my hair, he opens the door.

He stands in the doorway until his hair is damp from the steam.

"Are you coming in?" I ask him quietly.

"Yes."

My heartbeat races. We've been through so much, and I want to reconnect with him. I need to know if he feels the same.

He grabs the hem of his shirt and lifts it slowly over his head. I tip my head back, letting the hot water scald my scalp, streaming down my face as I stare at him. I blink.

His arm is cut and bleeding. There's a purplish bruise forming on his other arm, and yet, he's never looked so handsome.

He steps out of the rest of his clothes, letting them fall to the floor. There's something about being naked in front of each other that feels like a new beginning. I like it. As he steps toward me, I lazily look over every inch of him. A few feet away from the shower, he pauses. I swallow and lick my lips, reaching for the bar of soap and lazily soaping my breasts. It satisfies me immensely to see the way his erection grows while he watches me.

"You're so fucking beautiful," he whispers. "And you're mine."

I've never been one to enjoy possessive language, but something about the way he says it ticks every one of my boxes. I love it. I love *him. I want him.*

"Oh yeah?" I tease. "Is there something I'm supposed to do with that information, Mr. Romanov?"

I hold his gaze with mine, challenging him.

"Not at all," he says quietly, watching me as I soap my pussy. Little bubbles trail down my legs, and I rinse my hand. I put the soap down, run water over my fingers, and glide them to the top of my pussy.

The way he growls makes my skin prickle. "You leave what's mine for me, Renata. You know what I expect."

I do, which is why I'm touching myself, teasing him. This is a dance between the two of us, and I know the steps so well. I love that he leads, and he expects me to follow. While others may have instant connections, he and I have fought for what we have. And now that we've survived, now that we've made it to the first finish line of what I am sure will be many more, I feel as if we need this victory.

"Don't you dare," he says, his eyes blazing into me, daring me. Begging me. "That's *my pussy*," he whispers.

I don't know how he can say that and still maintain over-the-top masculinity, but it's so hot. I swear, I'd laugh at any other man who said it.

"Come in here, then," I say, backing up. "Come take what's yours."

He steps into the shower and reaches for me. I gasp a second before our mouths clash together. My hands are in his hair, my legs around his waist, he grips my ass almost painfully. Hot water cascades over our bodies, drowning us in rivulets, and we don't stop kissing. His tongue meets mine, and his passionate, male groan makes every nerve in my body ignite. I moan, grinding my pussy against his hot erection. He slaps my ass hard.

I swallow, my pulse racing as he lifts his mouth off mine, only to send a trail of kisses down my neck. He licks a seam of water that runs down my chest and moves his mouth to my nipple. Bending, he suckles it into his mouth and nips it with the edge of his teeth. My head falls back, and I moan. The bundle of nerves between my legs pulses. I need him. I want him. I love that he feels the same about me.

Our bodies entwine, arms and legs tangling as he worships my breasts. With me in his arms, his cock presses up against my pussy. I raise my hips, and he thrusts. I'm so full, so stretched, I groan with satisfaction. I swallow a moan, my mouth dropping open in ecstasy.

I love the feel of him. I love the way he holds me—possessively, powerfully—as if he's willing to carry me over hot coals and through blazing fire, through hell and war.

Maybe he already has.

My need for him climbs with every groan he utters, every touch of his rough hands and tender mouth. His fingers dig into my hips. His cock throbs inside me. My pulse races as he swallows my gasps and pounds into me. Pleasure wraps around me like a warm cocoon, and my body shatters at the same moment he groans, his hot come lashing into me.

We ride our pleasure, our bodies as one. I've never felt so light and so full all at once. His hot seed spills out of me as the water from the shower pounds into my skin.

My head falls onto his chest, and he holds me as if we've finally found each other.

Wordlessly, we soap each other off. My legs are shaky, so he holds me to him, brushing my hair out of my eyes and tipping my head back to rinse me off. Then it's my turn to lather his body. I kiss each inked mark and scar and guide my hand down the length of his back, rinsing off suds.

He shuts the shower off and reaches for a towel, quickly wraps it around himself, then gets a second one for me.

Silently, I step out of the shower and into the towel he holds out for me, into the warm protection of his arms. My legs are still shaky as he guides me into the bedroom.

It feels as if we've washed off the past and stepped into the future. Into the space of infinite possibilities and a love that knows no bounds.

CHAPTER TWENTY-EIGHT

Ollie

I WAKE up the next morning feeling like I might be the luckiest guy in the world. I have the most beautiful woman I've ever seen lying curled up beside me, one leg over mine, her delicate hands folded under her head. I savor this moment. I don't know what we'll face next, so I don't want to take one minute with Renata for granted.

"Hey," she says in a husky whisper. "Good Morning, Ollie."

I bend and kiss her gently. "Morning."

"Polina brought King Arthur up to you. She said something about him house-training like a champ and pulling a sword out of a stone in the garden? Maybe he'll be more than a little fluff-ball after all."

Renata grins and sits up, her face lighting up in delight when King Arthur bounds onto the bed and licks her face. "Now, off the bed before Daddy loses his mind," she says, putting him back down.

Daddy.

I've never imagined myself married, much less with a family. It almost makes me want to pinch myself. I let the word linger, testing its weight. I never thought I'd want to hear anyone call me that.

"Why the sad look?" she asks, sobering.

"I'm not sad. I'm stunned. Every time I wake up beside you, it hits me all over again—you're mine. In this world of chaos, I still get *you.*" I shake my head. "And when you said *Daddy,* I just... it made me think about kids. I never thought that far ahead."

Nodding, she reaches for my hand and gives it a little squeeze. "I get it. Me neither. There's no space for thinking of the future when you're in survival mode."

That's exactly it.

"But we're past that now," she says quietly. "And while I don't think I'm ready for kids *yet...* I will be someday."

I nod. "Someday" feels like a luxury I've never had.

"What were you doing on your iPad last night?" she asks, stretching. "Ohhh. You had breakfast brought up. Thank you, I'm *starving.*"

"Figured you would be." I wink at her. "You worked hard last night."

She gives me a sly look. "It takes two."

She sits up, and I put the breakfast tray between the two of us. I butter her toast, and she pours me coffee from a carafe.

We eat in amiable silence. It feels natural, and I fucking love it.

"I can't wait to cook our first meal together in our new home," she says with a smile. "I'll learn, eventually."

"You don't have to. I mean, I could just hire someone."

She shakes her head. "I want to."

I squeeze her hand. "Me too." Maybe people take domestic tasks for granted. I can't fucking wait to have a lawn to mow and a fridge to fill.

"How are you feeling?" I ask when we're done with breakfast and the tray's been pushed aside.

"I'm alright," she says quietly as she checks me over. "How are you? Are you hurt?"

I shrug. "I've got a few injuries but nothing that really bothers me. I'd have taken a hundred times worse than this for you."

She strokes my arm and kisses my bare shoulder. "I know. And I love you for it."

"I love you too."

She smiles. "Nice twist there." The way her eyes twinkle and a little hint of a dimple forms in her cheek makes my heart turn over in my chest. "I love you," she says, her voice husky with emotion.

I squeeze her hand.

A beat passes before she continues thoughtfully. "Ollie, I think I want to talk to someone. Therapist or something, you know? I think I need to heal. Not just from what happened with Carlos, but everything. I need to learn how to be...*me*... but without all that...fear." She sighs even as her eyes glisten.

I squeeze her hand, so damn proud of her. "I think that would be an excellent idea. Nikko's Vera has a friend who works with us. Or did you have someone in mind?"

"No, that would be great. Thank you. I just... I know I'm mourning my brother's death, but I've really been thinking about what you said. I'm not as sad about his death as I thought I would be, and I think it's because I've already mourned who he once was, if that makes sense."

I kiss her cheek. "It does, beautiful. And I'm proud of you."

King Arthur circles the door and gives a little *yip*, effectively ending our conversation as we race to pull on clothes and take him outside. It's a little overcast and cloudy, with a slight drizzle. Renata inhales the clean air. "Wow, it's beautiful out, isn't it? I never thought a day like this—cloudy, raining—could feel *hopeful*. But it does."

I smile at her and look to where the clouds break and light streams from the heavens above. I love that she looks at an overcast day like this and sees beauty. I see it too. "Yeah, baby," I say, my voice soft but sure. "It's beautiful."

We walk forward, hand in hand, our fingers tangled like the past we leave behind. As long as we're together, whatever comes next doesn't scare me. Because the future is *ours*. Our promise. Our story.

EPILOGUE

Ollie

"THIS ONE." Renata stands on the front stoop of the seventh home we've looked at in as many days. Nestled in a tree-lined neighborhood thirty minutes from The Cove, it feels like a private oasis. Set back from the road, shadowed behind imposing pines, it's secluded and homey, and I knew before she claimed it by the look in her eyes that we've found our forever home. Some people buy their first home just to move to the next bigger option later, but we want to settle. Put down roots. Grow a family.

"Yeah, baby," I say softly, surprised to find my voice husky with emotion. It's nothing extravagant like the homes I grew up in, the ones our realtor took us to, but it's homey. Comfortable.

"I can see us here," she says, gesturing at the woods. "Running around on the grass with our kids. Maybe we'll have a little... swing set or something. I don't know. But it's just so—"

"Peaceful," we both say at the same time. Wordlessly, we walk up to the porch, the floorboards creaking under our feet. The air is tinged with the scent of pine and cut grass. A gentle wind brushes her hair against my arm as I hold her to me. A bird tweets in the distance.

And what we don't have to say out loud is that it's such a dark contrast to the turbulence we left behind, it feels right.

"I'm going to ask you to do something, Ollie, and I want you to think about it." Her chestnut eyes bore into mine. She's so cute when she thinks she can intimidate me. "Don't just snap off an answer without thinking like you usually do."

I shove my hands in my pockets and can't help but smile.

"I don't snap off answers, you know that."

"I mean," she says, wagging her finger at me while shaking her head. "You are a very determined man, but you happened to be married to a very determined woman."

Jesus, don't I know it.

She goes on, her voice tremulous. "And I want to... I want to buy this house with my money. For a couple of reasons." I'm surprised, but I don't interrupt. I listen. I owe this to her, and the truth is, I don't care if she spends her money or mine. It's all ours, anyway. We're one now, a unit. A family. But this matters to her, so I listen.

"I don't want that money sitting around. I want to put it into a house and I don't want a mortgage. I want to know that I, Renata Romanova, purchased this house with my own money." Her chin thrusts out and she holds my gaze. "That *nobody* can take it from me."

She's come so far, such a long way, confident and independent now. I know this means a lot to her. This isn't just a house in a peaceful neighborhood, it's more than a place to live. It's a declaration of who she's become, of what we've fought for. She's forged her way past a life of instability where peace was fleeting. No one can take this from her. Not now, not ever, and I'll fight for this peace for her until the day I draw my last breath.

"Of course you can," I say with a shrug. "Doesn't matter to me, Renata. Everything I have is yours. *Everything.*"

And I do mean everything. I reach for her and she fits in my arms, nestled in as if we were carved from one piece, and now we've finally, *finally* made our way back to each other.

We fought hard for this. We'll fight harder still.

I kiss her forehead as the click of the realtor's high heels sounds across the porch. "Two acres of land and a reservation in the back, there's even a little creek where people even fish," she says. She pulls out a pair of reading glasses and continues to read down a list. She goes on and on about hot water and utilities, the local schools, the square footage, the exterior a blend of modern and classic blah blah blah, but I barely hear her. My woman's pleased as fuck and that's all that matters.

"This place is not far from the city," she continues, "but just enough away that people have to come a ways to visit you," she adds with a wink. Thirty minutes away from my parents, my brothers, and their families. It's just enough. Because we need something of our own.

"The kitchen may need some renovation," she begins with a little frown. "You may be able to negotiate the—"

"We'll take it," Renata says. The realtor, who worked with my family before, looks to me for approval. She quirks a brow.

"Mr. Romanov?"

"Why are you asking me? Do as my wife tells you," I say, my voice carrying a note of threat. She will not question Renata.

"Of course," she says with a smile, turning to face Renata. "Would you like to negotiate the price down for kitchen renovations?"

Renata shrugs. "No. I like the way it is. That kitchen island can function as a breakfast table, and I love that view of the garden outside the dining area." She turns to me. "Do you agree?"

I shrug. "I need a place to make a pot of coffee and a burner to scramble some eggs, and some place to put my protein shakes. The question is, are you happy?"

My brothers would rib me mercilessly but I don't fucking care. I know what my life's goal is, what my purpose is, and she's standing right in front of me with stars in her eyes.

"Excellent. You're a woman who knows her mind." She smiles broadly at Renata, who flushes a little. Of course she is. I squeeze her hand, and when the realtor goes inside to put in a formal offer, Renata claps her hands like a little girl and bounces on the balls of her feet. As I look at her, I can't help but think about the chaos we escaped, the dangers we faced. This moment is worth every goddamn battle I ever fought. I nestle my face in her hair and inhale, breathing in the familiar, grounding scent.

"Oh, Ollie," she says. She doesn't say more than that, but she doesn't have to. Just those two words. *Oh, Ollie.* They hold a world of meaning in them.

We're together. We're safe. We're doing this, the two of us, forging our way through hellfire to make a place of our own. We're going to raise a family. We're going to stay connected to mine, branch out, and make one of our own.

We celebrate with dinner at a steakhouse in town. I watch approvingly as Renata tears into a 20 oz. T-bone steak with a side of caramelized onions, a baked potato the size of King Arthur, and shoves her green beans aside. "Those are not my favorite," she says. I reach out to her and squeeze her hand. I run my thumb along her knuckles.

"What is your favorite?"

"You, of course," she says with a smile.

"Oh, that's not cheesy at all."

"As if I give a fuck about cheesy," she says with a grin. She sobers, chewing her food thoughtfully. Swallowing her bite, she chases it with a gulp of wine before she asks her question. "Ollie, has there been any word from the cartel? Have you heard anything from Colombia?"

I shake my head. "No. It seems as if things are at peace for now." *For now.* Isabella and Lev have their men combing every inch of the city, and they have taken great risks to make sure that there's no blowback.

"Thank God."

"It's quiet for now, Renata," I say. I don't want to break the spell. I don't want to be negative. As much as I want to believe that the peace we found is real and lasting, I can't shake the feeling that danger still lurks. Maybe it's all I've experienced haunting me. Maybe it's legitimate, I don't know. But I do know the La Sombra Roja cartel may be quiet for now, but they're not gone. I glance at Renata and push the thought away.

For now, I have to live in this moment. For her. For *us*.

"I know," she says quietly. "There is no lasting peace, is there?"

I shake my head. "It just means that we live in the moment, that we appreciate everything we have now. Everything we worked for. Everything we earned. Everything we felt. We appreciate this. We take nothing for granted."

I can see it, just like she can—the laughter echoing across that yard, scooters and bikes askew by the drive. Lazy afternoons spent by the creek, teaching our kids how to fish or climb trees. I want that. We both do. But it's still foreign to me to think about a future that's not just survival.

"I like that. Take nothing for granted. Maybe that's what all that bullshit about living in the moment actually means. Maybe we already have everything we need, right here."

"Polina's safety?" she asks, liberally buttering a roll.

"She'll be married," I say simply.

"Does Mikhail have plans for that yet?"

"No, he wants to give us time to see what La Sombra Roja next move is first."

For one second, I'm pulled back to the smell of gunpowder thick in the air, Renata's hand in mine. I don't know if I'll ever forget the fear in her eyes. I don't want to. Seeing her here, full of hope and joy, I renew my conviction to keep her safe, to never give her reason to cling to me with fear ever again.

"So we're not out of danger, but maybe it won't be... It won't be terrible," she says hopefully.

I grin at her and she smiles back. Hope mixed with realism, and just a touch of rose-colored glasses. I like that, though.

"Dessert? Cordial?" the waitress asks.

Renata winks at me. "This one's on me," she says magnanimously, spreading her hands across the table. "Order anything you want. The cake? An after-dinner cordial?"

I shake my head. "I let you buy the house. *This* is on me."

The waitress's eyes go wide. I don't give a shit.

"Can you wrap this up, please?" Renata says sweetly, pushing her plate toward the waitress. She ate less than half of it.

The waitress leaves with her leftovers when it dawns on me. "Wait a minute. Don't tell me you're planning on feeding your steak to the dog," I say with a groan. "You got the biggest steak on the menu only to bring it back home to him, didn't you? *Renata.*"

"King Arthur is a good boy," she says in a little singsong voice. "Potty trained now and so obedient. Of course I'm giving this to him." Her eyes flash with a hint of flirtation. "And don't you try to stop me, Ollie. Do you think I missed that bag of doggie treats on the front porch? I didn't buy those."

"Whatever." I grunt. "They had a buy-one-get-one-free sale."

"Admit it. That playful, sweet pup has stolen your heart."

"Sure. He *is* a good boy."

Renata can't set foot out of our bed or head to the bathroom without him obediently following by her side. He growls and barks when people knock at the door until we tell him to heel. When she walks out to get the mail, he is glued to her side. He *is* a good boy.

"I like to see you with him," she says softly. "Laugh all you want, but it shows me that you'll be a good *daddy*."

"I guess, I mean if you think about it—" and then I realize her eyes are twinkling mischievously at me.

Did she say daddy? Did she mean that the way I thought she did? "Renata. Is there something you need to tell me?"

My heart breaks a little as I watch her. She's too beautiful for words. Her hair cascades over her shoulders, her eyes bright as starlight. She smiles as the waitress brings a huge piece of chocolate cake to our table.

"What do *you* think?" she says, grinning at me. Then she turns to the waitress. "Maybe you should make that *two* pieces of cake. One for him... and one for me and the baby."

THE END

BONUS EPILOGUE

Want to read more of Ollie and Renata story? Scan the QR code below to get a free Bonus Epilogue for *Savage: A Dark Bratva Forced Marriage Romance*!

CHAPTER ONE

I stare at the cold, empty altar in front of me. I demanded simplicity, fitting for nuptials in a godless church and a loveless union.

A vase of fading white roses, their petals curling at the edges, sits on the marble altar, the cloying scent nearly nauseating. Shadows cling to the high, vaulted ceilings, cast by candles that flicker in iron sconces. Above, darkened stained glass depicts saints and martyrs in muted colors, their hollow eyes staring down through fractured light.

A faint trace of incense lingers from Sunday mass, mixing with the damp smell of old stone and earth. Here, walls seem to absorb sound, muting every breath, every heartbeat.

Every secret.

The priest my uncle summoned stands before me, his face pale in the half-light, almost skeletal in the shadows. His fingers tremble around the ancient leather-bound book he holds to his chest; its gilded edges tarnished with age. His eyes dart between me and the altar as though he expects some divine wrath to strike at any moment.

He looks as if he's about to faint. Coward. They should have appointed someone more powerful to be in charge of a place aptly named The Cathedral of the Eternal Martyrs, nestled in the heart of my family's hometown of Zalivka, a stone's throw from Moscow. I can almost feel the reproachful looks from their images in stained glass windows of forest green and blood red.

"Relax, Father," I say, my voice resonating in the cavernous church. I look away. "It's not your fault she pulled this stunt. I won't blame you." He blows out a breath as if I granted him a boon. Hell, maybe I did.

I can't help that my reputation precedes me. Sometimes I wish it didn't. Would make shit easier.

Eh, maybe not.

I can see the whites of his eyes and don't miss the way he's cleared his throat seventeen times in the past five minutes while I waited for my bride. She isn't coming. Not now, not ever.

The small crew of loyal friends and family who showed up to witness the ceremony sit still. No one dares to move. It looks like they're hardly breathing. Makes sense. They don't know if I'll burn this church to the fucking ground or call a mob to go after her.

Even I don't know how to react to being stood up by my future bride.

Mocked. Humiliated.

Disobeyed.

My hands clench into fists. When I find her... when I track down my bride and drag her back to me, I won't unleash my rage on her. No. I'll demand *penance* from her. Absolute surrender, body and soul, until she's broken and bound to me.

Out of nowhere, the raucous sound of someone pressing down on an organ breaks the silence. I turn abruptly, my gaze fixed on the choir loft, where a red-faced, flustered organist shakes her head.

"I'm so sorry, Mr. Kopolov. I stumbled. I'm sorry, sir. It won't happen again."

I shift away from her, dismissing her with a flick of my wrist. My fingers trace the edge of my cufflinks, an old family heirloom that once belonged to my father, and his father before him, and his father before him. I barely notice Semyon until he's already there, a quiet shadow moving into my peripheral vision.

Semyon stands just a few feet away, his lean frame blending into the dim lighting near the altar. I see the faint gleam of his glasses as he watches the room, his gaze sharp and calculating, missing nothing. He waits, a small shift of his gaze the only sign that he's asking permission to approach. Always the strategist, his mind whirs with the next step, cold and watchful. I jerk my chin in his direction, a signal. He ascends the three steps soundlessly, his calmness a stark contrast to the silent storm brewing inside me.

His footsteps echo on the marble floors as he walks up the three steps to where I stand by the altar. Younger than I am by a few years, he resembles me but with a leaner build.

"She isn't coming," I confirm in a low whisper. His eyes, ever unreadable, flicker toward me, then back to the entrance. I gave explicit instructions for her father to send her alone. I didn't want a ceremony, a big to-do. This was a transactional agreement, no more, no less.

Anissa fucking jilted me.

"Predictable," he murmurs, a faint edge of disinterest in his tone. He's always had a gift for neutrality I envied, a calmness that can unsettle even the most seasoned. His icy glare a promise of retribution. The Kopolov family will always stand as one.

I look away from him and stifle a curse. The air in the church is cold, musty, reminiscent of the catacombs I visited when I was a child. It was my favorite place to go, away from the hustle and bustle of family life. Away from my father's cruel, relentless oppression and my mother's quiet dignity.

The church seemed bigger then. Hell, everything did, even my father.

I wonder what it would feel like standing before him now if he were still here.

I look at Semyon and hold his frigid glare. My jaw locks, every muscle in my body conditioned to control, but underneath the calm, my rage claws at me like a beast ready to break free. *No one* fucks with the Kopolov family, and the fact that Anissa made a mockery of it will not go unpunished.

My jaw tightens, my gaze calculating, but underneath it all, turmoil churns. I stare at the empty pews in the back of the church and watch as my brothers give each other quick, anxious glances, uncertain of what to do next.

I'll make her wish she hadn't. I'll make her wish she'd come like the obedient little girl she'll learn to be.

I'll make her regret the day she disobeyed me.

Why did she run?

How did she get away?

Only the sound of distant whispers and the faint rustle of clothing breaks the silence.

"If I can assist in any way..." the priest begins. One look from me, and the words die on his lips.

A low, dark, irreverent chuckle comes from the pews. I glance at my youngest brother. Where Semyon embodies cold precision, Rodion is the unpredictable wildfire none of us can fully control—to be honest, nor do I want to. It helps to have someone like him on my side. Leaning back with his arms spread along the back of the pew, that ever-present smirk on his lips and glint in his eyes promise me that one word is all it would take from me and he'd happily burn torch this church to the ground—and roast our enemies in the flames with glee—if I asked him. His loyalty borders on madness. He left his motorcycle parked outside and probably has more weapons on him than he has tats, and that's fucking saying something.

I shake my head, give Rodion a meaningful look, and turn back to the priest. "That won't be necessary, thank you."

The only people who will "assist" in what I have to do next are already here before me. Armed and ready.

My bride was here earlier. I saw her from a distance. I'm not supposed to see the bride before the ceremony, and even I'm not going to fuck with tradition. As my grandfather says, "Superstitions may be for children, but adults are old enough to follow them."

So I did my duty when I came here. I wouldn't tempt fate and look at my bridge before the ceremony. I turned away when I saw the flurry of white fabric and a gauzy veil, when I heard the click of heels on the marble floor in the foyer. There were only two strangers here—my fiancée and her bodyguard.

She was here though. And now she's gone.

"Did anyone see her leave?" I say in a low voice to Semyon. I narrow my eyes on the doorway. "Is it possible that she was taken?"

Would somebody dare to take the bride I was about to marry? If anyone touched her, if anyone touched one hair on her fucking head—

"She wasn't taken," Semyon says. "We just found video surveillance from the basement. She left on her own. Paid off her guard, ripped her dress off, and ran."

Jesus.

I look to the priest. "You didn't tell us there was video surveillance in the basement, Father."

His heavy book falls to the floor with a clatter. He stammers as he tries to make an excuse. "I didn't know there was," he says. "That's not what I handle here. I'm sorry. If I knew, I would've told you—"

I shake my head. "Even I won't bring down the fury of hell by harming a hair on a man of the cloth in front of an altar, Father," I say quietly. "But don't test my patience. Or God's."

He clamps his mouth shut, his thin lips forming a perfect O before he swallows hard. Good. A wise man knows that sometimes silence speaks much louder than words.

I turn to face my family, my voice booming. "I'm calling an end."

My youngest sister, Zoya, jumps in her chair, though my sister Yana sits ramrod straight and doesn't move. She holds my gaze and gives me a slight nod of encouragement. Steadfast and loyal with sharp eyes that seem to take in everything around her, Yana has an aura of calm and stillness, though underneath, she is always thinking. Resilience is her middle name.

Zoya, however, is delicate and sensitive, and I feel like a dick for making her jump. Her kind, wide eyes are fixed on me. Shit. She's the only one who can make me feel guilty for raising my voice.

When she gives me her small, little smile, I swallow hard and nod, asking her forgiveness. She inclines her head, and her eyes grow soft—granting it.

One family, one fight—never apart.

I don't miss the way her fingers tighten on the small matteblack purse she carries, her own family heirloom. If I don't marry, I'll have no choice but to marry *her* off since Yana's already married. The thought fucking kills me. She's seventeen years old and still a child in my eyes. I can't do that to her. I fucking *won't*.

It is for her—it is for *all* of them—that I'm even here.

Beside her, my grandfather sits, his back ramrod straight, but his eyes warm with reassurance. One gnarled hand rests atop his cane, the other on Zoya's shoulder. His gaze tells me everything I need to know—he has total confidence that I'll handle this.

I stare out the stained-glass window, a brutal yet somehow beautiful depiction of the beheading of St. John, and past it to the graveyard where my life changed forever.

It was there that I witnessed the burial of my parents. There that I buried my youth. There that I became the guardian of my siblings, inherited my family's wealth and every one of their enemies.

I made a vow that day that I would be buried alongside my parents before I would allow anyone to break our family apart.

And now Anissa has done that very thing. What would cause her to run from me, knowing my wrath was inevitable?

My knuckles whiten where I clench my fist, aching for the chance at retribution. I blow the breath out through my nose when footsteps approach me, and a heavy hand comes to my shoulder.

"We'll find her, Rafail."

I know it's my uncle based on the smell of his cologne before I even turn to see. His wife loves to doll him up like he's her personal plaything. Fuck, maybe he is. "We will. No one can hide from us in this city."

I turn and face the priest, pinning him to the spot, determined to maintain civility and control. "Tell me what I owe you for this farce, Father."

"No, no," he says magnanimously. "No charge, Mr. Kopolov. I didn't perform the duty that you hired me for."

I shake my head. "I appreciate that, Father, but it is exceptionally bad luck not to pay for services rendered by the Church. Even debts to God have to be paid, or we know the repercussions."

When he begins to protest, I hold my hand up, palm facing him, and his words die on his lips. "And you don't have to give me that whole thing about not performing any services yet. I won't bring down superstition on my house." I give him a humorless smile, reach into my pocket, and take out my wallet. I peel off a thick stack of bills and hand them to him. "I'll be making a donation to the food pantry as well."

Good luck comes from donations to the Church. I don't tempt fate.

"Thank you, Mr. Kopolov," the priest says, his voice trembling. The bastard probably expected the roof to cave in—or maybe expected me to hit him. He doesn't have to worry about that. I don't touch a man of the cloth unless he proves himself to deserve it.

"Thank you, thank you. And when you find your bride," he says, unnecessarily cheerful, "let me know right away, and I will perform the ceremony you came here for. I promise," he adds with a smile.

I nod and turn abruptly.

"Everyone back to the house," I say, unbuttoning my cuff-links and rolling up my sleeves.

It's time to get to work.

My enemies circle like predators, sniffing for blood. And as soon as word gets out that I was jilted at the altar, they'll close in.

Our plan was to go back to my home and have dinner in the dining room. Now, instead of a celebratory dinner, we'll plan our next move. Not an attack but a strategy.

"We'll go back to my house. The food is ready. We'll discuss our options, scan through footage, and call in our allies. I want everyone to assemble within the hour."

My uncle bows his head to me. "Wise move. I would do the same," he says as if that should somehow console me. Right.

I snap my fingers, and my brothers rise, their movements swift, ready for war.

"Let's move."

Want to read more? Pre-order your copy of *Unleashed: A Dark Enemies to Lovers Romance* (Polina's Story) by scanning the QR code below (available November 15, 2024):

Fueled by dark chocolate and even darker coffee, USA Today bestselling author Jane Henry writes what she loves to read – character-driven, unputdownable romance featuring dominant alpha males and the powerful heroines who bring them to their knees. She's believed in the power of love and romance since Belle won over the beast, and finally decided to write love stories of her own.

Scan the QR Code below to receive Jane's Newsletter & be notified of upcoming new releases & special offers!

Be sure to visit me at www.janehenryromance.com, too!